THE LUCK UGLIES

PAUL DURHAM

HarperCollins *Children's Books*

First published in hardback in Great Britain by HarperCollins *Children's Books* in 2014
HarperCollins *Children's Books* is a division of HarperCollins *Publishers* Ltd.
77–85 Fulham Palace Road, Hammersmith, London, W6 8JB.

Visit us on the web at
www.harpercollins.co.uk

2

Text copyright © Paul Durham 2014
Map copyright © Sally Taylor 2014
Paul Durham asserts the moral right to be identified as the author of this work.

978-0-00-752690-1
Printed and bound in England by Clays Ltd, St Ives plc

MIX
Paper from
responsible sources
FSC **FSC® C007454**

FSC™ is a non-profit international organisation established to promote
the responsible management of the world's forests. Products carrying the
FSC label are independently certified to assure consumers that they come
from forests that are managed to meet the social, economic and
ecological needs of present and future generations,
and other controlled sources.

Find out more about HarperCollins and the environment at
www.harpercollins.co.uk/green

For Caterina and Charlotte, whose magic makes dreams come true. And for Wendy, who stayed in the ring.

CONTENTS

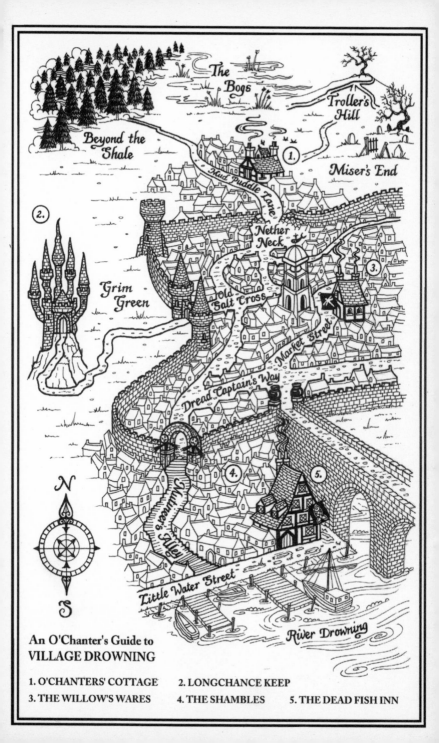

The Bogs

Troller's Hill

Beyond the Shale

Mud Puddle Lane

Miser's End

①

②

Grim Green

Nether Neck

Old Salt Cross

③

Market Street

Dread Captain's Way

④

⑤

Shambles

N

S

Little Water Street

River Drowning

An O'Chanter's Guide to
VILLAGE DROWNING

1. O'CHANTERS' COTTAGE   2. LONGCHANCE KEEP
3. THE WILLOW'S WARES   4. THE SHAMBLES   5. THE DEAD FISH INN

A WORD ABOUT VILLAINS...

Mum said the fiends usually came after midnight. They'd flutter down silently from rooftops and slither unseen from the sewers under a Black Moon. Luck Uglies, she'd call them, then quickly look over her shoulder to make sure they weren't listening. Father said the Luck Uglies weren't monsters. Outlaws, criminals, villains, certainly, but they were men, just like us.

I still remember the night the Earl's army marched through the village, forcing them north into the toothy shadows of the forest. Soldiers were sent to follow, but none ever returned. With time, the Luck Uglies faded into ghosts, then whispers. And finally, after many years, it was as if they had never existed at all.

Anonymous Villager

THE GARGOYLE

RYE AND HER two friends had never intended to steal the banned book from The Angry Poet – they'd just hoped to read it. In truth, it was nothing more than curiosity that had brought them to the strange little bookshop wedged between a grog shop and the coffin maker. But the shop's owner overreacted so strongly that they fled without thinking, the illicit tome still clutched under Rye's arm.

The accidental thieves tore back out on to Market Street, bouncing off villagers who shared the winding, cobblestone road with horse-drawn carts and pigs foraging in the sewers for scraps. The street was narrow and congested at the noon hour, its alleys clogged with foot traffic blocking their escape. The poet himself, hefty and determined, ploughed through everything in his path. With a quick nod as their unspoken signal, the children changed course. Their escape turned vertical as they scattered in different directions, each searching for footholds in the jagged bricks and mortar of the Market Street shops.

Rye had never been comfortable on the rooftops. They had scaled them once or twice before, but only as an avenue of last resort. She scrambled up the steeply pitched timbers, darting between the twisted chimneys, scowling gargoyles and leaking gutters of Village Drowning. Black smoke billowed up from the shops and markets, fogging her cloak with the smell of cured meat and birch bark. She didn't pause to look back at her pursuer – she'd been chased enough times to know better than that. Clearing the ridge of a gable, her momentum plunged her down the other side, legs churning uncontrollably to keep up. She stopped hard at the edge of the thatch and shingle roof, peering down past the toes of her oversized boots to the unforgiving cobblestones far below.

In front of her was freedom. Quinn Quartermast had already made it across a narrow alleyway on to the neighbouring roof. He was all arms and legs, built perfectly for jumping.

Somewhere not far behind Rye was a poet with bad intentions, one who had proved to be a remarkably agile climber for someone of such large proportions.

"I don't think I can do it, Quinn," Rye said.

"Of course you can," Quinn yelled and waved her on.

"No, really. I'm not very good at this sort of thing."

Rye looked out at the village around her. Drowning was more of a sprawling town than a village, one built on a foundation of secrets, rules and lies, but mostly just mud. It straddled the edge of the brackish River Drowning, close enough to the sea for residents to smell the tide in the mornings and watch the brash gulls waddle into the butcher shop and fly off with a tail or a hoof. North of the river and the town's walls were creeping bogs blanketed in salt mist, and beyond that was the vast, endless pine forest rumoured to harbour wolves, bandits and clouds of ugly luck. Villagers referred to it only as Beyond the Shale. Nobody respectable believed it to be full of enchanted beasts any more, but old rumours died hard, and there was still a general notion that the great forest teemed with both malice and riches for those brave or foolhardy enough to go looking.

Footsteps pounded the roof behind Rye. They belonged not to the angry poet, but to a small, cloaked and hooded figure that stormed right past her, arms pumping. It leaped into the air and landed with a thud and a barrel roll on the opposite roof next to Quinn. The figure popped to its feet and pulled off its hood to reveal a crazy nest of hair so blonde it was almost white. Her big blue eyes shone like marbles.

"He's right behind me," Folly Flood said between gasps.

"Just run and jump," Quinn said to Rye. "It's really not far."

"You've jumped that distance a hundred times on the ground," Folly added.

"Yes, but this is different," Rye explained, looking down again. "Something will happen. It always does."

"You can make it. Come on," Quinn said.

"I've been told that I'm a little bit clumsy."

"Nonsense," Quinn said, without conviction.

"Absurd," Folly scoffed unconvincingly. "Now jump."

"He's a poet," Rye said. "How bad could it be?"

"He's angry," said Quinn.

"And big as a humpback," Folly added.

As if waiting for just such an introduction, the poet in question pulled his ample belly on to the far side of the roof. He was indeed angry – for a variety of reasons, Rye supposed. For one, nobody paid much attention to poets any more. Most villagers wanted to hear words sung over harps or stomped out by actors in tights and feathered caps. Plus, as far as Rye could tell, books weren't exactly flying off the shelves in Drowning, its residents more partial to fishing, fighting and fortune hunting. In fact, the Earl who oversaw the affairs of Drowning had not only banned women and girls from reading, but went so far as to outlaw certain books altogether. None was more illicit than the book Rye now pressed close to her body, *Tam's Tome of Drowning Mouth Fibs, Volume II* – an obscure history textbook that had been widely ignored until the Earl described it as a vile collection of scandalous accusations, dangerous untruths and outright lies. Even an eleven-year-old could work out that meant there must be some serious truth to it.

The Earl's soldiers had collected and destroyed every copy they could find. Rye had heard rumblings that the poet kept a copy of *Tam's Tome* in a secret back room. On certain nights he would hold private readings for rebellious nobles with inquisitive minds. Rye and her friends had no silver shims to buy their way in, so they had held their own secret reading in the shop's broom cupboard. Unfortunately, the poet had picked an inopportune time to sweep the floor.

The poet seemed none too pleased that they'd now made off with *Tam's Tome*, accidentally or not.

"Come on, Rye," Quinn and Folly yelled together. "Now!"

Rye took a deep breath. "Here goes."

She took five steps back to prepare for her run. She adjusted her leggings. She puffed her cheeks, clapped her hands together and then made a critical mistake.

She glanced over her shoulder.

The poet had cleared the ridge behind her. The roof shook with his heavy footfall as he steamed towards her, and Rye narrowly escaped his lurching grasp as his momentum carried him right past her. Rye froze wide-eyed as the enormous man hurtled to the edge of the roof, flailed to regain his balance, teetered on his toes and somehow managed to avoid plunging off the side. He glared accusingly at Rye.

Rye turned and darted over the next gable to the village's tallest bell tower. Its rusted whale weathervane loomed over her as she crouched among the stone gargoyles and grotesques under the tower's shadowed eaves.

Quinn's and Folly's urgent calls were muffled by the throbbing pulse in her ears. The gargoyles stared with gaping mouths as they waited for her next move. A rook perched on the shoulder of one gargoyle, grooming its inky-black feathers with a sharp grey beak. This was no place to hide for long.

Rye could hear the wheeze of the poet's gasps as he made his way towards her. She knew she had to move. She wiped her damp hands on her leggings, but her muscles refused to budge.

The solitary rook cocked its head at her and made a clicking sound with its beak. Rye twisted her face into a scowl and shook a fist, hoping to threaten it into silence. Drowning was overrun with the ugly black birds. The locals had taken to calling them roof rodents.

That was when she noticed that the bird's perch was not like the other gargoyles. If this gargoyle had wings, they fell over its shoulders like the folds of a cloak. Its angular black eyes and long pointed nose jutted forth from its cheeks, its face more leathery than stone. Like a mask.

Rye did not come from a home with many rules, but the ones she lived by were absolute and unbreakable. The first House Rule flashed through her mind.

House Rule Number One: Don't stop, talk or questions ask, beware of men wearing masks.

Rye swallowed hard. An agitated warble vibrated in the rook's throat. Then, inexplicably, the gargoyle raised a gloved finger to its masked, lipless mouth, as if to tell the bird, "Shh."

Now that got Rye moving.

She burst from the eaves, the poet himself jolting in surprise as she rushed towards him. Throwing *Tam's Tome* at his feet, she sped past and called to her friends.

"Folly! Quinn! I'm coming! Get ready to catch me!"

Rye heard Folly's shriek and the throaty caw of the rook. She timed her jump as she ran and, with great focus and concentration… snagged her boot and fell off the side of the roof.

2

THE WILLOW'S WARES

RYE WAS AN expert when it came to falling. Landings, not so much. They could be bone crunching if you slipped backwards on to frozen ground. Or piercing if you tumbled headfirst into a thicket of thorns. They were seldom soft. Falling from such a height, Rye assumed this landing would be her last. Much to her surprise, it was just wet.

Rye swallowed hard to make sure her heart wasn't actually in her throat, and promptly coughed up a mouthful of run-off that tasted worse than bog water. Dragging herself to the edge of the shallows, she hiked her dripping dress past her leggings and up round her chest. The first clothes line had left an angry red welt straight across her belly. She quickly looked above her. For the moment, neither poet nor gargoyle had followed.

"Riley, put your dress down, please," a woman's voice scolded. "The whole village can see your business."

Luckily for Rye, her fall from the rooftop was slowed by several clothes lines full of laundry before she landed in the foul-smelling canal that drained swill from the village to the river. Not so luckily, that's where Mrs O'Chanter had found her. Rye dropped her dress back into place and tried to flash a smile as the thin green stew flowed around her feet. Mrs O'Chanter frowned and extended a hand.

Mrs O'Chanter suspected that Rye must have swallowed a horseshoe as a baby – she would have been a cripple ten times over if not for her otherworldly luck. She took the opportunity to mention this to Rye once again on their walk back to her shop, The Willow's Wares. Rye glanced warily at the rooftops as they went.

After Rye had changed her clothes and was good and dry, and just when she began to think she was out of hot water, Mrs O'Chanter sent her down to catch the basement wirry that haunted the crawl space under the shop. Rye didn't believe in wirries, and neither did Mrs O'Chanter from what she could tell. Still, she seemed to assign Rye this task once or twice a week, often after Rye had cartwheeled into a shelf of glassware or asked one too many questions about the jug of cranberry wine kept under the counter. Apparently, stealing from local merchants and plummeting from rooftops amounted to a similar offence.

Rye left her dress in a neat pile and opened the trapdoor to the dark crawl space below the floorboards. She wore her sleeveless undershirt and tight black leggings so she wouldn't further scrape, bruise or otherwise scar her well-worn shins. She tied her hair in a short ponytail and stuffed it under a cap to avoid accidentally lighting it on fire with her lantern. That was something you didn't want to happen more than once. She insisted on wearing the damp leather boots that had belonged to her father when he was her age – in case she stepped on anything sharp or hungry. They were far too big and probably contributed to some of the scars on her knees, but she filled the toes with fresh straw each day and wore them everywhere she went. Sitting on the edge of the trapdoor, she dangled her boots into the darkness as bait, an iron fireplace poker at the ready. In the unlikely event that an awful beasty really was running around down there, she fully intended to impale the little fiend.

Rye spent most of her afternoons helping out Mrs O'Chanter at The Willow's Wares – the finest jewellery shop in all of Drowning. Of course, The Willow's Wares was the only jewellery shop in Drowning, and more of a curiosity shop than anything else. It was not the type of place you would find the noble class shopping for golden heirlooms or silver wedding goblets. In fact, the only nobles who turned up in Drowning were usually hiding, and were quite often followed by whoever was trying to lock them in a dungeon or lop off their heads. Instead, Drowning attracted wanderers, rapscallions, rogues and other adventurous souls who were long on courage and short on sense. The Willow's Wares offered the charms and talismans these mysterious travellers needed – or thought they did, anyway.

It had been an hour, and Rye had caught four spiders, a blind rat and something that looked like a worm with teeth, but no wirries. Rye's boredom was interrupted when she heard footsteps overhead. She put her wirry-hunting tools aside and set off to investigate. The Willow's Wares' customers always had tales of misadventure or, at the very least, some good gossip to share.

The hawk-nosed man in the shop had watery eyes and stringy hair and did not look particularly adventurous. He looked like someone who spent most of his days locked in a room full of books. In fact, he had brought one with him. He hovered over the black leather journal he'd laid out on a workbench, a quill in hand. The two soldiers who accompanied him milled around, thumbing the hilts of their sheathed sabres and looking suspiciously at the curiosities lining the shop's shelves.

"And what is your name, boy?" the man asked, in a voice that creaked like an old iron chest.

"I'm a girl, thank you very much," Rye said. She was still in her tights. Her arms, legs and face were covered in basement grime.

"Oh. Indeed you are," he said, eyeballing her disapprovingly.

"R-y-e," Rye spelled. "Rhymes with *lie*."

Mrs O'Chanter frowned and gave her a harsh look.

"Sorry," Rye said. "Rhymes with 'die'."

That didn't improve Mrs O'Chanter's mood. She

scowled at Rye as the man carefully made markings in his book.

He raised a thick eyebrow and looked up. His eyebrows resembled the grey dust balls that accumulated under Rye's bed.

"The girl can spell," he noted. "Interesting."

"Of course I can spell," Rye said.

"I see," he said and made some more markings.

"What she means," Mrs O'Chanter interjected, "is that she knows how to spell her name. You know how children are these days, Constable Boil. Always curious. You need to indulge them sometimes otherwise they won't leave you a minute's peace."

"In my house," the Constable said, "I find a good thrashing on the tail does the trick."

Mrs O'Chanter did not seem at all pleased with the conversation. She stared out at the soldiers from the pile of black hair on top of her head, held fast with a simple blue ribbon and two wooden pins that had come from the shop. One soldier fingered a display of charms made from beeswax and alligator hide. He wasn't gentle. Rye knew that Mrs O'Chanter hated it when people touched with no intention to buy and she could be downright scary about it – but she said nothing this time.

"Mrs O'Chanter," the Constable continued, then paused to look her over. "Is it still Mrs or do you finally go by Miss now?"

"It's 'Mrs', thank you very much."

"How patient of you. Well then, there was quite a disturbance at The Angry Poet today."

"Was he reading those off colour limericks again?"

"No, Mrs O'Chanter. There was a robbery. Children no less."

"My goodness," Mrs O'Chanter said, without alarm.

"Indeed," Constable Boil said. "They took a bag of gold grommets and two flasks of rare wine."

Rye's ears burned. She knew that was a lie. She picked her fingernails as she listened.

"Gold grommets?" Mrs O'Chanter said. "Who would have thought the poet was doing so well? I can't say I've ever seen anyone actually go into that shop."

Mrs O'Chanter placed a hand on Rye's shoulder. Rye stopped picking her nails.

"Yes, well, nevertheless," the Constable said, eyeing

Rye, "Earl Longchance takes the upbringing of the village's youth very seriously. Wayward children must be moulded early. Tamed. The Earl's sweat farm has been known to do wonders for the strong-willed child."

Mrs O'Chanter just stared at the Constable without blinking.

"This child," the Constable continued. "Where has it been today?"

Rye began picking her fingernails again behind her back.

"She has been with me since first light this morning. Working here in the shop."

Rye held her breath.

"All day you say?"

"Indeed."

"I see," Constable Boil said, tapping his bony chin. "Well, do keep your eyes open, Mrs O'Chanter. Roving bands of child thugs are a pox on us all. I shall certainly keep my eyes out for you."

"Thank you, but that won't be necessary."

"No bother. It will be my pleasure," he added with a leer.

The Constable turned to leave. Rye started to sigh in relief, but she caught her breath when the Constable stopped and pivoted on his heel.

"Oh, yes," he added, "since I'm here – it occurs to me that although Assessment does not officially commence until next week, I might as well have a look around now – to save a trip. You don't object, Mrs O'Chanter."

It couldn't possibly have been mistaken for a question.

"No, of course not," Mrs O'Chanter said.

"Splendid."

The Constable strolled around, hands behind his back as if shopping. He paused in the doorway and faced the street.

"As you know, it's illegal to feed pigs on Market Street. That's a fine of ten bronze bits."

"That's a bird feeder," Rye whispered to Mrs O'Chanter.

Mrs O'Chanter nudged her to stay quiet.

Constable Boil leaned outside and cast his watery eyes up over the door. Of all the weathered grey shops that lined Market Street, each adorned with drab and unremarkable signs, The Willow's Wares was the only one that flew a colourful flag. Colours had once been used as signals by certain unscrupulous characters, and the Earl now frowned on their overuse by anyone other than his tailors. That day, The Willow's Wares' flag was a rich forest-green, adorned with the white silhouette of a dragonfly.

"That flag is too bright," the Constable said, pointing to the green flag over The Willow's Wares' door. "Fifty bits."

Fifty bits! Rye's ears burned again.

Constable Boil shambled back inside. He approached Mrs O'Chanter and studied her closely, squinting under his dustball eyebrows.

"No woman may wear any article of blue without the express permission of the Honourable Earl Longchance."

Rye looked at the ribbon in Mrs O'Chanter's hair.

"Two shims," the Constable said, his tone severe. Then he smiled, revealing a mouth of nubby yellow teeth. "And you shall remove it."

"He's making that up," Rye whispered to Mrs O'Chanter too loudly.

"Riley," Mrs O'Chanter scolded under her breath.

Rye fumed. "This is—"

"Riley," Mrs O'Chanter interrupted, "why don't you go and clean up in the back until I finish."

"But—"

"Riley, now."

Rye heard the finality in Mrs O'Chanter's voice, so she turned and marched towards the storeroom. She gave Boil and the soldiers a glare as she passed through the curtain in the doorway. As soon as she had made it through, she quickly turned and peeled back a corner.

Normally, Mrs O'Chanter only sent Rye to the back when she was about to do something she thought Rye shouldn't see. Maybe she would loudly chastise the Constable and soldiers, letting everyone on Market Street know what they were up to. Rye hoped she would chase them out of the shop. Even though it was against the Laws of Longchance, Rye knew that Mrs O'Chanter kept a sharp boot knife strapped to her thigh under her dress. She called it Fair Warning. Rye had watched her chase away a gang of thieves once – one of them had almost lost a thumb. That was a lot of fun.

Instead, she heard Mrs O'Chanter say, "Of course, Constable Boil."

Rye frowned as Mrs O'Chanter untied the blue ribbon and handed it to the Constable. She removed the pins too and her dark hair fell past her shoulders as Boil pressed the ribbon into his pocket. Mrs O'Chanter unlocked a small chest and emptied a pouch of bronze bits into his hand.

Rye pulled away from the curtain and slumped down in a corner. She crossed her arms and her ears went scarlet with anger.

Even after all these years, it seemed her mother could still surprise her.

3

THE O'CHANTERS OF MUD PUDDLE LANE

THE O'CHANTERS' cottage was the largest on Mud Puddle Lane, which is not to say that it was big or fancy, just that it had three rooms instead of two, and an attic Rye wasn't allowed in any more, ever since the time she fell through the ceiling and nearly crushed her sister. It also had a secret workshop Rye wasn't supposed to know about, but did.

Mud Puddle Lane was on the northernmost side of town, which made for a long walk to Market Street and The Willow's Wares. It had a view of the salt bogs and, from the roof where Rye kept her pigeon coop, you could see the edge of Beyond the Shale, where towering, centuries-old pine trees swayed in the winds. Mud Puddle Lane was the one village street outside the town's protective walls.

An accident had destroyed its section of wall many years before and, for one reason or another, it was never rebuilt. Rye's mother wasn't a fan of walls anyway.

Many people wouldn't appreciate a view of the bogs, and most would prefer to live as far away from the forest's edge as possible. Mud Puddle Lane was known to be the first stop for any hungry beast that might crawl, slither or lurch from the trees. Bog Noblins were the most vile and malicious of the lot. Their jagged teeth and claws dripped with a disease, making their bites poisonous. Three heads taller than a full-grown man, with bulging, runny eyes and lice infested, red-orange hair in all the wrong places, they could bury themselves deep in the bogs and mudflats during the coldest days of winter and go months without eating. Unfortunately for Drowning, with spring came the hungry season.

Rye was too young to remember the last time a Bog Noblin ran loose in the village, but she'd heard the tales. It had begun with the disappearance of a few reclusive woodsmen and stray travellers – easily written off as a hungry bear or pack of wolves on the prowl. The livestock on remote farms went next, followed by the farmers themselves. Then the village children began to disappear. In some parts of town – all of them. None were ever seen again.

Luckily, that was all long ago. Nevertheless, once, after some implausible stories from her best friend, Folly Flood, Rye couldn't help but ask, "Mama, what about Beyond the Shale? Shouldn't we worry about monsters?"

To which Abby O'Chanter had replied, "Riley, have you ever seen a monster come out of the forest?"

"Well, no."

"There you go," Abby had said. Then, she'd added with a wink, "Besides, if one did, wouldn't you rather be the first to see it coming?"

"I suppose you're right," Rye had said. And that had been the end of those worries.

Still, that night at supper, Rye wasn't feeling particularly thrilled about where they lived, or anything else for that matter. She sat with her mother and her little sister Lottie at the big table by the fireplace, picking at the fleshy white meat in the cracked shells on her plate. Her place setting was remarkably tidy. Typically, when Rye was hungry, the table and floor looked like a pantry raided by squirrels.

"Sea bugs again?" Rye said. "I wish we could have something else."

Sea bugs washed ashore in piles each morning. They were brown and grey until you threw them into a boiling pot, then they screamed, turned red and fought with each other to escape. Rye felt no gratitude towards the deranged person who had first strolled along the sand and eaten one.

"Cackle fruit!" exclaimed Lottie, banging her spoon on the table. Rye wondered if Lottie would outgrow the banging – and the yelling and fussing – when she turned three. That was coming soon, but not soon enough.

"Eggs are for morning," Abby said. "Besides, something's been troubling the hens. They haven't laid all week."

"Uh-oh," said Lottie, bending her head over the big claw on her plate. As she pecked at it, her nest of red hair bounced and coarse strands flew out in all directions like a barn fire. Her hair was nothing like Rye's, which was brown and chopped short above her shoulders, or their mother's, which fell long, thick and black down her back.

"As for you," Abby said, pointing a spoon at Rye, "be thankful we have sea bugs and bread. You know we can't afford to eat beef or chicken every night."

"Well, we could…" Rye mumbled.

"And what do you mean by that?"

Rye bit her lip. "Nothing."

Abby always seemed to know when something was weighing on Rye's mind. Rather than cuff her, or warn her not to talk back, Abby usually tried to help. It wasn't easy being Rye. Abby seemed to know that.

"What is it, Riley? You've been upset all day."

"It's just… the Constable. He lied to us today. You knew he was making up laws and you didn't say anything."

Her mother nodded.

"Why not?" Rye said. "You let him treat us like we're stupid."

"Me no stupid, me Lottie," Lottie said. She made an angry face and pounded her fist on the table.

"Of course, Lottie," Abby said and patted her red tuft.

Abby looked back at Rye. "The Laws of Longchance, Riley. You know that we – women, girls – we're not supposed to know those things. We're not supposed to know how to read or write."

Unless you were a Daughter of Longchance, Rye thought, *in which case none of those laws applied*. Her mother had told her that there were other places where girls and women could do anything they wanted. Abby had grown up in one of those places. When Rye asked why they couldn't move there, Abby told her it was complicated. When she asked again, Abby said there were worse things than not being allowed to read or write. The third time, Abby sent her down to catch the basement wirry under The Willow's Wares.

"Those are stupid laws," Rye grumbled now, her ears turning pink.

"They are stupid, old-fashioned, terrible laws that need to be changed," Abby agreed. "And, as you know, I refuse to follow them—"

"L-O-T..." Lottie began, spelling her name. Abby pointed to her as if to say, see.

"But," Abby said, "that does not mean we should flaunt it. No good can come of letting the Constable or anyone else like him know what we do and do not know."

"But they took our coins."

"It's for Assessment, Riley. The fines are pooled for the good of the village," Abby said, without conviction.

It seemed to Rye that the 'good of the village' seldom

spilled over on to Mud Puddle Lane. They couldn't even get street lamps after dark like every other part of town.

"It's just a few silver shims, Riley. It could be much worse. Remember why the Constable came to the shop in the first place."

Rye crossed her arms. Her mother had a point.

"Now, enough of this talk in front of your sister," Abby said.

"Fine. But if I eat another bite of this sea bug I'm going to grow claws."

Rye frowned at the ugly, beady-eyed head staring at her from her plate.

"So be it," Abby said. "Give it to Shady."

Nightshade Fur Bottom O'Chanter was the thick ball of black fur curled up by the fireplace. Everyone called him Shady for short. He slept so close to the fire that Rye worried an ember would jump from the flame and set his bushy tail alight. Rolled up like that, you might easily mistake him for a bear cub, but Shady was in fact a cat, the largest and furriest anyone had ever seen. His fur was such a thick, luxurious black that he shone like velvet, and he was as warm as a wool blanket when he curled up on the girls' laps on a winter night. Shady didn't know his own strength, and sometimes, when he got too excited, had a tendency to play a little rough. All the O'Chanters had the scars to prove it.

"Shady go outside?" Lottie asked.

Shady opened a big yellow eye at the sound of that, peeking out from his fur as if he understood what the littlest O'Chanter had said.

"No, no, Lottie," Abby said, wagging a finger. "House Rule Number Two. Shady must never go outside."

"Why? Cats go play," Lottie said.

Which was true. Most cats roamed the streets and alleys of the village, skulking through the night, hunting all sorts of vermin.

"Too dangerous," Abby said. "No, no."

"No, no, no," Lottie said, wagging a finger at Shady who, foiled again, stretched and slunk off into the shadows.

"That's right, girls. Now, what's the rule? Say it with me," Abby said. And they did.

House Rule Number Two: He may run and he may hide, but Shady must never go outside.

"Good," Abby said. "Shady, get your whiskers out of there." She pushed his fluffy face away from her glass.

They all raised their drinks for the nightly toast.

"Welcome what tomorrow brings us," Abby said.

Abby drank cranberry wine out of her favourite goblet. Rye and Lottie drank from smaller matching ones, leaving big goat milk moustaches over their lips.

Getting Lottie O'Chanter to bed each night was no easy task. It took a lot of screaming and temper tantrums, and that was just from their mother. Finally, Lottie pulled on her nightdress and clambered into the bed she shared with Rye in their small room at the back of the house. She would never agree to sleep if she knew Rye was staying up, so Rye had to change into her own nightdress, climb into bed, and pretend she was going to sleep too.

Abby leaned over and kissed each of her girls goodnight.

"Mona, Mona," Lottie said, thrusting forward the worn doll she slept with every night. Mona Monster was a little pink hobgoblin with red polka dots. Abby had stitched it herself and stuffed it with straw straight after Lottie was born. Mona and Lottie had been inseparable ever since.

Abby kissed Mona on her toothy pink lips. "Bedtime, Lottie."

Lottie made Rye kiss Mona too.

"Now get some sleep," Abby said. "Don't let the bed bugs bite."

Lottie chomped her teeth and clutched the thin leather choker round her neck. A silver dragonfly charm and some runestones were strung on the black leather strand.

Lottie touched her finger to an identical choker round her mother's neck. Abby smiled.

"Yes, I have one too," Abby said.

Rye also wore a matching choker. They were usually well hidden under the clothes the O'Chanter girls wore during the day. Even Shady had a similar collar. The chokers were the subject of yet another House Rule.

House Rule Number Four: Worn under sun and under moon, never remove the O'Chanters' rune.

"Cherish it with your heart," Abby had told Rye many times. "It carries the luck of the O'Chanters and our ancestors. It will keep you safe when times are darkest."

"Time for sleep," Abby whispered now, gently folding Lottie's arms round Mona Monster.

Abby leaned over and whispered in Riley's ear, "I need to tend to some things outside. You listen for Lottie."

"OK, Mama," Rye said, and Abby blew out the beeswax candles. The room glowed from the light of the fireplace.

It took quite a bit of tossing and turning, a little foot in Rye's belly and a round bottom in her face before Lottie finally fell asleep. Rye slipped from under the covers and went into the main room of their cottage, where she sat by the hearth on the sweet-smelling herbs and grasses that her mother spread over the floorboards to keep the insects away.

Shady settled in her lap and Rye rubbed his big ears, covered with tufts of fur inside and out. These quiet times – sitting alone when Lottie was sleeping and Abby was off catching up with one task or another – were the hardest for her. Abby had been taking care of the girls by herself for as long as Rye could remember. Rye had no memories of her father. Abby said he was a soldier for the Earl. Ten years ago he had marched off with the army into Beyond the Shale. For a few months there'd been messages and letters, and then, one day, they stopped. Abby never said more about it, but Rye was old enough to know what that meant.

Lottie was a different story. Nobody seemed to know

who her father was. Nobody except their mother that is – and she wasn't telling.

The girls and the shop were a lot for anyone to handle alone, and Rye worried about her mother. Abby had been spending a lot of time out of the house at night. Maybe the night air helped clear her head. Rye knew Abby didn't like her venturing outdoors after dark, but Rye thought her mother might appreciate the company. She kissed Shady and placed him on the floor.

"You smell like wine," she said, wiping his whiskers. "Stay here."

She put on her cloak and pulled the hood over her head. She creaked the door open and peeked outside. In a neighbourhood of drab, grey houses, their shiny purple door always stood out. It was etched with a carving of a dragonfly that changed colour as the sun hit it at different times of the day. The dragonfly was black now, the street dark except for light from the thinnest sliver of moon.

"Stay here, Shady," she said again and pointed a finger at him. "Don't you dare wake up Lottie."

Rye carefully closed the door and slipped behind her house. Their goat and hens were asleep in their pens. In the distance, the bogs came to life as vapour rose off the water like ghosts. Her mother wasn't back there either.

Rye was about to climb the ladder to her pigeon coop to see if she had any messages. Rye and Folly had taught the pigeons to fly back and forth between their houses and sometimes they wrote messages and tied them to the birds' feet. But something stopped her in her tracks. Her heart nearly jumped out of her chest. Someone was already on the roof.

She stepped off the bottom rung of the ladder and pressed herself against the side of the house. She looked up again. The figure was in a cloak like hers. It was her mother. She was staring at the forest Beyond the Shale. She was perfectly still. It was like she was watching... waiting for something.

Abby didn't seem to see her. Rye held her breath as she tiptoed back towards the house, slow and easy. Then there was a loud, terrible sound. Rye jumped and looked for a place to hide. The sound was far away but not far enough. It was a cross between the shriek of a wild animal and the wail of a baby. She looked up. Her mother had heard it too. Abby leaned forward ever so slightly, looking through the mist, but remained in place.

The sound again. It felt like a thousand insects running up Rye's spine. She scrambled inside as fast as she could and slammed the door behind her.

SCUTTLEBUTT AND SECRET ROOMS

YE AND QUINN sat on the split-rail fence in front of the O'Chanters' house and watched the commotion on Mud Puddle Lane.

"Have you ever seen anything like it?" Rye asked, carefully wrapping her arms and legs round the rail.

"Not since they spotted that school of sharks in the river a few years back."

The village had woken up that morning to find the streets filled with wild turkeys. Hundreds of them, at least six flocks, had come out of the bogs during the night. Mud Puddle Lane buzzed with villagers. Armed with nets and axes, some using only their bare hands, they chased the lumbering, feathered creatures up and down the roads and alleys. Nobody on Mud Puddle Lane was about to let a free meal run away.

The neighbourhood rooks perched on a cottage roof and watched in disapproval, almost as if they were embarrassed by the whole unseemly affair.

"Do you think anyone will catch one?" Quinn asked.

"I'd think someone will. Sooner or later," Rye said. She flipped herself upside down, now dangling by her arms and legs from the fence like an exotic pet she'd once seen by the docks. The sailor who owned it called it a sloth.

"Shall we try?"

"My mother said not to bother. She left for The Willow's Wares early this morning. Brought Lottie with her. She seemed a little distracted."

Rye wondered how many nights her mother had spent sitting up on their roof. Had the terrible wail from the bogs rattled her the same way it had Rye? Rye found it easy enough to push the sound out of her head this morning, with the light of day and the routine of her regular chores, but her mother's nervous energy and the commotion in the streets had her thinking about the eerie noise again.

"Did you hear anything strange outside last night?" Rye asked.

"With my father's snoring?" Quinn said. "I can't even hear the roosters crow. Why, did you?"

"I thought I heard something screaming. Or crying. Hard to say."

"It wasn't Lottie?"

"Not this time."

One of Rye's neighbours leaped for a turkey and fell chestfirst in the mud. The big, clumsy bird flapped its wings and landed on the man's roof. Rye and Quinn laughed. Rye's laughter broke her grip, her flailing legs found Quinn's ribs, and they both crashed to the ground.

"Are you OK?" Quinn said, rubbing his side.

Rye rolled over and struggled to catch her breath. "Fine," she wheezed.

They both looked at each other, then back to the turkey chasers, and began laughing again.

Rye's laughter trailed off as she considered what might have inspired the turkeys to leave the bogs and take their chances with the villagers' carving forks.

"They're hopeless," Quinn said. "Let's go and read – I brought a surprise."

*

Paintings of mermaids, adventurers and monsters covered a wall by the O'Chanters' fireplace. As proud as Abby was of her daughters' talent, she hung the girls' paintings for another purpose. The artwork covered a hidden door that slid open if you pushed it in the right way. The door led to a few shallow steps and Abby O'Chanter's secret workshop. At least Rye assumed it was secret, because her mother never mentioned it to her and she had never, ever, seen her mother go in. Then again, Abby had never told Rye to stay out of the workshop, so technically Rye wasn't breaking any House Rules. Regardless, Rye certainly wouldn't be telling Lottie about it any time soon; her sister ruined all the best hiding places.

Rye and Quinn sat at the heavy wooden table that nearly filled the small, sunken room, careful not to disturb the tools, beads and half-finished jewellery. Shady was curled up in a big black ball underneath it. If it hadn't been for him, Rye would never have known about the workshop in the first place. One day she had seen Shady sniffing the floor and pawing at Lottie's sketch of Mona Monster in a princess dress. Then, right in front of her eyes, he disappeared into the wall as if it had swallowed him up. It was amazing what kinds of surprises your own house could hold.

Rye and Quinn huddled round a lantern and a thick book – *Tam's Tome of Drowning Mouth Fibs, Volume II*. Quinn said that the angry poet had collected *Tam's Tome* after Rye had dropped it, but he'd been forced to stash it in a chimney before climbing down to answer the Constable's questions. Quinn had taken it upon himself to save *Tam's Tome* from nesting birds and chimney fires. Rye was impressed. That was like something she or Folly might try.

"What do you think the poet will do when he finds out it's missing?" Quinn asked.

"No idea," Rye said. "He didn't get a good look at us, so he can't just come knocking on our doors. It wouldn't be safe to report it missing, so I doubt he'll risk telling anyone."

"Probably not," Quinn said, chewing his lip.

"We should keep it safe," Rye said. *And read as much of it as we can*, she thought.

"I guess so…" Quinn said.

"Good," Rye said, before he could change his mind.

"We'll keep it at your house," she added quickly.

Quinn and his father lived just three cottages down from the O'Chanters. Their walls were already bursting with Quinn's books and his father's cluttered assortment of weapons that could crush your bones or separate you from your limbs. Angus Quartermast was a blacksmith with hammer-forged arms and a brow that seemed permanently furrowed, but he always had kind words for Rye and her mother. Quinn had lost his own mother to the Shivers years before and neither Quinn nor his father had turned out to be much of a housekeeper. At the Quartermasts' house, there was always a fine line between hidden and lost.

Quinn, unlike his father, was still so skinny that he had to use a rope belt to hold up his trousers. He had a tendency to forget things, like his lunch, or the shopping list, or sometimes his way home. But Quinn was also kind, and he was one of Rye's best friends in the whole world. Three times a week, he brought over a book and helped her with her reading.

Now, with time to examine *Tam's Tome* more carefully, they noticed that many of its pages were burned, torn

49

or missing completely, and its binding was covered in soot. Its contents, however, were like no book they had ever seen. Page after page was hand-scrawled in letters of varying sizes. Throughout the book, the text was packed so tightly that the thin slivers of parchment not covered by ink seemed to form phantom images all their own. Rye tried to make them out, but it was like spotting faces in storm clouds – lose your focus for just a moment and they were gone.

"We should see if there's anything about cries from the bogs," Rye said, and by 'we' she meant Quinn. She was still learning to wrestle with ordinary-sized letters.

Quinn sighed as he squinted to read the actual words. "This is going to take some time."

Fortunately, the maze of prose was occasionally broken up by the most detailed and lifelike drawings Rye had ever seen, and Rye and Quinn spent their time studying the illustrations. There were portraits of people she didn't recognise and maps of places she had never been. Creatures, both whimsical and menacing, seemed to leap off the page.

One image, however, plunged them both into silence.

It was vaguely human, its orange hair hanging in long, knotted ropes from a skull that looked to have been broken and carelessly reassembled. Sickly skin clung to its ribs and hung in loose folds from its face. Cold eyes conveyed anger and sadness, and there was something both ancient and childlike in its expression. Dwarfed in its bony fingers was a child's tattered rag doll; around its neck was a string of small, shrivelled feet. A Bog Noblin!

Rye shuddered and turned the page quickly, pressing her hand against the opposite side, as if the awful image might claw its way out. Quinn didn't object.

They had been leafing through *Tam's Tome* for much of the morning when Shady's ears perked up and he lifted his furry mane. Someone was coming. Rye and Quinn cast wary looks at Shady, then each other. Quinn hunched forward and tried to shield *Tam's Tome* under his arms.

The secret door opened. Rosy cheeks and big blue eyes beamed in the lantern light.

"Folly," Rye said with relief, "where have you been? There are some amazing things in this book."

"It's been a crazy day," Folly said, pulling up a chair. "Did you know turkeys have taken over your street?"

"They came out of the bogs last night," Quinn said.

"It's really busy at the inn," Folly said. "I had to help my mum get ready for tonight's Black Moon Party – got to hang Wirry Scares on the street."

Folly's family owned the Dead Fish Inn, the most notorious tavern in the Shambles. It was rumoured that, with enough grommets, you could buy anything at the Dead Fish. The Floods lived on the third floor over the guest rooms – Folly being the youngest of nine children, the rest of them boys. Her brothers were said to be the toughest in the village, which was good, because patrons of the Dead Fish were infamous for fighting, carousing and causing all sorts of commotion. Rye envied Folly. The Dead Fish was far more exciting than Mud Puddle Lane, and all the wild turkeys in the world couldn't change that.

Folly slapped her hands on the table. "You'll never guess what I heard over breakfast."

As usual, she didn't wait for them to guess.

"Two men came into the Inn this morning. They weren't villagers. They looked dirty and tired, and they had weapons. Lots of them. They said they hadn't slept in days."

Rye and Quinn's ears perked up.

"I heard them telling my father that they'd just come in from Beyond the Shale. While they were there they saw…" Folly paused, the words stuck in her throat.

"They saw what?" Rye asked.

"What was it?" said Quinn.

"A Bog Noblin," Folly gasped, with a heaping of alarm and a smidge of excitement.

"You're just winding us up," Rye said. "They're extinct."

"It's true."

"In the forest?" Quinn asked.

"No," Folly said. "Out there."

She tilted her head in the direction they all knew the bogs to be. Rye and Quinn looked at each other in disbelief.

"Stop it, Folly," Rye said. "That's bogwash. You're just trying to get us in a twist."

But Rye knew Folly wasn't teasing them. She heard the concern in Folly's voice.

Quinn now wore his worry on his face. He flipped the pages of *Tam's Tome* and pointed to the open page. The Bog Noblin with the necklace of feet stared back.

Quinn frowned like he'd swallowed a damp mouse.

"Ugh. He's a knotty-looking one, isn't he?" Folly said.

The drawing made Rye's stomach hurt. She closed the book. "It's just tavern talk, Folly," she said matter-of-factly. "There's no such thing as Bog Noblins any more."

The three friends were quiet. Quinn squirmed uncomfortably in his chair.

"You'll still come to the party tonight, won't you?" Folly asked Rye finally.

Rye had always wanted to go to a Black Moon Party. She'd heard that villagers roamed the streets in garish clothes, carousing until sunrise. Of course, these days the Laws of Longchance brought curfews, fines and floggings, which put a damper on celebrations of the first new moon each month. And there was also that pesky O'Chanters' House Rule Number Three.

House Rule Number Three: Lock your door with the Black Moon's rise. Don't come out until morning shines.

"Maybe," Rye said. "I'll have to wait for my mother to leave the house."

Her mother had arranged some sort of Black Moon sale at The Willow's Wares for special customers that night.

She'd told Rye she'd need her to watch Lottie and Shady after they had gone to bed, but that she would be home as quickly as she could. If her mother was breaking the House Rule, so could Rye.

"You have to," Folly implored. "This is no ordinary Black Moon Party. I heard—"

Rye and Quinn prepared for another tall tale.

"—that there's going to be a secret meeting about…" She looked over her shoulder as if someone might be listening. "The Luck Uglies," she mouthed.

'Luck Uglies' was a name whispered around the docks and darkest taverns, places where men played fast and loose with the laws and their lips. Calling someone a 'cockle knocker' or a 'shad' might get a child's tongue tamed with a horse brush. But 'Luck Uglies' uttered in the wrong company could earn you a week in the stocks. Of course, like all children, Rye had heard Luck Ugly stories – usually round a fire after dark, or at a graveyard's edge as the salt mist crept over the tombs – but never from her mother. Folly's older brothers told one about a Luck Ugly who sharpened his teeth into fangs with a grindstone and fed on village vagrants after dark. Quinn's father once told him that he'd better eat his cabbage or the Luck Uglies would come to take his dog while he slept.

It was the Luck Uglies who, ten years before, finished off the last of the Bog Noblins shortly before disappearing themselves. Neither group had been particularly missed.

"Luck Uglies?" Rye repeated quietly.

Folly nodded with great enthusiasm. "Maybe it has something to do with the Bog Noblin."

Quinn rolled his eyes. "When is the meeting to discuss witches and sea monsters?" he asked with an uneasy chuckle.

"I'm coming," Rye said, making up her mind. Talk of Bog Noblins and Luck Uglies, real or imagined, was too good to miss.

"What about you, Quinn?" Folly asked.

"I don't think my father would like that."

"Parents aren't supposed to like what we do," Folly said. "That's their job."

Quinn bit his lip and thought hard, but shook his head.

"Are you sure?" Rye asked him. "We could go over together."

She hoped for the company. She'd never been to the

Shambles after dark, but she'd heard… things. The Shambles was the one part of town where the Laws of Longchance weren't enforced – the one place where the Earl's soldiers dared not tread. Nobody really lived there except the transient shadow brokers who were laying low, biding time or hatching plans, and people like the Floods who profited from them.

"I don't think so," Quinn said.

"What's wrong, Quinn?" Folly said. "Are you afraid the Luck Uglies might get you?"

"No," Quinn said quickly. "There's no such thing as Luck Uglies any more, right, Rye?"

"Right," Rye mumbled, not sounding particularly convincing.

"Of course there isn't," Folly said. "Just like there are no more Bog Noblins." She squinted and eyed Rye and Quinn carefully. "You're positive you haven't seen anything out in those bogs?"

"Nothing," Quinn said, his eyes wide. "Have you, Rye?"

Rye shook her head. She hadn't seen anything. But she was sure she had heard something last night. A sound like nothing she had ever heard before.

5

BLACK MOON RISING

THAT NIGHT, LOTTIE went down without a fuss. Rye couldn't have been more surprised. Lottie snuggled up with Mona Monster and began snoring fitfully under the covers as soon as Abby blew out the candles. Rye didn't even need to lie down with her. Abby stoked the fire in the girls' fireplace and they both slipped quietly from the room.

Shady, on the other hand, was not in a restful mood. He paced the house like a caged bugbear, pawing at the floor and yowling. He climbed up their legs with his long claws. Finally, Abby locked him in her own bedroom.

When Abby returned from her room, she was dressed in her heavy cloak, ready to leave.

"I don't know what's got into him," she said.

Rye watched her mother throw a thick pack over her shoulder. Abby had washed her face and tied her hair in a neat ponytail. Rye held back a smile – Abby had used another blue hair ribbon. Rye thought her mother was quite beautiful despite her old age – she was almost thirty-one. The way folk around the village looked at Abby, they must have thought so too.

"Whose shoes are these?" Abby asked.

"Quinn's," Rye said.

"How does someone forget his shoes?"

Abby didn't wait for an answer. Rye could see in her mother's body the same anxious energy that was setting Shady on edge tonight.

"Now, Riley, I need you to listen for Lottie, understand? If she wakes up, you take good care of her."

"Yes, Mama."

Abby was preparing a lantern. "It's very important that you stay inside. This is not a night for children to be traipsing about, not even in the yard. Don't go and fuss with those pigeons. What's House Rule Number Three?"

"*Lock your door with the Black Moon's rise,*" Rye sang,

rolling her eyes. "*Don't come out until morning shines.*"

Abby smiled and knelt down.

"I do realise I'm telling you to stay inside while I pack a bag," she said. "But this is an important meeting with some very special customers. They only make it around this way once or twice a year. I'll be home as soon as I can."

Rye furrowed her brow. "Just… be careful."

Abby smiled and touched Rye's cheek. "I'll be fine, my darling. There's nothing to worry about."

"You're not worried about…" Rye's voice trailed off.

"About what?"

Rye picked her fingernails. "Folly said someone saw a Bog Noblin in the bogs. Could it be true?"

"I adore Folly as much as you do, but you must admit she's never heard a story she couldn't embellish."

Her mother's answer was no answer at all.

"But," Rye said, "is it possible? I thought there were no Bog Noblins left."

"You were still crawling the last time a Bog Noblin threatened this village. Don't fret over them now."

Rye wanted to ask about the terrible noise she'd heard but, given what she had planned for the evening, she thought it better not to mention that she'd been in the yard just the night before – well intentioned or not.

Abby was almost ready now. Rye had run out of fingernails to pick. Something else remained on her mind.

"Mama," Rye said. "What about the Luck Uglies? Are you worried about them?"

Abby flinched, as if Rye had pricked her with a pin. She seemed to catch herself and resumed lacing her boots.

"Riley, dear, why would I be worried about them?"

"Well, the Black Moon. Isn't that when they come out?"

"Where did you hear such a thing?"

Rye shrugged. "I don't know... around. I think I read it somewhere."

She hadn't got to that bit in *Tam's Tome* yet, but everyone knew the Luck Uglies once prowled the village on Black Moons, the darkest nights of every month. They wore frightening masks to conceal their real identities, stalking the streets in small packs or flying from the rooftops like bats.

"Darling, you don't need to worry about any Luck Uglies any more," Abby said, standing up. "They're gone. Forever. Earl Longchance made sure of that." Her voice was flat.

Still, Rye was worried. She vividly remembered her fleeting glimpse of the masked gargoyle on the rooftops. She harboured no illusion that it was a statue come to life, nor a mere figment of her imagination. Could it have been a Luck Ugly?

Abby picked up her lantern and pulled the cloak of her hood over her head.

"Riley," she said, "follow the House Rules and I assure you that no Bog Noblin or Luck Ugly will ever trouble this family."

The way she said it, Rye couldn't help but believe her.

Abby opened the front door and carefully covered her lantern with a sheath to dim the light. A chilly wind rushed in from outside. In her cloak and hood, Rye's mother was almost unrecognisable. The pinched rise in her shoulders seemed to soften. Her eyes flickered with excitement under her hood. In Abby's room, Shady scratched at the door furiously.

"You may want to leave Shady in there. I don't know what's got into him."

She blew Rye a kiss with her hand. Rye pretended to catch it.

"Be good, my love," Abby said, and disappeared into the night.

"I don't know about this," Quinn said.

"Don't worry about it," Rye said. "Lottie's fast asleep. She never wakes up once she's gone down."

Rye was determined to meet Folly at the Dead Fish Inn, but didn't want to leave Lottie alone. It had taken a lot of convincing, but Quinn had agreed to come over and stay at the O'Chanters' house until Rye returned. Rye and Quinn had signalled to each other with their lanterns when Abby had gone and Angus was asleep, and then Quinn ran down the street.

"Aren't you afraid to go out?" Quinn said.

"You made it, didn't you?" Rye said.

"I'm only three houses away. You're going to the other side of the village."

"I'll be fine," Rye said, trying to convince herself. She pulled her cloak round her shoulders and her hood over her head. "Thanks for your help, Quinn."

"You owe me. And hurry back. How am I going to explain this if your mother gets home before you?"

Rye grabbed her lantern. "I won't be late. Remember, don't let Shady out."

Rye herself had never been out on the Black Moon. It was forbidden for women and children under the Laws of Longchance. Normally it was a half-hour walk to Folly's house. Rye intended to go as fast as she could to minimise her time on the streets.

Mud Puddle Lane was dark under the best of circumstances, never mind with no moon in the sky. Rye kept her lantern lit at first, although she planned to cover it as soon as possible. She could hear voices and laughter behind the doors, but the dirt street was empty. She could smell tangy-sweet hickory fires from the chimneys; someone was cooking a celebratory treat.

When she reached the end of her road, she stepped carefully over the crumbled section of the village's wall, now overgrown with weeds and moss. Rye and Quinn played on the wall every day, so she was able to navigate it well, even in the dark.

After Mud Puddle Lane, she crossed into Nether Neck and Old Salt Cross, where the open spaces between houses closed and the cobblestone streets narrowed. In Old Salt

Cross the second and third floors of buildings jutted over the streets like tree limbs in a dense forest. Street lamps, though sparse, lit the corners and she was able to dim her lantern. Rye stayed in the shadows, darting from one alley to the next. Other people roamed the village, although most moved silently and alone. Rye avoided everyone. If someone approached, she stepped into a doorway until he passed. There were short cuts to Folly's, but she intended to stay away from Market Street at all costs. Running into her mother would be scarier than getting snatched by a Bog Noblin.

Rye picked up her pace as she grew more comfortable with the darkness. Skipping from cobblestone to cobblestone, she imagined herself leaping across the rooftops. She gave herself a shiver, wondering whether there was a masked gargoyle up there watching her right now.

She leaped over puddles and flew from an alley on to Dread Captain's Way when the tall figure stopped her in her tracks. Rye fell backwards on to her bottom and her lantern hit the ground with a rattle. Its flame flickered and died.

The figure loomed over her in its dark robes, orange eyes glowing like fire.

6

THE WIRRY SCARE

RYE PROTECTED HER face with her hands and peered through her fingers. Spidery wrists stretched from billowing black sleeves, long claws poised to pluck out her eyeballs. Its sharp-toothed mouth scowled down at her from its pumpkin head. Its face was carved like that of a feral cat, with whiskers and angular eyes whose glow came from the candle inside.

Rye lowered her hands. The claws were nothing more than branches, the menacing figure just a Wirry Scare mounted on a tall wooden frame. Apparently wirries weren't the only things these stickmen frightened. It meant she wasn't far from the Dead Fish Inn. Maybe Folly helped put up this one herself.

Rye straightened her clothes and scolded herself for

being so easily spooked. Before she could rise, she heard the shuffling of boots, the clinking of metal on stone, and a voice yelling, "Did you hear that? It came from over there."

The source of the voice hurried towards her. Rye looked for somewhere to hide. She lurched forward and rolled under an abandoned farmer's wagon filled with rotting hay. It wasn't a moment too soon, as three figures emerged from the alley she'd used.

Rye pressed herself flat on the cold, damp cobblestones. Villagers were not the tidiest folk. She was surrounded by rotting vegetables, other rubbish and an old shoe. She pinched her nose and peered through the spokes of the wagon's one large wheel.

A man in a brown cloak led the way, scurrying out of the alley like a crab. He was bent and bow-legged, but moved much faster than one would expect given his rickety looks. Behind him lumbered two heavily armoured soldiers, one carrying an enormous axe over his shoulder. They wore the black and blue crest of the House of Longchance on their shields – an iron fist and a coiled, eel-like serpent displaying a gaping maw of teeth. Their armour sounded like Lottie when she got loose amongst Abby O'Chanter's pots and pans. Rye had never seen, or heard, soldiers armoured so heavily in the village.

The man in front peered through the shadows.

"Bring the light," he called. "Where are you, rat?"

From the alley, a much smaller person appeared carrying a large lantern. The link rat's light rattled as he ran. Rye had never met a link rat before, but she'd heard about them from Folly. Link rats were children – usually orphans – paid to guide travellers through Drowning's streets after dark. It sounded like terribly dangerous work for a child, but if one got lost, hurt or stolen, well, there was always a replacement. Orphans weren't hard to come by in Drowning. Rye knew Quinn had suffered from nightmares about becoming a link rat ever since he'd lost his mother. It was why he clung so tightly to his father's side.

When this particular link rat caught up with the other men, Rye saw that he was not much taller than her. His clothes hung in tatters off his narrow shoulders and his straight black hair fell past his ears. Rye also got a better look at the first man's face squinting in the light. She recognised the dustball eyebrows. It was Constable Boil.

"Over here," the Constable said, waving to the link rat. "What's that?"

The link rat moved forward, casting the lantern light on the Wirry Scare. Boil's feet scuffled forward and the clank of armoured boots stopped less than a metre from Rye's nose. From under the wagon, Rye could only see their legs.

"Another one," Boil growled. "Superstitious simpletons. Chop it down."

Rye watched one of the soldiers brace himself and listened to the chop of the axe. She flinched as the Wirry Scare creaked and splintered.

"You," Boil said to the other soldier, "keep your eyes peeled. I heard noises over here."

Rye held her breath and watched the soldier's feet circle round the wagon. The link rat seemed to have noticed something on the ground. Constable Boil's feet shuffled round the wagon in the opposite direction. She was surrounded on all sides. When she turned back, her heart nearly jumped out of her chest.

The link rat was just a boy, probably not much older

than Rye. His eyes stared into hers without blinking, irises reflecting strange colours in the dim lantern light. Then he looked towards Rye's own lantern, which lay on its side where she had dropped it, in plain view on the street not far from where the Constable and soldiers were now searching. He turned back towards her again. Rye shook her head, placed her palms together and pleaded with him silently. Her efforts seemed lost on him. It was like he wasn't looking at her, but through her.

Finally, the boy lifted his index finger as if he was going to point her out to the Constable. Instead, he raised it to his lips – for quiet. With his foot, he gently slid Rye's lantern under the wagon, hiding it out of sight.

"Boy!" yelled the Constable. "Don't just stand there, bring the light round."

The link rat glanced in Rye's direction one last time and then moved on, following the Constable's instructions.

There was another chop, then a loud crack, and the Wirry Scare collapsed into a heap on the street. Its pumpkin head rolled off its frame and landed centimetres from Rye's face. It exploded with a splat as a soldier's steel boot crushed it with a mighty stomp. *Blech*, Rye thought.

It was going to take forever to wash pumpkin guts out of her hair.

"Let's go," Boil barked. "There are plenty more of those dreadful stickmen to be found."

Rye listened as Boil and the soldiers continued down the street. Only when they sounded far enough away did she crawl out from under the wagon. She watched the link rat's lantern light disappear as the patrol turned a corner. She wondered why the boy had put himself at risk to help her. What a terrible way to spend the night, trudging around in the cold being bullied by the Constable and those two knot-headed soldiers.

Rye considered turning round and going back home to Mud Puddle Lane. But she was closer to Folly's house than her own. She wasn't going to waste any more time sneaking around in the shadows. Rye grabbed her lantern, looked both ways, and ran right down the middle of Dread Captain's Way as fast as her legs would take her.

Mutineer's Alley wasn't an alley at all, but a set of steep stone steps that led down from Dread Captain's Way in the village proper to the dirt streets, shops and taverns of the Shambles. Ordinarily, it was hard to find unless you were looking for it. But on the night of the Black Moon, two Wirry Scares beckoned from either side of the archway and open torches lit the entrance. Paper lanterns trimmed into grotesque faces lined each step, creating a sinister glowing path down to the banks of the River Drowning.

Rye took a deep breath and started to go down. There was no turning back now.

The main street in the Shambles was a mud walkway called Little Water Street that ran parallel with the river's bank. It was much busier than the streets Rye had travelled in the village itself. People milled about alone or in groups, both men and women, and no one seemed surprised to see a young girl walking alone after dark. Rye remembered some advice her mother had given her once: *Walk strong, act like you belong, and no one will be the wiser.*

Rye pulled her cloak and hood tightly round her and moved with purpose. Catching the eyes of a passer-by, she nodded curtly and kept walking.

Those on the streets of the Shambles wore colourful cloaks in hues Rye almost never saw in the rest of the village – bold reds, rich greens and vibrant purples. People kept to themselves, which is not to say they were quiet. She heard a woman laugh as she and her companion stumbled arm in arm into a dark alley. A gimpy man dragged a wooden leg behind him with a *step-tap-step-tap*.

The shopkeepers were busy even at this late hour, their windows flung open to entice customers in. An artist with a needle tattooed the enormous back of a shirtless man, who grimaced and sipped his ale with every pinch. A shyster played a shell game for bronze bits, making a small blue stone disappear and reappear under halved coconut shells through sleight of hand.

The commotion grew as Rye reached the end of the street. Wandering into the dense crowd, she looked up. In the shadow of the village's most impressive structure – the great arched bridge that spanned the River Drowning – rose a brooding building made of heavy timber and stone. Candles burned in each window and the revellers spilled down the front steps and caroused in the glowing street. Rye had never seen the Dead Fish Inn this busy before. Boisterous conversations floated through the air and over the river, where Rye could see lights bobbing on the water. Boats and rafts filled the docks tonight. Given all the unfamiliar flags, Rye suspected they'd sailed from towns far upriver to join the festivities.

Wind gusted off the water into Rye's face and set the black flag flapping over the inn's massive, iron-studded doors, the white fish bone logo swimming against the breeze. Rye always found it curious that an inn would need doors so thick. Two hulking guards stood watch at the front, joined together from the waist down by some dark magic. Their identical faces, under thick mops of white-blond hair, scrutinised all who tried to pass. Rye knew the intimidating guardians to be Folly's twin brothers, Fitz and Flint, who, since birth, had shared a single pair of legs. They had the final say over who was allowed passage in or out of the Dead Fish. With their keen eyes and quick fists, there was no sneaking past them. Fortunately, Rye knew another way inside.

She slipped unnoticed down a darkened walkway and tiptoed through the alley behind the inn, taking care to be quiet until she tripped over a body on the ground.

"Ouch," a voice grumbled, and a dirty hand grabbed Rye's leg.

"Baron Nutfield?" Rye whispered. "Is that you?"

"Yes!" The voice smelled of ale and onions.

"Let go of my leg and go back to sleep," Rye said.

He did.

Baron Nutfield was the old man who lived in the alley behind the Dead Fish. He actually lived in a guest room, but the Flood boys threw him in the alley whenever he failed to pay his bill. He spent more time outside the Dead Fish than in it. He claimed to be a nobleman in a county far to the south, but he never seemed able to find his way back there.

Rye reached down and picked up a pebble. She looked up at the third floor and counted three windows over from the left. Taking aim, she threw the pebble and it bounced off the glass with a rattle.

Nothing happened.

She picked up another, larger stone and tried again. This time it went clear through the glass.

"Pigshanks," Rye whispered.

Her mother would scrub her tongue with soap if she heard her use language like that, but Rye was pretty sure Baron Nutfield didn't mind.

"Hey!" an angry voice called from above. A man's head

jutted out of the broken window, but he couldn't see her in the dark.

Maybe it was three from the right, Rye thought.

"Here," Baron Nutfield said. He reached up and handed Rye another stone. "Put a little more arc on it this time."

Rye tossed the stone at the window three from the right.

A lantern blazed to life. The window creaked open and a rope ladder slowly slid down the wall.

THE DEAD FISH INN

"You're filthy," Folly said.

"It was a long walk."

"Is that sick in your hair?" Folly asked.

"Pumpkin. Long story," Rye said. "I like your dress."

"Thanks," Folly said, and did a little twirl. "Mum let me wear it for the Black Moon Party."

It was dark-green velvet with gold trim. Like Rye, Folly didn't wear dresses very often.

Folly's room was small, but it was her own. She didn't have to share one like her brothers did. It was decorated with glass bottles of all shapes and sizes, each filled with a colourful concoction of potential ingredients – frogspawn, belladonna blooms, dollops of earwax. Folly was always trying to make magical potions. They never worked, but

Rye gave her credit for trying. Folly's parents didn't seem to mind. With eight sons and a whole inn to run, they hardly noticed the chemical fires and pungent fumes wafting from their daughter's room.

"Are you ready?" Folly asked.

Rye nodded. This was going to make the whole trip worthwhile.

"OK," Folly said. "Stay close to me and try not to draw attention to yourself. My father will be too busy to notice, and nobody else will care that we're here."

"Got it," Rye said.

Folly opened her door and they stepped into the hall. Sound and heat roared from below. The four-storey inn was open from floor to ceiling, with a central staircase leading from one level to the next. Rye and Folly walked to the edge of the railing and peeked down. Hanging from the beamed ceiling, fixed with an anchor chain, was a chandelier fashioned from the sun-bleached skeleton of some long-extinct sea monster. Its bones were covered with hundreds of beeswax candles that bathed the inn in the glow of soft light.

All the tables were filled and people stood shoulder

to shoulder at the bars. Barmaids pushed through the crowds, delivering trays of mugs and goblets that seemed to make everyone happier. A huge black shark roasted on a spit over the stone fireplace. Its jaws, filled with sharp teeth, were wide enough to fit a person inside. Every now and then a barmaid would cut off a piece, slap it on a plate, and deliver it to a hungry patron. With each cut, the juices of the shark steak dripped into the fire, sending flames shooting into the air, and everyone would cheer.

"Come on," Folly said, and they took the stairs down to the second floor.

The second floor was busier than the third. Guests made their way in and out of their rooms, some disappearing behind latched doors. Over the noise of the crowd, Rye could hear music. There were drums, maybe a lute. Rye was spellbound by the festivities. She crossed her legs and leaned her head against the railing, soaking in the sights and sounds.

The Dead Fish drew an unusual crowd. Unlike most villagers, these people looked like they had been places and done things. Gambling was everywhere – drinkers bet on who could empty their mugs the fastest, or who might fit the most spiders in his mouth. A card game was heating up at a table in the corner. A man with slicked-back hair and a small black monkey on his shoulder seemed to be doing most of the winning. The monkey shuffled the cards and collected the bronze bits after every hand the man won. At one point someone accused the monkey of cheating. Insults were traded. Someone got bitten.

Folly's father, Fletcher, served behind the main bar, which made him the most popular person at the inn. His hands never stopped working and his gap-toothed smile never left his face. He strung grommets, shims and bits on the leather coin belt round his waist as quickly as the customers dropped them on the bar. On the shelf behind him, the bottom chamber of a tall hourglass slowly filled with black sand. Rye had never seen anything quite like it. On what kind of beach could you find black sand?

If Fletcher Flood was the most popular person at the Dead Fish, it seemed to Rye that the man at the Mermaid's Nook wasn't far behind. The Mermaid's Nook was the best table in the house. It was the closest to the main fireplace and it sat higher than the others in a semi-private corner with a view of the entire inn. Folly told Rye it was her favourite because of the beautiful, life-sized mermaid that was carved into the wooden table top.

The man at the Mermaid's Nook had a short, stubbly beard flecked with grey, and dark hair that was long but not unkempt. His nose, though bent, seemed at home between his cheeks. He had more than a few scars. Several ran through his eyebrows and another across his throat. His eyes flashed with delight, or was it wariness? Rye's eyes followed the man's as they scanned the inn, seeming to take inventory of everything in it. His eyes found Rye's, and she looked away until she felt them move on.

The woman at his table had her back to Rye. Her dress, the colour of fresh cranberries, showed off her soft, white shoulders. Rye watched as every few minutes someone would stop at the Mermaid's Nook to greet the man and his companion. Visitors would shake his hand, heartily slap his back, or almost timidly touch his shoulder. When he waved or reached across to say hello, Rye could see the green tattoos that began above the leather bracelets criss-crossing his wrists. They snaked their way up his forearms and disappeared beneath his sleeves. His silver rings and the chains round his neck glinted when they caught the light. He seemed apologetic after each visitor left, and he would lean forward and whisper something to the woman at the table.

"Folly, there you are," said a voice. "Oh. Hello, Rye."

It was Fifer Flood, the nicest of Folly's brothers.

"Hi, Fifer," Rye said.

Fifer was thirteen and, for some reason, Rye always found herself blushing when he was around.

"Folly, be a love and bring these down to Mum, would you?" Fifer asked. He handed her an armful of bar rags. "I need to get back to cleaning room seven. The sword swallower had a terrible mishap. There'll be no second show this evening, I'm afraid."

Folly crinkled her nose and took the rags.

"Thanks," Fifer said. "You two stay out of trouble."

Rye shadowed Folly's steps down the last flight of stairs to the main floor of the inn. A young, straw-haired bartender spotted them, but just smiled and waved them over. It was Jonah, a friend of the twins. He was always kind to Rye and Folly and let them sip the honey mead when no one was looking.

"You two up to mischief?" he asked.

Why did everyone always jump to that conclusion?

"No. Well… maybe," Folly said with a smile. "Don't tell my dad."

Jonah pursed his lips and buttoned them with his fingers. "I doubt he'll notice anyway," he said. "This is the busiest Black Moon we've seen in years. The Bog Noblin chatter has everyone on edge. Folk get thirsty when their nerves are frayed."

"Are you nervous, Jonah?" Rye asked.

"I'm scared they'll string me up if we run out of ale. But scared of Bog Noblins? No, not me." He raised an eyebrow. "Did you come here to talk about them too? Try over there." He pointed to where a small crowd had gathered round a tall man in a corner.

"Jonah," Folly said, a hint of conspiracy in her voice. "Has anyone said anything about… Luck Uglies?" Out of habit, she peeked over her shoulder when she said it.

Jonah snorted and tugged the tuft of beard on his chin. "People are saying all sorts of foolish things. We've been down that road before. Asking the Luck Uglies to solve your problems is like letting wasps in the kitchen to get rid of your flies. Once the flies are gone, who do you think the wasps will sting?"

He snapped a bar rag at them playfully. Rye and Folly giggled nervously as they moved on.

"What was that supposed to mean?" Rye asked Folly when they were beyond earshot.

"Beats me, but I'm staying out of the kitchen for a while," she said, and they both giggled again.

Folly and Rye darted between hips and thighs as they worked their way towards the corner Jonah had indicated. They stopped at the smaller side bar where Faye Flood rinsed dirty goblets at a furious pace in a trough of brownish water.

"Here, Mum," Folly said.

She dropped the stack of dirty rags on the bar.

Faye flipped back the lone streak of grey in her blonde hair, which hung down in front of her face. She gave a quick smile and a wave and returned to her chores. Her face was round and pretty, but Rye noticed that the years of scrubbing had left her hands thick and weathered.

Eventually, they found their way to the corner where a tall, bearded fellow with some miles under his boots was addressing a small crowd of patrons over his mug.

"The sickly skinned cockle knocker lurched out at us from the muck while we was eating," he said, raising a hand like a claw.

His audience seemed transfixed by his story.

"Fortunately, I kept my wits about me," the man continued. "Made eye contact with it – like they says to do." He paused for dramatic effect. It caused everyone to stop their drinking and hang on his words – not an easy task. At last he thrust his fist forward.

"Then I gave it a stiff punch in the snout!"

The men roared their approval. Several women gasped. Over the din, a voice called out dryly.

"Rubbish."

"Who said that?" the tall man asked.

"Bogwash," the voice said again.

Several patrons stepped aside and Rye saw that it was the man with the monkey. He sat in a chair with his legs crossed, glaring over his fingers, which he'd folded into a pyramid on his chin.

"You's saying I'm a liar, gypsy?"

"If you actually saw a Bog Noblin," the man with the monkey said, "which I highly doubt, I suspect you wet your knickers and threw your chicken leg at it. If you had tried to punch it in its snout, you wouldn't be standing here at all."

The storyteller took a menacing step forward. The man with the monkey stood up. The monkey put up its fists. The men who stepped between them were soon pushing and shoving one another, and before long everyone seemed to forget who had started the trouble in the first place.

Rye and Folly dashed away, disappearing into the forest of legs. Someone stepped on Rye's foot. Someone else bumped an elbow and accidentally spilled wine on the girls' heads. They shrieked, then looked at each other and laughed.

"What do we do now?" Rye asked.

"Are you hungry?" Folly asked.

"I could eat."

They worked through the crowd and positioned themselves near the swinging doors that led to the kitchen. Before long, a barmaid hurried out, balancing a heavy tray of food. Folly reached up when the barmaid wasn't looking and grabbed two grey-black lumps of meat. Folly and Rye skipped back into the crowd before the barmaid could notice the empty plate.

"Try one," Folly said. "They're hot."

Rye took a tiny bite and chewed. She chewed some more. It was salty.

"What do you think?" Folly asked.

"Rubbery," Rye said, finally swallowing. "What is it?"

"Sea lion," Folly said.

They didn't eat sea lion back on Mud Puddle Lane... or anywhere else Rye could think of. She examined the dark meat between her fingers. Suddenly she felt like she'd been kicked in the stomach. The pain made her drop the rest on the floor.

"I think I'm going to be sick."

"More for me," Folly said, dangling her share over her lips.

"No, really, Folly." Rye clutched her side. "I'm going to be sick."

Folly tossed the sea lion aside and grabbed her hand. "Well, don't do it here. Come on, let's get upstairs."

"Hurry, Folly," Rye said, turning green.

The girls ran through the crowd, Rye's insides on fire.

They were almost to the stairs, Folly pulling Rye, when

Rye crashed into someone's leg. She bounced off and stumbled into a barmaid, who dropped an entire tray of empty mugs. There was a crash, then a roar of cheers from the crowd.

Rye was about to stop, but Folly just pulled.

"Keep going," she said.

When Rye glanced over her shoulder she saw that she'd run into the woman in the cranberry-coloured dress. The one who was sitting at the Mermaid's Nook. The woman was apologising to the barmaid. She never saw who hit her.

Rye noticed that the woman had soft features and dark-black hair tied into a ponytail with a simple blue ribbon. She held a goblet of wine in her hand and, round her neck was a black choker strung with runestones. It looked just like Rye's.

"Pigshanks!" she said, slamming to a halt. "It's my mother!"

Rye and Folly were lying on their bellies in the third-floor hallway, staring through the railing down into the inn below. It was the only position that made Rye's stomach feel better. The sea lion had already come back to visit her three times, along with her supper from earlier that day. There was nothing left in her belly, but it still felt like she'd swallowed an old boot.

"Are you sure she didn't see you?" Folly asked. Her voice was sleepy, her eyes half closed.

"Yes," said Rye. "Believe me, if she had, sea lion would be the least of my worries."

Abby O'Chanter was back at the Mermaid's Nook with the tattooed man. They were speaking quietly to one another across the mermaid's body, but Rye couldn't tell if Abby was happy or sad. One thing she did know was that she'd never seen her mother wear a dress like that before. She'd never known her to show so much of her shoulders and neck in public.

"Do you have any idea who that man is?" Rye asked.

"No," Folly said. "It seems that other people do, though."

"My mother said she had a special sale for customers at The Willow's Wares," Rye said. "What's she doing here?"

"Maybe she's finished her business," Folly said, drifting off to sleep. "Or maybe he's one of the customers."

The inn began to spin and Rye thought she was going to be sick again, but she realised it was just the massive chandelier bobbing in front of her eyes. A rook hopped among the bones and candles, trying to keep its balance with its creepy little feet. Rye crinkled her nose. The filthy creature must have flown in through a window. A black bird that flies by night was considered bad luck. The worst kind. In its beak was a large, metal fish hook that glinted in the candlelight, its barb still slick as if the bird had plucked it fresh from some mackerel's mouth.

Rye jumped as the rook spread its wings and dived down from its perch. It swooped unnoticed over the heads of the partygoers before passing over the Mermaid's Nook, where it lost its grip on the hook. The hook dropped straight on to the table. The bird flapped awkwardly upwards and disappeared into a dark corner of the rafters.

Rye leaned forward. Her mother had pushed herself back from the table, but her companion picked up the hook and seemed to examine it with great interest. Unbelievably, he held it under his nose and sniffed it.

Rye's concentration was broken by a loud ringing below. Folly's father had mounted the bar and he now clanged a brass ship's bell. He kept it up until the crowd grew quiet. He cupped his hands to his mouth.

"Last call," he bellowed. "Last call."

There were rumbles and hisses. Fletcher Flood pointed to the large hourglass behind him. The black sand had almost run its course.

"Finish your cups and be gone," he yelled, "or the doors get locked and you drink 'til dawn!"

There was a roar of approval. Then the crowd raised their glasses and broke into a chant.

"*The Black Moon rises, thick with thieves! No one enters, no one leaves!*"

"Folly," Rye asked. "What's going on?"

Folly was snoring.

"Folly!" Rye jabbed an elbow in her side. "What's going on here?"

"Huh?" Folly said. "Oh. On the Black Moon the doors get locked at midnight. Everyone is free to go or stay, but once the doors are locked, no one gets in or out."

"What? It's midnight already? Why do they lock the doors?" Rye asked.

"I don't know; tradition?" Folly said. "Most people stay.

It can get really crazy in here after the doors are locked."

Rye looked back towards the Mermaid's Nook. Abby and the man were now standing. Even from this distance, Rye recognised the lines of worry on her mother's brow. Abby flung her everyday cloak over her shoulders, extinguishing the striking cranberry dress like mud on a fire. The man had one too, black as the charred shark on the spit, and when he turned, Rye noticed two sheathed swords strapped to his back. They made their way with haste to the front of the inn with a handful of others.

"Wait," Rye said. "Where's she going?"

Fitz and Flint stood to the side of the thick doors with both sets of arms crossed. Rye's mother and her escort pulled their hoods over their heads and disappeared with the small crowd into the night. Rye noticed that the man with the monkey was part of the group. He had slipped in behind them unnoticed. Fitz and Flint used their shoulders to close the heavy doors behind them, and dropped a thick iron bar across to bolt them shut. The latch echoed just as the sand ran out of the hourglass. The crowd broke into louder cheers.

"Folly!" Rye cried. "I can't get locked in."

"Don't worry," Folly said. "You can sleep in my room."

"No, Folly, listen." Rye grabbed her by the shoulders. "My mother's going home. I have to get out!"

8

CURIOUS BEASTS

RYE DROPPED DOWN from the rope ladder and landed hard in the alley. She had climbed out of Folly's window so fast she'd forgotten her lantern. There was no time to go back for it now. She was careful not to step on Baron Nutfield, but he was nowhere to be found. Maybe they had let him inside.

Rye tried to ignore the protests of her stomach as she darted through the alley and on to Little Water Street, worried that she might run straight into her mother once again. But something was different. Terribly different. The street was dark and lifeless. Another solitary rook pecked at a string of festive beads now discarded on the docks. It regarded Rye with its dark coal of an eye before flying off, disappearing under the bridge. There were no lights on the River Drowning and no more boats offshore. The river was still, its water black. The shops were all shuttered. She looked up at the Dead Fish Inn. Even the candles in its windows had been darkened.

Rye breathed hard. It had grown colder. She could see her breath. From the corner of her eye, she thought she could see things moving in the shadows of the buildings. Then, when she would look, they'd be gone.

Rye began to run.

Rye wasn't the fastest runner on Mud Puddle Lane, but she could run for the longest. Whenever she raced Quinn from her house to Miser's End Cemetery, Quinn would always win. When they raced to the cemetery and back again, Quinn didn't stand a chance. Rye's big lungs and strong legs served her well on the night of the Black Moon. She tore through the streets, falling twice over loose stones. She picked herself up and kept going.

By the time she reached the broken wall, her chest pounded and her hood stuck to the sweat on her forehead. Her head was spinning worse than her stomach now, but she was greatly relieved to make it to Mud Puddle Lane without anyone seeing her, grabbing her, or otherwise scaring her out of her wits. She was even more relieved when she opened the door to the O'Chanters' cottage and found it to be quiet. Rye had managed to make it home before her mother.

Then she realised the problem. Nobody else was there either.

"Quinn?" Rye called.

The door to her mother's room was open. Rye poked her head inside, but found it empty.

"Quinn!" Rye called again. She opened the door to her own room. The covers were off and Lottie was nowhere to be seen.

Rye picked her fingers as panic set in. She ran to the main room and threw open the front door, about to run to Quinn's house to see if he'd taken Lottie back with him. A thought made her pause. She quickly walked to the wall by the fireplace and pushed on a painting of Mona Monster's belly button.

Quinn was in the secret workshop, pinned to a chair by Lottie. Her arms were round his neck, her mop of red hair buried on his shoulder. She snored like a hive of lazy bees. Poor Quinn looked frightful. His hair was as wild as Lottie's and his face was covered with blue paint.

"You said you'd be right back," he said.

"I'm sorry," Rye said.

"You said she never wakes up."

"She doesn't," Rye said. "What happened?"

"She said she had to do a wee."

"Did she?" Rye asked.

"Not a wee," Quinn said.

"Oh," Rye said. "Did she use her Pot?"

"No," Quinn said glumly and pointed to his shoes in the corner.

"Ugh," said Rye.

"It was awful, Rye. What do you feed this girl?"

"I'll clean your shoe."

"She was screeching about a lazy glue wagon," Quinn said.

"A baby blue dragon," Rye corrected.

"And magic narbles," Quinn said, shaking his head. "She refused to sleep until I gave her a magic narble. Where on earth do I find one of them?"

"A magic *marble*," Rye said. "They're just beach pebbles.

Lottie gets one every time she uses her Pot. When she fills her goodie jar, my mother says she can have a baby blue dragon."

Rye had no idea where they might acquire a baby dragon of any colour. But Lottie didn't seem particularly enthusiastic about potty training anyway. She was just as likely to go in her mother's vegetable garden, or a saucepan, or poor Quinn's shoe. She had only collected three marbles so far. They still had plenty of time to sort out the details.

"And that one," Quinn said, pointing to the corner, "has been unbearable all night. I thought he was going to rip down the door."

Shady paced the floor restlessly. He looked over his furry shoulder as they spoke about him.

"He scratched me," Quinn said. "Twice."

He held up his arm. There were four long red welts.

"Sorry, Quinn," Rye said. "Where else did he get you?"

"I'm sitting on it."

Shady blinked his yellow eyes and chattered, quite satisfied with himself.

"Quinn," Rye said. "Why did you bring Lottie in here? She's going to tell my mother."

"I didn't," Quinn said. "I was chasing her. Trying to get my shoe. She knew where the door was – ran back here and hid. I was shocked myself."

Just then the flame in the lantern flickered from a draught.

Shady noticed it too. His ears perked up and he darted from the workshop.

"Pigshanks," Rye said. "The front door."

The front door was open, but not because Abby was home. In her haste to find Quinn and Lottie, Rye had forgotten to close it. Rye ran back into the main room from the secret workshop just in time to see the fluff of Shady's black tail disappear out of the door.

"Shady, no!" Rye yelled, with no effect.

Quinn followed her from the workshop, shoeless, with Lottie hanging upside down from his arms, still fast asleep.

"Quinn, stay here. I have to go after him," Rye said.

"No way," Quinn said, shaking his head. "You're not going to leave me here alone with her again."

"Please, Quinn," Rye said and didn't wait for an answer.

Rye ran back into the night. She stood in the middle of

Mud Puddle Lane, calling for Shady in a whisper at first, then more loudly. With his black fur, he'd be invisible in the shadows. Rye thought about what she would do if she was a cat let outside for the first time. Cats were cautious, so she would probably take her time and look around. After that, well, she'd probably try to catch a bird. The hens?

Rye rushed round the side of the O'Chanters' cottage towards the yard. She didn't see anything at first, but she could hear the hens rustling in their coop. The goat was bleating in its pen. Everything seemed restless on the Black Moon. Then, low in the grass, by the side of her house, she saw a strange, pale-blue glow.

She squinted in the dark. Could it be a wirry? It was very still. She crept closer. As she approached, she saw that the blue glow was attached to two glistening eyes. They were yellow. It was Shady. He was crouched low on his belly staring out at the yard and beyond. Maybe she was right, he was getting ready to explore the henhouse. The blue glow came from the collar round his neck. The runestones had taken on an otherworldly light.

Rye pulled at the collar of her cloak and craned her head to look down at the choker round her own neck. It had the same strange pale glow. She had never noticed that before. It certainly didn't glow when she was asleep in bed. Had it been doing that all night?

She tiptoed carefully, whispering compliments and sweet words as she approached Shady. She was just about to pick him up when he darted into the yard, faster than she had ever seen him move. All she saw was his blue collar speeding past the henhouse. She ran to follow, but the collar kept going, over the wattle fence of their yard. Rye's words were no longer complimentary or sweet.

She hurdled the fence and watched the collar now well ahead of her. Shady was heading up the path along Troller's Hill. Once he got to the top he would have two options. To the right was Miser's End Cemetery – a forgotten old graveyard that everyone said was haunted. Rye hoped he would go that way. Her heart sank as she saw the blue glow stop at the top of the hill. Shady chose to go left, and headed down towards the bogs.

The bogs were not pleasant under the best of circumstances, and Rye tried to avoid them even during the day. They were damp and full of moss, hip-deep in places. It was easy to get stuck if you weren't careful.

Snakes and blood-sucking insects made it their home, and if the beasts didn't bite you the plants would. Carnivorous bog plants trapped and ate things with their leafy mouths – frogs, birds. Folly said her brothers found one so big it nearly ate one of their hunting dogs. Rye didn't quite believe that. Of course, that wasn't the worst thing Folly said someone saw in the bogs.

Chasing after Shady, Rye didn't have time to think of any of those things. She knew if she lost sight of the glowing collar he would be gone forever. He still had a healthy lead and pulled further away as she splashed through the dark, knee-deep water. The salt fog was rising, making the light difficult to follow. She was shivering, her clothes soaked from the spray of her footsteps. She pushed herself as hard as she could, but her feet stuck in the layers of moss and muck until she could barely move. The blue light faded away.

Rye stopped and threw her arms to her sides in frustration. Running was pointless. Her stomach churned as if she might be sick again. The night had left her head dizzy and disorientated. She listened. Frogs. The hum of a thousand insects, even this late in the season. Somewhere in the distance she heard a splash.

"Shady!" she called in despair, as loudly as she could.

The bog went silent. The frogs – even the insects – stopped humming. Rye felt a shiver run up her spine. Then it went up the back of her neck. It was a centipede. Yuck. She swatted it off.

Then she saw something. A faint glimmer on the ground in the distance. She couldn't tell if it was blue, but it was most certainly a light. Rye pushed through the muck as best she could. As she approached she realised the light was coming from a mound of earth, dry ground sitting up out of the wetness of the bog. Carefully, she crept up to the clearing. It was a small, smouldering fire, made with loose twigs and logs and encircled with stones. Over the fire, some sort of animal cooked on a crude spit.

Rye had a horrible thought, but quickly determined that it wasn't a cat. Maybe a big hairless rat or weasel. It looked even less appetising than the sea lion. Someone must have been hungry, as there were already large bite marks in its haunches.

The fire appeared to be recently abandoned. Rye looked around for any clues as to who might have made it. There wasn't much of a camp, but in the dim light she could see a small leather pouch no larger than her fist lying next to the fire. It was tied shut with a horsehair rope. She crept forward and carefully picked it up. She untied the cord and peeked inside. The three items there were quite unusual. Rye was inspecting them so closely that she didn't notice the long, nasty-looking club on the ground beside it. The one with the bent iron nails jutting out in all directions.

There was another splash. Rye peered into the darkness. Five or six metres from the camp, two eyes flickered at water level. Something was bent over, using its hand like a cup and drinking from the bog. One of the eyes, independent from the other, suddenly looked over in Rye's direction. The second one followed, and they both rose up from the water as it straightened at the waist. Even stooped over, the eyes came to rest at the height of a fully grown man. As it stood, Rye knew immediately that this was no man. She was about to run, but was too late.

The creature covered the ground between them in three strides. It had leathery grey skin and large ears, with a pointed nose turned up at the end like a pig's. Its chest was covered in thick hair and, although tall, it was bony.

Rye could see its ribs between its shallow breaths. Under its distended jaw, a long orange beard was plaited like rope and tied at the end with a child's shoelace. The top of its head was knotty and elongated like a pine cone, with a tuft of coarse hair that matched its beard and would have reminded Rye of a carrot if she had been in any mood for silly thoughts. The miserable beast had metal fish hooks through each ear and another through its nose and, at the corner of one furrowed eyebrow, a small red puncture seeped and oozed. Round its neck was the most horrible necklace Rye had ever seen. Strung on a brass chain were three pairs of what looked like human feet.

Rye had time to observe all of this because, unfortunately, she wasn't going anywhere. The terrible knot-headed creature had snatched her up by the collar and was examining her closely with its most terrifying feature – its eyes. They were small for its head, but they bulged like someone was squeezing it by the neck. Each eye rotated in a different direction as it studied Rye. The creature lapped at its lips with a long, black tongue, leaving spittle in the hair on its chin.

After a moment, the creature's two eyes apparently

reached a consensus and fixated on Rye's throat. With its free hand it pushed aside the collar of her cloak with a crooked finger.

Rye thrashed her arms and legs in an effort to break free. She couldn't.

The creature's eyebrows furrowed. Its eyes squinted closely and its mouth opened. Rye could see its jagged misshapen teeth.

Suddenly, its left eye darted in one direction and grew wide. The right one quickly joined it. The creature let out a horrible scream, a cross between an animal in pain and a baby wailing. Rye threw her hands over her ears.

She saw a dark flash out of the corner of her eye and then she was falling. Rye's shoulders landed hard in the mud. The back of her head followed closely behind, bouncing off earth that was moist but not soft.

Her world went dark.

9

WATCH WHAT YOU EAT

Before Rye opened her eyes she knew she was somewhere warm and familiar. She heard the crackle of a fire and felt the comfort of soft sheets. She turned her cheek and saw a toothy, pink hobgoblin staring at her from the other pillow. Mona Monster.

She felt the pressure of something moving on her chest. She lifted her neck to look, but it hurt her head. It was Shady. The big black pile of fur touched her chin with his wet nose and gave her a lick. There was someone else moving in the room. Rye assumed it was her mother, but when she turned her head she would have jumped out of bed if she'd had the strength.

A man stood over her. He was tall, with longish dark hair to his neck. He had scars on his cheeks and nose.

She could see them through the stubble on his face. He seemed surprised to see her awake and studied her carefully with his dark eyes. He was familiar. Rye had seen him before – at the Dead Fish Inn. That could have been hours or weeks ago. Her memory was fuzzy and dull round the edges.

The man reached towards Rye and she could see his green tattoos. Rye shuddered as he touched her, but when he put his big hand gently over her eyes, everything went dark again.

When Rye next woke, it was to a great commotion.

"Mine, mine," Lottie was yelling.

"Lottie," Abby said, "put that sword down this instant."

"No!"

A door slammed.

"You'll lose a foot playing with that thing," Abby called. Then, more quietly, "Riley, you're awake?"

Abby came and sat on the side of the bed. She placed a cool hand on Rye's forehead.

"How are you feeling, my darling?" she said.

Rye tried to talk, but she couldn't summon a voice. She just touched her throat.

"Yes, your voice," Abby said. "Don't worry, it will come back soon enough."

There was a loud crash in the other room, followed by Lottie's cackle. It sounded like a small army was going to battle with the pots and pans.

"In the meantime, we could do with some quiet around here," Abby said. She got up and fetched a cup of steaming liquid from a kettle boiling over the fire. "Here. Peat tea. It will help."

Rye sat up and took a sip. The tea was bitter, and a little too hot going down, but it seemed to help her catch her breath.

"A man," Rye said, in the loudest voice she could muster. It was little more than a whisper. "He had a scar on his face and…"

Rye ran her fingers up her forearms. It was easier than trying to say 'tattoos' with no voice.

Her mother seemed to think for a moment before answering. She gave her a tight smile.

"He's a friend, Riley," she said finally. "He comes here from time to time. Don't worry. He's harmless."

"Mama…" Rye whispered, but couldn't force out any

more words. She took another sip of tea. "Mama… there was… a Bog Noblin. I saw it."

Her mother put her hand on Rye's cheek and shook her head.

"I did," she whispered, "in the bogs."

"I believe you," Abby said. "We found you collapsed and feverish on Troller's Hill. It's a good thing Quinn was able to tell us where you'd run off to, or you might have been out there all night." Rye thought she saw a tremble in her mother's reassuring smile.

"It breaks my heart that you had to experience something like that," Abby said. "But you're safe now, as safe as you could ever possibly be."

"Mama," Rye said, pushing her mother's hand away from her face. "We need to tell the soldiers. Before it, it…" Rye shuddered, "…comes back."

"Darling, quiet now." Abby eased her back down. "Your close call is something best kept to ourselves. Bog Noblin attacks attract attention. The Constable – and the Earl – would be eager to speak to you. That's not the type of attention we want."

Rye didn't understand.

"But what about the rest of the village?" she said, with the last of her voice.

"Riley," her mother said. "Listen to me carefully. I'll make sure the right people know what happened. But at the moment, you need to rest. Your encounter in the bog was not the only trouble that befell you on the Black Moon. You were poisoned."

Rye stopped. Her eyes grew wide.

"That's right, my love." Her mother gave her a knowing look. "You must watch what you eat at places like the Dead Fish Inn."

Rye swallowed hard, for a variety of reasons.

"That sea-lion cake you ate was laced with Asp's Tongue. It's a deadly poison – intended for someone other than you of course. You just happened to pick the wrong plate to sample. More than one or two bites would have been fatal. As it was, it caused you fever and turned your stomach inside out. That, plus what must have been quite a thump on your head, put you in bed for days."

Rye was stunned. She didn't know what to say.

Her mother smiled again. She leaned over and kissed Rye on the forehead.

"Don't fret too much, darling." She stood up. "We will talk about this after you are feeling better. We have a lot of talking and explaining to do, don't we?"

Rye nodded. Abby nodded back.

"Good," she said. "In the meantime, some people have been waiting very patiently to see you. I promised them fifteen minutes once you were awake. But no more than that. You need your rest."

"Rye," Quinn said, "your mother is going to throttle us if she sees we let you get up."

"He's right, Rye," Folly said. "Quick, under the blankets before she comes back."

Rye was standing in her nightdress by the fire, refilling her cup with peat tea from the kettle in between every breathless word. She couldn't help it. There was so much she had to talk about. So much she had to make sense of.

"How long was I asleep?" Rye whispered.

"Four days," Quinn said. "You woke up from time to time, babbling about monsters, gargoyles in masks... Fifer Flood."

"What?" Rye gasped, and her pale cheeks blushed with colour.

"Don't mind him," Folly said. "He's just teasing about Fifer."

"Is it true, Folly? I was poisoned?"

"Afraid so," Folly said. "It's a good thing you have such a weak stomach – must have got most of it out before it had a chance to take. One of the kitchen dogs just licked the plate and keeled right over."

Rye's gut turned sour at the thought. That part she remembered.

"My father and brothers are all up in arms," Folly said. "We have our share of trouble at the inn – it's part of the charm, Mum says. But, as you can imagine, poisoned guests are never good for business."

Rye scowled. "Wouldn't want my near-death to get in the way..."

"You know I didn't mean it like that."

"Do they—" Rye began to cough. "Do they know who the poison was meant for?"

"My father and brothers have been tight-lipped about that," Folly said. "I know they haven't worked out who did it yet. The twins are looking into it, though, and I wouldn't want to be the culprit when they find him. There aren't many places to get Asp's Tongue around here."

"I need to sit down," Rye said, climbing back into bed. She handed Folly her cup of tea.

"I'm not surprised to hear there was poison in the sea lion, though, considering how you reacted," Folly said. "I mean, sea lion is really quite delicious once you've acquired the taste. This, on the other hand, is awful."

Folly peered into the cup she'd just sipped from.

"Can I take some home for an experiment?" Folly asked.

"Go ahead," Rye said. Her throat felt like she'd swallowed sand.

There was a loud purr from the floor and Shady jumped on Rye's bed, settling into her lap. It was such a relief to rub his ears. The last she remembered, she feared she would never see him again. She fingered the runestone collar round his neck. It wasn't doing anything particularly unusual at the moment.

"Quinn," Rye said, "what happened on the night of the Black Moon? How did I get home?"

"Your mother showed up just after you went looking for Shady," Quinn said. "I didn't have much choice but to tell her where you'd gone. She told me to stay with Lottie. It was quite a while before she returned with you and Shady. Shady seemed fine, but you were in a pretty bad way. She took you into the bedroom and told me to go home. She made me a deal. She said if I never spoke of what happened, she wouldn't tell my father."

"That was all?" Rye said.

"Yes," Quinn said. "Well, that and I'm not allowed to help you with any more of your ridiculous plans."

"Are you sure you didn't see anything else?" Rye said.

"Well, there was one thing," Quinn said. "When your mother came back with you – she wasn't alone."

"What?" Folly said, interested now. She had been examining the moss floating in the tea.

"Who was with her?" Rye said.

"A man. I'd never seen him before. He was the one carrying you."

"Did he have scars on his face?" Rye said.

"Was he handsome?" Folly asked.

"Folly!" Rye said.

"What about tattoos?" Folly said. "Did you see any tattoos?"

"Well, now that you mention it," Quinn said, "I think he did have some marks on his face. And there were tattoos on his arms."

Rye and Folly looked at each other. It was the man from the Dead Fish Inn. It was also the man Rye had seen here in her room.

"One minute," Rye's mother called from outside the door.

There was so much Rye needed to talk through with Quinn and Folly. She hadn't even covered the most important part.

"Folly. Quinn," she whispered. "That night in the bog. I saw it. The Bog Noblin."

"Rye," Folly said, touching her arm like adults often did when they didn't want you to feel stupid, "your mother told us your fever might make you say some crazy things."

"Yeah, Rye," said Quinn. "You were poisoned. Your brain was playing all sorts of tricks on you."

"No. It was real. It touched me. It grabbed me."

"If a Bog Noblin had really grabbed you, it would have eaten you," Quinn said.

"He's right, Rye," Folly said. "It would have made a necklace out of your feet and used the rest of you for stew."

"Listen, you two," Rye said, her voice returning now, even without the tea. "I have known you both my entire life and I have never lied to you. I saw a Bog Noblin and I can prove it."

Folly and Quinn looked at her sceptically.

"How?" Quinn said.

"Bring me my cloak."

Quinn retrieved Rye's cloak from where it hung by the fire. He handed it to Rye and she dug around inside it. From the secret pocket she had sewn inside, Rye retrieved a small leather pouch tied with a horsehair rope.

"What's that?" Quinn asked, his eyes wide.

"It smells like swamp cabbage," Folly said.

Rye untied the pouch and emptied its contents on her bed.

The three friends stared at a tiny skull, an iron anklet, a small wooden stick figure and a rotten yellow tooth tied to a string.

10

THE MAN IN MISER'S END

RYE WAS FEELING quite a bit better on the morning after Quinn and Folly's visit – or so she told her mother – and Abby felt comfortable enough to return to The Willow's Wares for the first time since the Black Moon. Abby seemed to be full of anxious energy, but still hadn't got around to talking about the Dead Fish Inn, not that Rye was in any hurry to bring that up. Fortunately, Abby took Lottie with her so Rye wouldn't have to look after her.

Abby had told Rye to rest when she kissed her goodbye that morning and Rye, of course, had promised that she would. In reality, she was desperate to find out more about Bog Noblins and the mysterious bag. She had managed to climb to the roof and send a message by pigeon to Folly with every intention of sorting out the mysteries of the past week. Unfortunately, Quinn was in a big hurry when he stopped by that morning.

"Sorry, Rye," he said, "I'm going to be late for reading today. Things are crazy at the shop and my father needs my help."

"What's going on?" Rye asked.

"I'll explain more later, but he can't keep up with the demand. Swords, arrows, shields – you name it."

"What? Why?" Rye said.

There was a loud bellowing of Quinn's name, followed by a not so nice demand of, "Now!"

"Bog Noblin," Quinn said quickly. "I'll be back this afternoon."

Rye raised her eyebrows. "What?" But Quinn was already on his way. "Don't forget *Tam's Tome*," she said in a loud whisper.

"Yes, yes. I have to go."

Rye pulled on her boots and stepped outside. The weather was turning chilly fast and the remaining leaves on the trees were burned the red and orange of autumn. There was no way she was going to stay cooped up inside.

There wouldn't be that many good days left before the first frost.

Mud Puddle Lane hummed with activity, with neighbours gathering in large groups to talk amongst themselves in an animated fashion. Some seemed to be stocking up on supplies. Others were hammering nails as they reinforced doors and windows. The adults were too busy to take any notice of Rye as she listened in on their conversations.

"The old Cider Mill was attacked last night – third farm this week," someone said.

"That's the closest one yet," another said.

Rye slipped away, joining another group of neighbours.

"What'd it take?" a neighbour asked.

"Two lambs, all the goats, half a cow."

Rye cringed. Did that mean the other half was left behind?

"The farmer see anything?"

"Don't know. Ain't no one seen *him* since."

Rye left that group and headed towards the village end of Mud Puddle Lane. Several neighbours stared silently at the broken section of the village's wall. A street sweeper in a black-and-blue tartan vest laboured with a brush and bucket at the wall. He unsuccessfully tried to scrub away an enormous smudge of tar larger than Rye herself. Rye pushed forward to get a better look. Despite the streaks the street sweeper had managed to make in the graffiti, Rye could still clearly make out the image.

Someone had smudged the shape of a black four-leaf clover.

"You sure you want to do that?" a villager asked the street sweeper.

He paused and wiped his brow. "Push off. I'm just doing my job."

No sooner had he said it, than a glob of white bird droppings painted the wall too. The crowd erupted in laughter. The culprit, a rotund pigeon, flew leisurely overhead. Rye turned and hurried back to her cottage as fast as she could on her still-wobbly legs. She climbed the ladder to the roof and reached into the coop where the bird had taken roost. Molasses, her favourite but slowest carrier pigeon, cooed at her, a folded note tied to his foot.

Can't come this morning. Madness at the inn. See you this afternoon.

Pigshanks. Folly was going to be late too. Rye rubbed the bird's grey head and placed him back inside. From the roof she could see the edge of the bogs. She wasn't inclined to return there any time soon. Still, her mother said they'd found her on Troller's Hill. Maybe she'd look around there to see if she could find anything that might jog her memory of the night.

Rye slipped through a child-sized hole in the wattle fence and worked her way along the path to the top of Troller's Hill. The sun was warm overhead, but the familiar spot now gave her chills. She carefully checked the length of path that forked down towards the bogs, as if that awful Bog Noblin might come charging up it at any moment. The wind rustled the colourful leaves on the trees, sending a few of them fluttering to the ground.

She looked down the other fork of the path, towards Miser's End Cemetery. She squinted to see if her eyes were playing tricks on her. Someone was sitting in the graveyard.

Miser's End was a very old and very small cemetery. There weren't more than two dozen overgrown gravestones, many of them in disrepair. No one other than Rye and her friends seemed to go there any more. The man in the cemetery sat on a headstone that had toppled over on its side. His arms and hands stretched out behind him, his chin back and his eyes closed. He seemed to be enjoying the warmth of the sun.

Rye approached the man cautiously, stopping when she was about three metres away. Eventually, he opened his eyes, noticed her, and gave her a small smile.

"Good morning, Riley."

"Good morning," Rye said.

"It's a fine day, wouldn't you say?" he said.

Rye nodded. "It seems nice enough."

He didn't say anything else. Finally, Rye said, "I know you."

"I suppose you do," the man said. "At least in passing, anyway. You can come closer if you like."

The man smiled. He had a scar across his bent nose and several more etched his cheeks and chin, but now, in the light of day, they seemed old and faded. Despite the scars, there was something not altogether unfriendly about his face. She took a few steps towards him.

"What should I call you?" Rye asked.

"What did your mother say?"

Rye thought for a moment. "She said you were harmless."

"Then that will do. Call me Harmless."

That seemed like a strange thing to call someone you'd just met, especially someone who looked like this. 'Harmless' would suit someone like Quinn just fine. But a man with more scars than all of Folly's brothers combined? It would be like calling Lottie 'Whisper'.

Rye pointed up the path. "Were you with my mother when she found me on Troller's Hill?"

"I was."

"Yesterday. You were in my room. You touched my head."

"I did."

He was a strange fellow, Rye thought. But at least he seemed willing to talk to her. Most adults couldn't be bothered, unless they were yelling at her for trampling on their gardens or demanding that she not dance so close to their breakables.

"Who are you exactly?" Rye said.

"I'm Harmless, Riley. We just introduced ourselves."

Rye was not amused. Harmless pushed himself up off

his hands and crossed his legs. He wore weatherbeaten boots and the same cloak he'd worn at the Dead Fish Inn. She could still smell charred shark from the Black Moon Party in its folds.

"I'm sorry, Riley," Harmless said. "I don't mean to tease. I am happy to answer all your questions about your misadventure that night, but you should speak to your mother first. The things to be discussed, well, it's really not my place to speak of them until she has had her say."

Now this was getting interesting, Rye thought. Even Harmless was afraid of her mother.

"I've never seen you here before," Rye said. "I've never seen you at all, well, except recently."

"Do you come to this cemetery often?" Harmless asked.

"I play here in summer," Rye said. "Old Lady Crabtree and some of the other spinsters say it's disrespectful. Mama says the dead don't mind. They probably enjoy the company."

Harmless chuckled. "I would guess she's right. If it were me, I'd certainly prefer the laughter of children over the tears of some old crones."

"They say this place is haunted," Rye said.

Harmless scratched the short beard on his chin. "Do they say it as if 'haunted' is a bad thing?"

"Isn't it?" Rye said. "I mean, they say restless ghosts of the dead wander the woods at night."

"Where else would you suggest they go?" Harmless asked.

"I don't know," Rye said. "A lot of people say they should be at peace. Return to where they came from."

"And where would that be?" Harmless asked.

Rye took a seat on a headstone and thought about it. "Well, I'm not sure exactly," she said. "No one ever really explains that."

"Hmmm," was all Harmless said, as if that explained everything.

"Where do you think they go?" Rye asked.

"Who?" Harmless said.

"The dead," said Rye.

"Oh, them," Harmless said. "Well, I can't say for sure. No one can. Although you'll meet plenty of people who will tell you otherwise. But, between you and me? I don't think they go anywhere at all."

Rye looked at the headstones they were sitting on. "You

mean, this is the end? They just stay in the ground where you put them?"

"Not exactly," Harmless said. "What I mean is, I think they stay right where they've always been. That's here." He touched his chest. "And here." He touched his temple.

Rye raised an eyebrow.

"In our hearts and in our thoughts," he said.

Rye just looked at him.

"I guess, Riley, that I'd say we're all haunted. Haunted by those we've loved but who are no longer with us. That's where the dead go. And the more people who you've loved, or who you've affected in some way, well, the more people you have to live on in. Forever."

"So what about the ghosts that haunt this cemetery?" Rye said. "Or the dungeons of Longchance Keep. Or the wine cellar at the Dead Fish Inn?"

"Maybe the ghosts who walk this cemetery are just lonely," Harmless said. "They don't have any hearts to go home to."

Rye thought for a minute, then nodded.

"Interesting theory," she said. "Interesting, but creepy."

"Your mother says that about me all the time."

Rye laughed nervously, stopping herself when she realised the familiarity that his words implied. She looked around at the stones.

"Did you know anyone buried here?" she asked more warily.

"I did," Harmless said.

Rye waited, but he didn't say anything more. Harmless just stared off into the trees. He looked like he was listening for something. Or maybe trying to smell something. Rye listened too. She couldn't hear anything unusual.

Rye was never good with long silences. She always lost the who-could-stay-quiet-the-longest game when she played it with her mother. She picked at her fingernails.

"Do you live out here?" she said finally.

"In the cemetery?" Harmless said. "Of course not."

"Where do you live?"

"Different places. I move around quite a lot."

Rye wondered if Harmless was like Baron Nutfield. He sure didn't seem like him. Everyone had been quite happy to see Harmless at the Dead Fish. No one tried to throw him into any alleys. Harmless smelled much better too, charred shark and everything.

"Would you like to come back to our house for lunch?" Rye asked.

"You're very kind to offer," Harmless said. "But I'm not allowed."

"Says who?"

"Your mother wouldn't like it."

"Why not? She said you were a friend."

"Yes, but that doesn't mean she likes me."

Harmless got up and stretched his arms over his head.

"I'm afraid I have some things I need to do," he said.

"One more question," Rye said.

"Yes?"

"Why do you have all those tattoos? Did they hurt?"

"That's two questions," Harmless said.

He pulled his sleeves up to his elbows. Both of his forearms were completely covered in green-black ink. He held them out for her to see. Rye could make out a skull, a mermaid, a woman's face, a crude map, a sword and shield, maybe a bouquet of shamrocks. There was more, but it was difficult to tell where one tattoo ended and the next began.

"They help me remember where I've been and how to

get back there," Harmless said. "They hurt, but no worse than a bite of a serpent or the pinch of a sea urchin's spine. These, on the other hand, were different."

Harmless opened the palms of his hands. Each was covered with a circular pattern of symbols and markings. They were runes.

"These," he said, "felt like flaming arrows through the chest."

Rye leaned forward and studied them closely.

"What do they—" she began to ask, but he held up a finger to interrupt her.

"You have more questions than your mother has moods," Harmless said. "I have certain affairs I must attend to now that cannot wait. But I'll be here in Drowning for a bit longer and will make you a bargain, Riley. I shall meet you here each morning and answer each and every question you ask of me. But this knowledge will not come free. I ask two things in return."

"Yes?" Rye said.

"First, you will bring me something for breakfast each day. It need not be anything special. A scrap of bread or an egg will do just fine, as long as you make it yourself."

Rye nodded. Easy enough.

"Second, these are dangerous times. There are things afoot you do not yet understand. You must promise not to go out at night again by yourself. If you do, trust me, I will know about it. And I will never return to this cemetery again."

That one was going to be harder, but Rye nodded. "Agreed," she said. "I promise."

"Splendid," Harmless said. He stood up and stretched.

"How long?" Rye asked.

"Pardon?"

"You said you'll be here a bit longer. How long?"

Harmless adjusted his cloak and kicked some mud from his heels.

"No longer than it takes. I find my boots gather moss if I stay in one place too long."

Rye wanted to ask how long *what* takes, but Harmless cut her off.

"It was a pleasure to meet you, Miss Riley," he said, and gave a little bow. "I look forward to seeing you tomorrow."

"Pleased to make your acquaintance, Mr Harmless," Rye said, and returned a wobbly curtsy.

With that, Harmless turned and marched off into the weeds and thickets surrounding Miser's End Cemetery. As he left, Rye again noticed the two short but nasty-looking blades strapped to his back, neither of which looked particularly harmless at all.

11

THINGS THAT GO BUMP IN THE NIGHT

RYE COULDN'T RECALL ever seeing soldiers on Mud Puddle Lane, never mind six or seven times in one day. But that afternoon the Earl's soldiers made no secret of their presence. A patrol of two fully armoured soldiers marched down Mud Puddle Lane and back every hour. By their third or fourth pass they seemed to be thoroughly bored by the whole process, and by the fifth trip they were downright rude. They threw stones at the foraging rooks and one peed in the weeds outside Quinn's house.

Rye, Folly and Quinn watched the soldiers as they stopped and picked an apple from the tree in Old Lady Crabtree's yard. Old Lady Crabtree was sitting on her doorstep, studying them with a wicked look from behind her stringy white hair. Crabtree was cranky, demanding, and most people found her entirely unpleasant to be around. For some reason, she and Lottie got along famously.

The soldier bit into the oddly shaped little apple and pulled a face.

"These apples are sour," he said.

"And poisonous," Old Lady Crabtree croaked with a little grin.

The soldier frowned and spat out the bite.

"Longchance needs to invoke the Treaty," she said. "Instead, he sends your useless lot to prance through the streets and plunder our orchards."

"Don't trouble yourself with the workings of the Earl, old woman," one soldier said. "There is no more Treaty."

"The Luck Uglies are the only ones who will save us," Old Lady Crabtree said.

"The Luck Uglies are criminals," the other soldier grunted. "We'll protect you – not that you deserve it."

"The Earl's soldiers couldn't protect this village from a house mouse with bad intentions," Old Lady Crabtree said.

"Mind your own business, crone," the soldier said, and threw the sour apple at her. "Tend to your skunk apples and be thankful we're even on this wretched street."

"We're doomed, you stubborn louts," Old Lady Crabtree said, pointing a crooked finger at them. "You'll see."

Rye, Folly and Quinn kept quiet until the soldiers had stalked past them.

"Folk in the Shambles are buzzing about Luck Uglies," Folly whispered as soon as they were out of earshot, but Rye interrupted with an emphatic shake of her head.

"Not out here," Rye said, and nodded towards her house instead.

The three friends slipped inside the O'Chanters' cottage and reconvened by lantern light round the table in the secret workshop. Rye brought Shady with them. Rye knew his keen ears would let them know as soon as Abby and Lottie, or anyone else, came within ten metres of the front door. For the moment, he busied himself by swatting at a pheasant feather he'd pilfered from Abby's supplies.

"I heard," Folly resumed, "that the village sent a runner to Longchance Keep. They're going to ask the Earl to invoke the Treaty of Stormwell – and call for the Luck Uglies."

"The Luck Uglies don't exist any more," Quinn said under his breath.

"Do you know that for sure?" Folly said, pursing her lips.

"No, not for sure," Quinn said. "But my father says we don't need that kind of trouble. The village is arming itself. He can't keep up with the demand at the shop. He actually let me use the forge."

Quinn held out his blackened hands proudly.

"What's the Treaty of Stormwell?" Rye asked, pulling a spool of red ribbon from Shady's teeth before he could devour it.

"It was an agreement between the House of Longchance and the Luck Uglies," Quinn said. "A deal to save Drowning from the Bog Noblins."

Tam's Tome lay open in front of them. Quinn flipped through its pages.

"Look," Quinn said, "it's all in here." He began to read. "Twenty years ago, the Luck Uglies struck up a loose alliance with the House of Longchance. They signed the Treaty of

Stormwell and agreed to rid the Shale of the Bog Noblins, who were terrorising the countryside and threatening to destroy merchant society. It took nearly ten years, but the Luck Uglies fulfilled their end of the agreement. Shortly thereafter, the newest heir to the Longchance line, Earl Morningwig Longchance, branded the Luck Uglies as outlaws, and they were forced to disband and scatter throughout the Shale and beyond."

"What good's a treaty with Longchance?" Rye said. "He makes his own laws anyway."

"I heard," Folly began, and both Rye and Quinn exchanged sceptical looks, "that the Treaty of Stormwell was signed in blood under a Black Moon."

"It would be pretty hard to read something signed in blood," Quinn said.

"And," Folly continued, ignoring the interruption, "there were only two copies. One's supposed to be in possession of the last High Chieftain of the Luck Uglies. The other is locked away in the treasure hole of Longchance Keep."

"My father says that's where our things go when I lose them," Quinn noted, then dropped into a perfect imitation of his father's booming voice. "Where's the wheelbarrow, Quinn? Let me guess – the Earl took it for his treasure hole?"

"But why did the Earl declare them outlaws?" Rye said impatiently.

Quinn looked up from the pages grimly. "It says in here that they kidnapped Longchance's bride."

"Which one?" Folly said, rolling her eyes.

"The fourth," Quinn said. "The mother of his daughter. They snatched her from her bed in the middle of the night."

"That is pretty bad," Rye said.

"It gets worse," Quinn said. "When the House of Longchance couldn't provide them with their ransom, the Luck Uglies chained her to a swamp oak in the bogs on a winter night. Nobody ever saw Lady Longchance again."

"That's awful," Rye said, shaking her head.

"It says that Longchance almost shed a tear in front of the entire village when he announced what had happened. He said that no villager was ever to speak of Lady Longchance again and then promptly declared the Luck Uglies to be criminals. He gathered an army and marched, driving every last Luck Ugly from Drowning. They called it the Purge."

Rye tried to process the information.

"But why, Quinn?" she asked. "Why would they do something so awful? Why would the Luck Uglies break their truce after going through all that trouble?"

"I don't know, Rye," Quinn said flatly. "As far as I can tell, they were not very nice."

"It just doesn't make any sense," Rye said.

Quinn's face had darkened. Even with all of his worrying, Rye had never known Quinn to be overly sensitive. Then it occurred to her. Quinn knew what it was like to lose a mother.

Quinn riffled through the thick stack of pages with his thumb. "Maybe there's more in here."

"What about the things we found in the Bog Noblin's bag?" Rye asked quickly, changing the subject in the hope it might brighten Quinn's mood.

The little bag sat next to *Tam's Tome*, each of the four items set out neatly on the table. They smelled of stagnant water and decay.

"Nothing really," Quinn said, crinkling his brow.

"I can't find anything on tiny skulls or anklets. There's something about cures for toothaches, but nothing about teeth on strings. And nothing at all about little wooden stickmen. It does say that Bog Noblins are extremely superstitious and believe in magic. They have a fascination with trinkets, charms and anything shiny."

Quinn looked up from the book. "Not much to go on."

"No," said Rye.

"But it's a big book. I'll keep looking."

Rye had another source she would try tomorrow. She hadn't said anything about Harmless to her friends. She wasn't sure why, but he was something she wanted to keep to herself. For now anyway.

Shady abruptly stopped shredding a roll of parchment. His ears twitched and he cocked his head. Rye, Folly and Quinn took his cue and went silent.

A moment later came the commotion on the street – a ringing of the bell they recognised as belonging to the Village Crier. Important news seldom reached Rye's neighbourhood. When it did, it was almost always bad.

"News," Quinn breathed.

"Let's go," Rye said, packing the four items back

into the leather pouch. "Hurry up before we miss the announcement."

The residents of Mud Puddle Lane poured out of their homes and gathered near the broken village wall. The street sweeper must have given up on the scrubbing because the wall was covered with a patch of fresh white paint, the black four-leaf clover now peeking through as muted grey. Rye, Folly and Quinn slipped their way to the front of the crowd. Neither Abby O'Chanter nor Angus Quartermast were there. Still at their shops, they would have already heard the news from the Market Street Crier. Mud Puddle Lane was always the last to know.

The Village Crier had arrived accompanied by Constable Boil and two of the Earl's soldiers. At the sight of Boil, Rye took a step behind a large villager, shielding herself from his view. Boil scanned the gathered residents from under his dust-ball eyebrows with a look that conveyed both suspicion and disdain.

The Crier unrolled a long scroll and cleared his throat. He was a tiny man with a voice as loud as a trumpet.

"Puddlers," the Crier began, which was how the Earl

always referred to the residents of Mud Puddle Lane, "this proclamation is delivered upon the order of the Lord of this county, the ward of this village, the wise and honourable, the fashionable and handsome–" the Crier rolled his eyes at that last part– "Earl Morningwig Longchance."

A disgruntled murmur came from the crowd.

"Denizens of Drowning," the Crier continued, "it is hereby confirmed that a semi-aquatic lowland Nobificus – more commonly known as a Bog Noblin – has been sighted by credible sources in or about the village proper."

The crowd groaned and shrieked. An old woman next to Rye looked like she might faint. The Constable held up his hands to silence the crowd. The Village Crier began again.

"A village-wide curfew is now in effect. Henceforth, any man, woman or child found roaming the streets after dark and not acting on official village business shall be subject to immediate arrest and imprisonment. Even during daylight hours, villagers should remain vigilant at all times. Any suspicious behaviour is to be reported to the constable of your local ward."

Boil puffed out his bony chest at the mention of his

status. The Crier continued.

"Typical Bog Noblin activities include clawing, biting, growling, consumption of humans and livestock, vandalism and recreational dismemberment."

There were more yells from the crowd. Folly and Quinn just looked at each other. Rye raised a well-picked fingernail to her mouth and began to chew.

"What about the Treaty?" someone yelled.

"We need the Luck Uglies!" cried someone else over the crowd.

"The Luck Uglies don't care about us any more than Longchance does," a third person objected.

"We don't need their brand of help," croaked a fourth.

A few other residents quietly cursed the Luck Uglies under their breath, but such contrarians were quickly shouted down.

The Village Crier cleared his throat loudly. "Your attention, please. As you know, the Luck Uglies have long since disavowed the Treaty—"

"Rubbish!" another voice called. "Longchance is afraid of them!"

"The Earl reminds all residents that the Luck Uglies

are and remain wanted criminals." The Crier looked at the scroll and read the prepared words carefully. "The Luck Uglies are outlaws, thieves, liars, scoundrels, ruffians, scallywags, turkeyholes and all round bad apples."

Someone nudged Rye on the shoulder.

"I guess the Earl won't be inviting them to his Winter Feast any time soon," he whispered.

Rye looked back. A hooded man stood behind her. Peeking from under the hood, he gave her a little wink. It was Harmless.

"And furthermore," bellowed the Crier. Rye turned back towards him. "For the avoidance of all further doubt, the illustrious House of Longchance confirms that it shall henceforth be the sole guardians of the health, wealth and welfare of the great northern county of the Shale, and the not-so-bad Village Drowning. By the Laws of Longchance, any resident found harbouring any Luck Ugly shall be subject to immediate imprisonment in the dungeons of Longchance Keep for a period of not less than one year."

The noise of the crowd was uncontrollable now. Folly gave Quinn a shove and mouthed, "I told you."

The Village Crier finished up quickly. "The Lord of this

county, the ward of this village, the wise and honourable, the fashionable and handsome, Earl Morningwig Longchance–" the Crier took a breath after spitting it out "–hereby bids you all a good day."

Constable Boil watched the restless crowd with a smug grin, revelling in their discontent. But as he studied their hovel-like homes and overgrown garden plots, Rye saw his cheeks go white and his face fall.

"What is that?" he yelled.

The villagers on Mud Puddle Lane did not hear him amidst their own commotion.

"Whose house is that?" he shrieked, loud enough now that the din subsided and Rye's neighbours took notice.

The Constable grabbed a soldier and thrust him ahead, pushing through the masses, stomping towards the far end of Mud Puddle Lane. They stopped at a ramshackle cottage at the furthest end of the street. Its windows were broken. Creepers grew in tangles over its collapsed roof.

"Whose house is this?" Boil screamed again, with a ferocity that couldn't be ignored.

"Nobody's," someone volunteered, which was the

truth. The cottage had been abandoned for as long as Rye could remember.

But now, over its hollow door frame, hung an ominous, tattered black flag and emblem – crossed swords behind a four-leaf clover.

"Get it off there," Boil commanded. "Pull it down."

A soldier gave it a hard tug and pulled the flagpole from the door, splintering it in two over his knee.

Rye turned round to ask Harmless what all this meant, but he was nowhere to be found.

That night, Rye curled up in bed with her head on her mother's shoulder. They both watched the fire crackle in the fireplace. Lottie snored between them, sleeping upside down so that her scratchy little toenails pressed against Rye's chest. Shady snuggled in a warm, furry pile at Rye's feet. The wind had started up outside, and the banging of loose shutters echoed in the night.

"Mama," Rye said, "are we safe from the Bog Noblin?"

Shady rustled around at the foot of the bed, licking a paw and cleaning himself. Abby smiled at him.

"The doors are bolted and the windows shuttered.

There's no safer place in the village than where we are right now."

"Then why aren't you sleeping?" Rye asked.

Abby sighed. "There are others I worry about. But there's nothing we can do at the moment. Let's both close our eyes and get some sleep."

Rye wondered if she meant Harmless. Her eyes were still wide open when Abby spoke again.

"Riley, tomorrow I'd like you to come with me to The Willow's Wares in the morning. I'm bringing Lottie too."

"OK," Rye said.

"It's been many years since there was a Bog Noblin scare in the village," Abby said. "You were just an infant the last time. Towards the end it got bad. Truly awful..." Abby's voice drifted off. Rye felt her mother's body shudder against her. "People can sometimes lose their heads. The shop, well, bad news tends to be good news for our business. Too good sometimes. I may need your help."

"Catching wirries?" Rye said.

"No, *real* help," Abby said with a chuckle. "Besides, I'll feel better knowing you and Lottie are close by."

They both closed their eyes. Rye wanted to ask her

mother if she'd seen Harmless again. She wished she could tell her mother about her conversation with him in Miser's End. But Abby had yet to speak another word about him. Why did Rye have to ask all the questions?

Rye resigned herself to get some rest. Eventually the gentle hum from her mother's nose told her that Abby was asleep, but the far-off banging of shutters kept Rye awake for a long time.

12

LONGCHANCE

"THIS ONE," HARMLESS said, pointing to the small white scar that peeked through his eyebrow, "came from the teeth of a fearsome beast."

"Really? What kind?" Rye asked, eyes wide.

"I was bitten by the family dog when I was about your age."

"That's not a very exciting story," Rye said.

Rye and Harmless sat on headstones in Miser's End Cemetery. Rye had brought him breakfast, as promised – a chunk of bread and some porridge Rye had slow-cooked in the fireplace embers overnight. She'd also brought a jug of fermented cider to wash it down. Abby had been preoccupied all morning and Rye was able to sneak it out without too much trouble.

Harmless rolled up his sleeves and showed her some smooth, pink welts round his elbows. "What about these? This is where I was set on fire."

"You jest," Rye said.

"I'm afraid not," Harmless said. "How about this one?"

He pulled the hair back over his left ear. More accurately, his left earlobe. The rest of it was missing.

"That one's from when I had to jump from a bell tower into a farmer's hay wagon," Harmless said. "Unfortunately, I missed the wagon and landed on his plough."

Rye cringed.

"It was a good ear. I'm not sure where it ended up – hopefully planted in a nice orchard somewhere. And then there's this."

He held out the pinky on his left hand. It was a centimetre too short.

"What happened to it?" Rye asked.

"Snarklefish. A whole school of them. Fortunately, that's all they got."

"What about that one?" Rye said, pointing to the one on his chin.

"Broad sword," he said.

"That one?"

"Shillelagh."

"And that one?"

"Copper kettle."

"A kettle?" Rye said.

"I once made an insensitive remark about a young woman's cooking. I won't make that mistake again," Harmless said. "By the way, this bread and porridge is quite delicious. Will you not join me?"

"I can't," Rye said. "My mother is leaving for the shop any minute and I need to go with her."

For once, Rye was actually disappointed to be going to The Willow's Wares. It was her first breakfast with Harmless and she wouldn't even be able to sit down and ask him all the questions she'd thought up. She had come to drop off his food so he would know that she intended to keep their deal. They hadn't covered all his scars, but Rye had learned you needed to ease into questions with grown-ups. Start them off with easy ones before you got to the good stuff.

"Have you ever broken a bone?" Rye asked.

Harmless laughed. "Most of them. Haven't you?"

"No," Rye said. Not that she could remember, anyway.

"I see a healer in Trowbridge – Blae the Bleeder," Harmless said. "He says I've broken all the major ones anyway. Legs, arms, ribs, my back, neck, cracked my skull – Blae says there are nine bones in my body that I haven't broken, shattered, bruised or cracked in some way."

"You seem to get hurt an awful lot," Rye said.

"What's life without a little adventure?" Harmless said.

Rye could hear her mother calling for her from the other side of Troller's Hill. Her eyes darted towards the hill and she shifted nervously from one foot to the other. Abby always looked for her at Quinn's first, then Miser's End. She turned back to Harmless, who raised an enquiring eyebrow.

"What is it you do exactly?" Rye asked quickly.

Harmless scraped the bottom of the porridge bowl with his spoon.

"Well, that varies. It depends somewhat on who's paying," Harmless said. "I've tracked things, trapped things, retrieved things, delivered things. Certain things I will only do during certain seasons. Piracy, for example, is strictly a summertime affair. Frozen in the ice with fifty unwashed sailors is not how you want to spend February, believe me. I could show you my toes from the frostbite—"

"Did you say piracy?"

"It's a broad term," Harmless said. "Most of the time, though, what I do is collect things. Then I look around until I find someone who might need them more than me."

"Do you ever *collect* things that belong to other people?"

"You mean steal? Pilfer? Rob?"

Rye nodded.

"Riley," Harmless said, his face aghast, "that would be wrong."

Rye was taken aback. Then Harmless raised an eyebrow, scratched his stubbly chin and asked, with a hint of a smile, "Wouldn't it?"

Rye was pretty certain he was teasing her. Still, it left just enough room for doubt that she hesitated to ask about the Bog Noblin's pouch.

"Yes," she said flatly. "I suppose it would."

Again, Rye heard her mother call her name – closer now. She knew there'd be big trouble if Abby had to call a third time, but she had one more question to ask. She stood up and adjusted her leggings.

"Shouldn't you be going?" Harmless said.

"So what are you doing now?" Rye said, ignoring him. "And I don't mean eating breakfast with me."

The cheerfulness in Harmless's tone seemed to drain.

"I'm following something," he said.

"Following?" Rye said.

Harmless nodded.

"What are you following?" Rye asked.

"His name is Leatherleaf."

Rye became very still. She had a pit in her stomach. Given all that had happened over the past week, the strange comings and goings, she just knew, deep in her gut, what Harmless meant.

"That's the Bog Noblin, isn't it?" she said very quietly.

Harmless nodded and reached into the folds of his cloak. He removed a large, steel fish hook and held it up between his fingers. Rye's mind jumped back to the rook at the Dead Fish Inn. She recalled the pierced, bleeding hole in the Bog Noblin's eyebrow – its face burned into her memory forever.

"It is, Riley. And between you and me, I'm afraid he may be the least of this village's worries."

"RILEY WILLOW O'CHANTER!" her mother yelled. She was standing at the entrance to the cemetery, her hands on her hips. "RIGHT NOW!"

"Pigshanks," Rye muttered to herself. Then, quickly to Harmless, "Return the bowl and jug whenever you can."

She turned and ran out of the cemetery. Rye wasn't sure who was getting the uglier look from Abby – her or Harmless.

Rye and Abby completed their long walk to The Willow's Wares in silence, Abby not uttering so much as a word about Harmless, or anything else for that matter. For Rye, her mother's silence was always a far worse punishment than being yelled at.

As soon as they opened up the shop, it became clear that Abby hadn't been joking about bad news being good news for business. The Willow's Wares was busier than Rye had ever seen it. Villagers filled the small shop, bumping one another to get to items that were rapidly disappearing from the shelves. They had already sold out of liquorice root and graveyard dust, two key ingredients in a home-made concoction said to repel Bog Noblins.

Rye's mother sent her out the back to fetch another crate of beeswax poppets, crude candles fashioned into the shape of a Bog Noblin to be lit at sundown and left on the doorstep overnight. Gentle snoring came from a little body curled on a pile of old sacks in the storeroom. Lottie was having her afternoon nap. The crates were heavy and the poppets were moving fast, and Rye loosened her collar to cool off.

When Rye returned to the shop, she saw her mother talking to a woman with three small children whom she had never seen before. The woman and the children were dirty and dishevelled, and their toes poked through their shoes. The woman was looking at the dragonfly jars. The Willow's Wares sold live dragonflies, collected from the bogs themselves. It was said that for as long as a dragonfly remained alive in its jar, no bog creature would harm a resident of the house. Of course, most people had no idea how to keep a dragonfly alive, and were back within a couple of days to buy another.

The woman clutched a few bronze bits, and Rye saw

her mother lead the family to a small corner of the shop that went largely ignored by most of the other customers. Abby O'Chanter handed the woman a tied bundle of sage and pine needles, and whispered a few instructions in her ear. Rye knew the sage was for smudging – burning it in each corner of the home and then smudging the ashes on the front door. It was one of the few items in The Willow's Wares she had ever seen her mother use in their own cottage. The woman held out the bronze bits again, but Abby gently closed the woman's hand without taking them, sending her and the children on their way.

"Oh good, Riley," her mother said when she saw her. "Be a dear and put those poppets on the shelf over there."

"What was that about, Mama? With the woman and those children?"

Abby smiled. "Oh nothing, darling. I just hate to see some people throw their money away."

Her mother was soon tending to another customer while Rye stocked the shelves with the beeswax poppets. As she did, Rye couldn't help but wonder if, of all these people scrambling in and out of the shop, she was the only one who had actually seen the Bog Noblin Harmless called Leatherleaf. No sooner had Rye finished her work on the shelves than Folly rushed through the front door of The Willow's Wares. Her cheeks were flushed from running.

"Have you seen him yet?" she asked.

"Who?" Rye said. "Did you run all the way here from the Inn?"

"Earl Longchance," Folly said.

Rye had forgotten it was Assessment Day, probably because The Willow's Wares had already paid through the nose during the Constable's visit last week.

The Earl almost never came down into the village from the old castle at Longchance Keep. Rye had seen him once or twice for big events – he'd had a procession through town after his fifth wedding. But each year, on Assessment Day, he made his annual pilgrimage to Market Street to check in on the merchants who kept his coffers well lined with gold grommets and silver shims. Occasionally he deigned to enter a shop or two and exchange pleasantries with the shopkeepers. He'd never taken much interest in The Willow's Wares, though.

"With all the Bog Noblin talk, I'm surprised he's

coming this year," Rye said.

"My father says he's trying to make a point," Folly said. "Show the villagers that it's still safe to walk the streets, go about their daily lives."

"Why would he care? My mother says the Earl has never been one to fret about the wellbeing of the villagers."

"My father says it's taxes. People are staying in, not spending money any more. Although you wouldn't know it here," Folly added quickly, looking around the busy shop. "I stopped by to see Quinn. The blacksmith's is doing well too, but that's about it."

Folly peered through a smudged windowpane. "Come on," she said. "Let's go and see if we can spot him."

Rye decided her mother could spare her for a few minutes and slipped outside with Folly. The place was already thick with people. They huddled in doorways and hung out of windows. The middle of Market Street had been cleared of horses and wagons and a dozen armoured soldiers had taken up posts on the corners. Rye and Folly stood in the doorway under The Willow's Wares' flag. Today her mother had hung a plum-coloured flag with a horseshoe logo.

From the far end of Market Street, rows of heavily armed soldiers marched on either side of the road. As they approached, Rye and Folly could see the two figures walking in a leisurely manner down the middle of the street. The Earl was tall and gangly, well over six feet tall, and he carried himself with an air of great importance. His shiny leather boots stretched past his knee and his clothing was made of fine fabric not sold by the tailors in Drowning, in rich, peacock-like colours they were discouraged from delivering to anyone else. He had an enormous belt buckle made of gold that matched the basket hilt of his sword. His cloak was made from the soft fur of gentle woodland animals.

The girl who was with him wasn't much older than Rye or Folly. She wore a black dress made of fabrics as richly appointed as the Earl's. Her jet-black hair was tied in an elaborately plaited bun on top of her head. Her skin was as pale as the moon on a winter's night and she wore a frown so tight it looked like her lips might crack.

The Earl gave half-hearted waves to the gawkers who lined the street while the soldiers glared menacingly at everyone.

"Easy to say it's safe on the streets when you have an army by your side," Folly said. "He still wouldn't go parading through the Shambles like this, though," she added, with a touch of pride.

"Is that the daughter?" Rye said.

"That's her. Lady Malydia Longchance," Folly said. "She looks like she sat on a pin."

It was well known that the Earl had been married five times but only had one child so far. Marrying Morningwig Longchance had proved to be a hazardous activity, as each of the five Lady Longchances had either disappeared or met a rather untimely demise. In fact, there was an illicit little rhyme that was sung around the Dead Fish Inn.

Anna was the first to wed,
she was a terrible cook and turned up dead;
Lady Gwendolyn, homely but proud,
was banished Beyond the Shale for snoring too loud;
Rory came third and seemed just right,
she snuck away after just one night;
Emma bore a child and tongue too loose,
then she was of no further use;
Finally there was Grace the Red;
let's just say she lost her head.

*

As the Earl and his daughter drew closer, Rye could make out more of his features. His hair was as black as his daughter's and tied up in its own loose bun on top of his head. He had two deep folds in his cheeks running from his nostrils past his mouth and the long tuft of black beard on his chin was tied into three little tails like the barbels of a cranky hornpout. He acted like he was taking a casual stroll through a meadow, but his nervous black eyes darted around like a lizard's. Rye was surprised he had been able to find one bride, never mind five.

The soldiers had now reached the stretch of Market Street in front of The Willow's Wares. Rye looked directly across the street at a familiar-looking boy sitting on the kerb, his arms wrapped round his knees. He tilted his head and looked towards the Earl and his daughter without blinking, his chin in the air. It would be hard to actually see the Earl from that angle. Rye realised it was the link rat, the boy with the lantern who had saved her from the Constable on the night of the Black Moon.

Rye was about to run across the street to talk to him, but a soldier gave him a hard kick in the hip.

"Clear the kerb, rat," the soldier grumbled, and the link rat quickly rose and disappeared into the crowd.

Rye craned her neck to see where he had gone. She was so preoccupied, she didn't notice that the soldiers – and the Earl – were heading for The Willow's Wares.

Rye and Folly managed to slip back into the shop just in time, but the soldiers followed and cleared out everyone who didn't work there, including Folly. Four soldiers took up positions on either side of the door. Rye stood close to her mother. She had no idea what was going on, but Abby placed a reassuring hand on her shoulder.

The door opened and the Earl had to duck to fit his tall frame through the doorway. He reached his long, silver-ringed fingers into a pouch held out by an attendant, and removed a wedge of orange fruit. He sucked the juice and pulp from the rind as he looked around, then reached back for the hand of his daughter and led her in. Rye could already tell she wouldn't like Malydia Longchance one bit. Malydia walked into the shop as if she owned it and began browsing the shelves without so much as acknowledging Rye or her mother's existence. She marched around and turned her pointy little nose up at everything she examined, as if the place smelled bad. True, the alligator root took some getting used to, Rye thought, but everything else smelled fine.

The Earl did acknowledge their presence at least, but once he approached, Rye wished he hadn't. He strode forward and reached for her mother's hand.

"Miss – ?" he said, sounding like a snake.

"*Mrs* O'Chanter, my Lord," her mother said, and offered her hand.

The Earl kissed it, lingering a bit too long for Rye's liking. Her mother didn't seem to care for it either. With that strange little beard, it must have felt like she was being gnawed by a goat.

When he was done, the Earl held up the chewed orange rind. "Care for an exotic fruit, Mrs O'Chanter? They are from overseas – and very expensive. I think you will find them to be quite sweet."

"I have tasted oranges before, my Lord. No, thank you."

"Very well," Longchance said with a frown, and threw the chewed rind on to the floor. He paid attention to Rye for the first time.

"Child," the Earl said, by way of acknowledgement and with far less enthusiasm.

Rye offered her hand as well. The Earl gave her an insincere smile. His teeth seemed rather yellow and crooked for a noble. He looked at her dirty fingernails and then carefully took her hand between his thumb and forefinger, wiggling it like a table scrap over a hungry dog.

"Charmed," he said, and quickly let her hand go. "Thank you for your hospitality," the Earl continued, as if they had been given any choice. "Lady Malydia and I were just enjoying our day in the village and she wanted to stop for a souvenir."

The Earl was wandering around now as he spoke, looking things over himself. Rye noticed that his dreadful little daughter was staring at her. When Rye caught her eye, Malydia Longchance quickly returned to frowning at some lodestones in a basket on the shelf.

"Your visit is quite unexpected, but of course welcome, my Lord," Abby said coolly.

"Yes, well, what better place to pick up a memento of our visit than your little curiosity shop, Mrs O'Chanter," the Earl said, looking around more carefully now. "These knick-knacks represent the simple, superstitious nature of the villagers so perfectly, don't they?"

Lady Malydia was fingering a beautiful beaded necklace – one of the more valuable items in the entire shop. It dropped on the floor and the chain broke, beads rolling everywhere.

"Oops," Lady Malydia said, tittering.

Rye felt her mother's hand tense on her shoulder, but Abby simply said, "No bother. Leave it. We'll clean it up."

"These insects here," the Earl was saying. "What do you call them?"

"Dragonflies?" Abby said.

The Earl picked up a jar and eyeballed the blue dragonfly inside. From the other side of the glass, his eye was magnified to the size of an egg.

"Dragonflies, yes," he said. "Do they work? I mean, for their intended purpose?"

He shook the jar. The dragonfly bounced off the glass helplessly.

"Oh, yes, my Lord," Abby said with a smile. "I highly recommend them."

He gestured towards a soldier.

"You. Take them all," he said. He turned back to Abby O'Chanter. "Not for me, of course," he said quickly, "but the children of the servants will appreciate them."

"Of course, my Lord," Abby said.

Rye could tell her mother didn't believe him either.

The soldier began to collect and juggle the various dragonfly jars in his arms. Lady Malydia had now turned her attention to Rye. She stalked closer, until she stood directly in front of her. She studied Rye carefully. Rye didn't appreciate the intrusion on her personal space, but her mother's grip on her shoulder told her to stay put.

"Malydia, my dear," the Earl said, "have you found anything yet? Perhaps something that's not the colour of soot for a change?"

Rye thought she saw Malydia crinkle her nose at her father's turned back. The look passed.

"Yes, Father," Malydia said, her voice high-pitched and unpleasant. "I believe I have found something."

Malydia was within a metre of Rye now. She was half a head taller than Rye and looked down at her intently. Rye noticed something too – Malydia's eyes. They didn't match. One was brown and the other was pale blue. Those eyes weren't looking at Rye's face, but her neck.

"Father," she said. "Look at this choker. I have never seen anything like it."

Rye's hand immediately went to her neck. Her choker peeked out from the collar of her shirt, where she'd absentmindedly loosened it while moving crates in the storeroom.

"I don't know," the Earl said, distracted by a beeswax poppet. "It seems rather drab."

"I don't think so," Malydia said. "I think it's rather extraordinary. What are those symbols?"

Malydia reached out to touch it with her finger and Rye pulled away. Rye looked up at her mother.

House Rule Number Four ran through Rye's head.

Worn under sun and under moon, never remove the O'Chanters' rune.

Malydia turned round. "Father, I want what she has. I want one of those."

"Certainly, of course," the Earl said with little interest.

"Unfortunately," Abby said, "that choker is one of a kind. It's not for sale. We do have some others you might be interested in, though."

The Earl slipped the beeswax poppet into his cloak and gestured to his attendant, who began collecting the rest from the shelf. He then stepped forward, Lady Malydia now getting his full attention.

"Mrs O'Chanter," he said, "would you deny a Longchance what she requests?"

For the first time, Malydia's frown turned into a tight little smile.

"I'm sorry," Abby said. "It's not for sale."

Rye stared hard into Malydia Longchance's different-coloured eyes. Her ears were burning. She clenched her fists. Oh, what she would have done to her if the little monster had been just another girl on Mud Puddle Lane. If Rye hadn't been so angry, she might have heard the commotion outside on the street.

"Of course," the Earl said and stepped towards Rye. His voice was steady but menacing now. "It's not for sale. I understand. It will have to be this little wretch's gift to my daughter."

The Earl lurched and grabbed Rye's choker. There were loud noises outside and Rye struggled as the door to The Willow's Wares flew open.

"My Lord!" It was a soldier in the doorway. His helmet was bent and falling off his head. With the door open, they could hear yelling in the street.

"Luck Uglies," the soldier coughed, trying to catch his breath.

"Impossible!" The Earl was in shock. He looked at the soldier and then to his own hand. It was bleeding. He clutched it tightly with the other. Rye's choker was still round her neck. With the distraction, Fair Warning's sharp blade was back under her mother's dress before anyone had even seen it.

"Where?" Longchance yelled at the soldier.

"Here," the soldier gasped. "On Market Street!"

13

UNMASKED

RYE TURNED TO her mother, eyes wide. Abby seemed equally surprised.

"Is there another way out of this place?" Longchance barked at Abby, without regard for his hand.

"There's a door that leads to the back alley," Abby said.

"Show us," Longchance said. "You," he said to a soldier, "get the girl."

The soldier reached for Rye.

"Not her, you idiot," Longchance yelled. "My daughter!"

Abby leaned down and whispered to Rye. "Do not leave this shop. I'll get Lottie. You stay inside."

Rye nodded.

Her mother led the Earl and his group to the back,

Malydia Longchance glaring at Rye one last time as the soldiers ushered her away.

Luck Uglies on Market Street? Rye's curiosity got the better of her, and she carefully crept to the front door and peered round the doorframe. The smell of smoke filled the air. A wagon burned across the street. Two horses galloped past without riders, spooked by the fire. Villagers ran through the alleys and took cover behind anything solid enough to protect them from the rocks and bottles that hurtled past their heads. Rye spotted cloaked figures climbing through shop windows, quickly emerging with armfuls of looted goods. One of the looters burst out of the front door of the unattended butcher's shop and Rye got a good look at his feathered and bejewelled face. Masks.

House Rule Number One echoed through her head as the masked thief fled down Market Street, dragging a string of blood sausage and a leg of lamb.

Don't stop, talk or questions ask, beware of men wearing masks.

She'd never fully pushed the masked gargoyle from the rooftops out of her mind. Maybe he was on the street right now.

Amid the chaos, Rye could see the looters' cohorts. There were at least a dozen. All wore masks of varying colours, some bent into laughing smiles, others looks of mock surprise. Those who were not ransacking shops pelted the soldiers with stones, old shoes and rubbish scraped from the cobblestones. No sooner would one fling his missile and disappear into a shadow than another would step forward and take his place, arm cocked and ready to throw. Rye watched in fascination. So these were the Luck Uglies.

Recovered from their initial surprise, the soldiers regrouped and advanced on their masked attackers now, indiscriminately smashing any villager, masked or not, who stood in the way.

Rye craned her head to the left and to the right, squinting through the smoke. Villagers clogged the street as they fled.

There was one person, however, who wasn't moving. A boy in tattered, dirty clothing stood in the middle of Market Street, his body jostled and pushed on all sides as villagers stormed past. Amid the smoke, noise and confusion, he held his hands in front of him as if trying to feel his way to safety. The soldiers headed straight for him as they advanced on a small group of Luck Uglies they'd isolated from the rest.

Rye's stomach dropped. It was the link rat.

Rye didn't think, she just shrieked from the doorway.

"You! Link rat! This way!"

The boy must have heard her. He turned and fumbled towards the sound of her voice.

"That's it! Come on!" She waved him on.

Two Luck Uglies were in the process of ransacking the village bakery, throwing heavy sacks of flour from the second storey down on the soldiers below. A sack just missed the link rat's head as he reached Rye and its contents exploded into a great white cloud at her feet. She wiped the flour dust from her eyes.

The boy was bigger than Rye, but she didn't give him a choice. She grabbed him by his shoulders, pulling him into The Willow's Wares. Rye and the boy fell into a heap in the doorway.

Rye looked at the boy's eyes – wide now with fear. They were mismatched, brown and blue, just like Malydia's.

"It's OK," Rye said.

The boy reached forward and touched her face with his fingers. When he pulled them back, he rubbed the flour between his fingertips and smiled.

That was when it dawned on her. The link rat was blind.

"What's your name?" Rye said.

"Truitt," he said, in a strong voice that took Rye by surprise. For whatever reason, she didn't expect it coming from a blind link rat.

Rye and Truitt scrambled to their feet.

The soldiers had cornered two Luck Uglies. The others had wriggled away and fled down the street, flinging off their masks as they went.

"Fools," someone declared sternly behind her. It was her mother. Fortunately, she was looking at the street, not at Rye.

Abby O'Chanter stepped into the doorway behind Rye and Truitt.

The soldiers dragged the two masked men to the centre of Market Street.

Rye looked up at her mother. "They've captured the Luck Uglies."

"Of course they haven't," Abby whispered through

gritted teeth. "Luck Uglies do not throw stones. These half-witted imposters have made a terrible mistake."

From the street, determined footsteps echoed on the cobblestones. Earl Longchance emerged from wherever he had hidden himself, and he stalked towards the now de-masked men held fast by the soldiers. Constable Boil joined him, shambling close behind. Curious villagers peeked from windows and doors. Rye was relieved to see Folly and Quinn watching from the doorway of the blacksmith's shop, tucked safely behind Angus Quartermast's thick forearms.

Longchance's venomous black eyes studied the captives. Rye noticed now that one was just a teenage boy, his cloak too big in the sleeves and dragging under his feet. He appeared absolutely terrified. The larger one Rye recognised as a regular barfly from the Dead Fish Inn – the tall, bearded one she'd heard sharing tall tales on the night of the Black Moon. He looked as if he'd already been at the grog.

"Who are they?" Longchance spat, without taking his eyes off them.

"The ugly one is Jameson Daw," the Constable said.

"Horse thief. Hustler. Cutpurse. He's seen his share of days in the dungeon."

The horse thief gave a little bow with a flourish and nearly fell over. The soldiers jolted him upright.

"This here's the son of the stable master," Boil said with a sneer. "We haven't seen him before, but it would seem that the manure doesn't fall far from the horse's behind."

Boil held up one of the colourful masks taken from the captives. He waved towards half a dozen more that had been discarded on the street and collected by the soldiers.

"Common party masks," he said to Longchance. "Sold all over town. They're just pranksters."

"Or opportunists," Longchance hissed.

Longchance slipped on a leather glove and took the mask from Constable Boil.

"So," he said, looking from the horse thief to the stable master's son and back again, "you like costumes, do you? Like playing jokes?"

The bearded man shrugged. The boy's lip trembled.

"You think it's funny to disguise yourself as criminals? To embarrass these fine soldiers with eggs and litter? To steal from your neighbours' shops?" He turned and faced the boy. "To steal from *my* shops!" he boomed.

The boy closed his eyes.

"Perhaps you and your friends have been decorating the village as well?" Longchance's voice was silky again. He beckoned to an attendant, who rushed forth from the mariner's supply shop with a small, steaming cauldron and a brush. "Tarring my walls with clovers?"

Jameson Daw sobered up quickly. "No, not us, my Lord."

"What about your fun-loving friends?" Longchance asked.

The attendant held the cauldron while Longchance carefully painted the inside of the mask with a sticky, boiling substance. He stroked the brush with care, as if at a canvas. Rye could smell the hot tar and began to squirm.

Daw shook his head emphatically. The boy still hadn't opened his eyes.

Longchance leaned in close to the boy's ear. "Boy," he cooed. "Boy. Open up."

He cracked one eye then the other.

"Are you mute?"

The boy shook his head. "No, my Lord," he said quietly,

and glanced fearfully at the mask in Longchance's hands.

"Good," Longchance said. "We'll need your tongue later."

Rye felt her mother's hand guiding her from the doorway into the shop. She checked to see if Truitt would join them, but he had disappeared as mysteriously as he'd arrived on Market Street.

"As for you, Mr Daw," Longchance said, examining his handiwork on the mask. "Since you are so fond of masks, let's make sure you don't lose this one again."

He raised the steaming mask towards the man's face. Daw gasped and struggled, but couldn't break the soldiers' grasp. Longchance stopped just centimetres from his chin.

"Then again," he said, lowering the mask. "We may need to hear what you have to say as well."

Longchance turned to a soldier. "Take them both to the thrashing stump. We'll find out who their cohorts are soon enough."

Abby and Rye stepped back into The Willow's Wares. Abby shut the door behind them.

Rye could hear the guards drag the prisoners off, the boy's pleas for help echoing unanswered in the streets.

14

LEATHERLEAF

RYE, ABBY AND Lottie returned from The Willow's Wares late in the afternoon. On their walk, Rye noticed more swatches of fresh white paint on the sides of buildings in Nether Neck. Abby ushered her along when she slowed to examine them for signs of black four-leaf clovers. By the time they arrived home, Folly had already sent several pigeons, sharing village gossip eavesdropped from the guests at the inn.

Flags on doors. Mum says old superstition.

Soldiers on every corner. Not the Shambles. We're on our own.

Earl's orders: Anyone wearing masks in public to be arrested on sight.

Rye folded the slips of parchment into her pocket as

she joined Abby and Lottie for supper.

"Mama," she said, as she helped clean up afterwards, "I thought the villagers were terrified of the Luck Uglies. The black four-leaf clovers, the flag I saw on the old shack at the end of the street – what do they mean?"

Abby sighed and paused from her toils.

"Years ago, when Luck Uglies freely walked the village, a black clover on a tavern or shop meant that Luck Uglies were welcome. Even then the Luck Uglies weren't well regarded everywhere, but villagers took a certain comfort in their presence when faced with the alternative." Rye knew Abby meant Bog Noblins.

"I think we are seeing some of the same," Abby continued. "Villagers' memories are short, and it's easy to welcome something when you think it might benefit you. That said, there are opportunists out there. People who will try to use the villagers' fear for their own gain. Those men today thought they could hide behind their disguises of masks and rocks."

Rye shuddered as she thought about the Earl's reaction.

"Given the Earl's display on Market Street," Abby continued, "I don't think we'll see any more pretenders."

Abby put away their plates and goblets.

"The night the Earl marched on the Luck Uglies, the soldiers destroyed every clover banner they saw. Shredded them with their blades so that they might never be hung again. That flag on our street – the ragged clover – it's the first I've seen in many years."

Abby paused for a moment and scratched Shady behind the ears. He rolled over so she could get to his belly too.

"Riley," Abby said, "until this Bog Noblin situation is resolved, I don't want you leaving here by yourself. Not even to go to Quinn's house."

"What?" Rye exclaimed.

"This isn't a punishment, Riley, it's for your own good. And that includes no more visits to Miser's End."

Rye was furious. "Why can't I see him? You said he was harmless."

"I don't want you sneaking around cemeteries with strangers," Abby said.

"Stranger? You sneaked out to see him at the Dead Fish Inn!" Rye said. "Why is it safe for you, but not for me?"

Abby's eyes flared. She opened her mouth, but couldn't seem to find the words. That didn't happen often. Rye shrank back – now she was going to get it. But instead, Abby quietly put the last of the plates away and went to get her room ready for bed without another word. Silence again – the worst reaction of all.

That night they all went to bed together in Abby's room. They exchanged 'goodnights' and 'sleep tights'. Nestled between Rye and Abby, Lottie fell asleep first. Rye found herself staring at her sister's delicate features. She tried to recreate Harmless's face in her mind. As unpleasant as Lottie could often be, Rye had to admit she was remarkably cute and scar free – which made for a tough comparison. Still, her mother's conspicuous silence had left Rye wondering how well Abby and Harmless really knew each other. She was determined to continue her morning visits – one way or another.

Shady rested on Rye's feet at the foot of the bed and began gently snoring. Rye couldn't tell if her mother was asleep yet, but she soon drifted off herself.

Rye didn't know how long she had been sleeping, but she woke to a heavy pressure on her chest. When she opened her eyes, two yellow orbs glowed centimetres from her face. It was Shady. His thick body stood on her chest, his big feline eyes wide and alert.

"Shady," Rye whispered, "what are you doing?"

A low growl escaped from somewhere deep in Shady's throat. Rye sat up carefully. Both her mother and sister were fast asleep.

"Why are you looking at me like that?" she said.

Rye slipped quietly from the bed and set her bare feet on the cold floor. She tried to pick up Shady in her arms, but he wanted nothing of it and wrenched himself free. Clearly it wasn't Rye he was interested in. He climbed to the head of the bed and stared intently at the window.

"What is it, Shady?" Rye whispered again. "Is there something out there?"

She put her hand on the shutter. Shady twitched with anticipation. Rye opened it quickly. Only darkness greeted her from the other side of the glass. The room was dark too except for the glow of embers in the fireplace.

"See, Shady," Rye whispered with relief. "There's nothing there."

Shady's tail stopped twitching, but he now made a clicking sound like he was grinding his teeth. He obviously didn't believe her.

"Maybe it's a possum or a skunk," Rye said and cupped her hands round her eyes as she pressed her nose to the window. She didn't see Shady's collar begin to glow.

A bulging, watery eye appeared on the other side of the glass, just centimetres from her own.

Rye screamed and nearly leaped out of her nightdress.

Outside, Leatherleaf unleashed his terrible, beast-baby wail.

Nobody on Mud Puddle Lane was sleeping any more.

The O'Chanters watched from behind their front windows as Leatherleaf stalked down Mud Puddle Lane. The moon was bright in the sky and cast enough light for them to see his hulking shadow, but little else.

Rye saw the light from candles and lanterns in other windows on the street, her neighbours keeping watch, just as they were, but no one ventured outside. Leatherleaf had already eaten two sheep and a chicken he'd plucked from a neighbour's yard, and tufts of wool and chicken feathers were matted in the thick hair on his chest. His appetite seemed to be satisfied for the time being, and he turned himself to another favourite Bog Noblin pursuit –

vandalism. He kicked over a wooden fence. He grabbed the trunk of the apple tree in Old Lady Crabtree's garden with both claws and shook it violently, until each and every apple had fallen to the ground. He then picked them up and proceeded to throw them in every direction.

Rye turned from the window and looked around the cottage. The doors and windows were firmly latched, but she had no doubt that Leatherleaf could knock them open in one or two blows if he was so inclined. Shady was doing his best to rip them down from the inside. He howled and yowled and threw himself against the door. That didn't work and he had now taken to clawing at it with his paws, his determination so fierce that he left deep grooves in the wood. Abby seemed to consider him for a long time. Finally, reluctantly, she hauled him scratching and thrashing into the pantry and shut the door.

"Not now, little warrior," Rye heard Abby say to the door, in a whisper that was barely audible.

She joined the girls at the window again. Lottie's chin barely cleared the sill, but she pressed her nose against the glass.

"Mama," she said, "bear outside?"

"Yes, Lottie. It's a bear."

Lottie scowled. "Mean bear. Throw Nanny Cab-Tee's apples. No, no, no," she said, shaking a finger.

Abby stared out of the window, never taking her eyes off Leatherleaf, watching the street.

Perhaps the most interesting thing Rye noticed was the pale-blue glow round all their necks. The O'Chanters' chokers, even Shady's collar before his banishment to the pantry, glowed a matching shade of blue.

There was a loud thump as an apple bounced off the house. All three O'Chanters jumped in surprise.

"Mean bear hit our house," Lottie yelled.

Outside, Leatherleaf had taken his vandalism to a far more serious level. He had climbed on to the roof of the cottage across the street. His weight alone buckled the thatch and shingle roof, but now he was digging into it with his claws and tearing pieces away.

"Mama," Rye said, "it's the Pendergills' house. There are babies in there."

"I know," Abby said quietly. "I know."

"Mama," Rye said, "we have to do something."

Rye started dancing from foot to foot, as she often

did when she was excited. It usually meant that her brain was about to stop working and she was going to run off somewhere and do something not-so-clever. Abby caught her by the arm and held it fast.

"Riley," she said, "you are staying right here."

"But, Mama," she said, "the babies."

Leatherleaf had managed to tear a hole in the roof. He stared down through it, his black tongue flicking wildly at his lips.

"Mama," Rye said, her eyes welling with tears, "he'll hurt them. Please, we have to stop him."

"Mean bear not nice," Lottie huffed, and stepped away from Abby's side.

Abby turned and reached for her. As she did, she lost her grip on Rye's arm.

"Lottie, wait – RILEY!"

"Humph!" Lottie said as she stomped to her room, angrily slamming the door behind her.

Rye didn't say anything at all as she unlatched the front door and rushed out.

Leatherleaf plunged his long, knotted arm through the hole up to his shoulder, fishing it around like a hungry cat's paw in a kettle of sardines. His face wore a toothy smile as if he had grabbed something tender and sweet, but when he noticed Rye, his jagged grin disappeared. He climbed down from the roof empty-handed and approached her.

She stood at the edge of her yard, now completely befuddled by what she had expected to accomplish. In her long history of bad decisions, even Rye had to admit this one might be her worst. She'd rushed headfirst into danger without thinking. Now she was alone, in the dark, with the same beast that had tried to make a meal of her once before.

Except this time she wasn't alone. She felt her mother's arms wrap themselves round her from behind and pull her close to her body.

Leatherleaf was less than three strides from them. He stared at them intently, his drippy, bulging eyes rotating in different directions. He stepped forward, then hesitated and took a step back. He paced back and forth, advanced and seemed to reconsider again. The smell of the bogs filled Rye's nose. Skunk cabbage. The same smell as the pouch she'd taken from Leatherleaf's camp.

Rye felt Abby draw her in tighter.

Leatherleaf snarled, pulling at his beard with a claw. He lurched forward, causing Rye to nearly jump out of her leggings, but he stopped short. Abby didn't budge.

"Stand strong," she said in a whisper.

Leatherleaf paced. He scratched at his face as if struggling with some enormous challenge, but Rye had no idea what it could be.

Rye looked up at her mother.

"No, no," Abby whispered without looking down. "Eyes right at him."

Rye noticed her mother's choker, exposed now from the loosened collar of her dress. It glowed even brighter than it had inside. Rye glanced down. Her choker beamed too.

Leatherleaf, on the other hand, was growing more and more agitated. He scuffled at the ground with his clawed feet like a bull ready to charge. He slapped at his own knobby head. His eyes rotated from Abby to Rye to the Pendergills' house and back again.

Rye felt her mother's hands move up to rest on Rye's shoulders.

Leatherleaf drooled. Mucus from his eyes ran down his cheeks.

With Abby guiding Rye by the shoulders, they took a collective step back towards their cottage.

Leatherleaf pitched his head towards the sky and let out the fearsome wail Rye had already heard too many times. But instead of following them, he turned angrily and faced the Pendergills' house. Rye's eyes grew wide. Leatherleaf started for the hole he'd already made. Rye opened her mouth to scream, but another sound froze him in place.

It was a long, low whistle that carried its way up Mud Puddle Lane.

Abby loosened her grip on Rye and they both looked towards the source of the noise. Leatherleaf's eyes darted nervously.

They had to squint, but there, at the far side of Mud Puddle Lane on the forested end of the dirt road, was a solitary figure. It was covered head to toe in a dark hooded cloak, and it was standing perfectly still.

Leatherleaf remained motionless, watching the figure, as if hoping that if he stared long enough, it might go away.

Neither of them moved for a long while, until finally the figure took a step forward. Then another. It approached

Leatherleaf at a slow and deliberate pace. Leatherleaf seemed to grow increasingly nervous and agitated as the figure neared, but did not advance one way or the other.

When the figure was about halfway down Mud Puddle Lane, it brushed aside the folds of its cloak and reached over its shoulders. Hands reappeared holding two sharp blades. There was something round its neck. Something that glowed intensely blue like flames in a white-hot fire.

Then Leatherleaf did something entirely unexpected. He began to run. In the opposite direction.

What happened next was a blur to Rye. No sooner had Leatherleaf cleared the Quartermasts' cottage than heavy netting engulfed him. The ropes of the net were as thick as a man's arm and each end was weighted with heavy iron anchors. While Leatherleaf struggled to free himself, dozens of armoured soldiers spilled on to the road from the village end of Mud Puddle Lane. They chopped at Leatherleaf's legs with clubs and flails. Leatherleaf let out his hideous wail. All the soldiers paused for a moment to cover their ears before promptly resuming their attack. The more Leatherleaf struggled, the tighter the netting became.

Rye looked back towards the other end of the street. The figure just stood there and, while she could not see its face, its body language seemed to indicate it was just as surprised as Leatherleaf at this recent turn of events. Abby took Rye by the arm and hurried to their house.

There were cheers and Rye looked to see the soldiers jumping up and down. They had managed to drag Leatherleaf to the ground. They continued to pummel him. Rye craned her neck towards the cloaked figure as Abby pushed her into the cottage, but he was nowhere to be found.

Over the next half-hour, the soldiers secured the Bog Noblin for transport. Leatherleaf put up a mighty struggle even on the ground, but after being beaten nearly senseless by a small army of soldiers – he'd managed to dispense with several even while caught in a net – he had no more fight left in him. An enormous cart pulled by a team of draught horses was brought to Mud Puddle Lane and Rye's neighbours began to venture out on to their doorsteps to watch the extraordinary proceedings unfold.

Abby leaned on the window in silence, her jaw tightening as she took in the spectacle. Rye wondered if her mother was angry with her, Leatherleaf, or something else entirely. Lottie had joined them. A copper pot rested on her head, serving as a makeshift helmet. She held the lid as her shield, a small garden spade as her weapon. She seemed disappointed to have missed the battle with the mean bear.

Rye noticed that Abby was clutching the collar of her nightdress, covering her choker.

"Mama," Rye said, "why do our chokers glow?"

"What's that?" she said, as if she hadn't heard.

"Our runes," Rye said, tugging at her own choker. "Why do they glow whenever the Bog Noblin's around?"

Abby glanced over. She stepped towards Rye and adjusted Rye's collar closed too.

"It's a warning," she said simply.

"They warn us when Bog Noblins are near?"

"Something like that, yes," Abby sighed. "But, more importantly, it warns *them* to stay away."

Rye shook her head in disbelief. Where in the Shale would chokers like these come from?

There was a great deal of hooting, hollering and armoured back slapping outside. With Leatherleaf finally secured to the enormous cart, the horsemen cracked their whips. The fleet of horses began pulling the cart and the vanquished Bog Noblin towards the village walls.

15

TROUBLE AFOOT

RYE WATCHED CAREFULLY as Harmless tossed the gold grommet straight up in the air and caught it in his right hand three times, the coin flashing in the sunlight. The fourth time he flicked it across his body and caught it in his left. But when he opened his left palm to show Rye, it was empty.

Rye shook her head. "I still don't understand. Where did it go?"

"Nowhere. It's still in my right hand," Harmless said, showing her. Indeed it was.

"But I saw you throw it."

"Your mind saw it, but it never really happened," Harmless said. "That's the illusion. Here, watch again."

Rye watched again, closely. Again, she saw the coin fly

from his right hand to his left. But when Harmless opened his palms, the coin hadn't moved.

"Your mind is a very powerful tool," Harmless said, "but it can be deceived with a little practice. Someone who learns to trick the minds of others is very powerful indeed."

Harmless tossed her the coin. Rye bobbled it and dropped it into the overgrown weeds of the cemetery. She quickly found it and picked it up. Harmless just smiled.

"Keep it for practice. Or spend it if you like. Whichever you prefer."

Harmless retrieved his bowl and spoon from the fallen headstone that served as their makeshift breakfast table. Rye was exhausted after her sleepless night on Mud Puddle Lane. She suspected the rest of the neighbourhood was weary too, although they all seemed greatly relieved now that the Bog Noblin had been captured. Despite her drooping eyes and dragging feet, there was no way Rye was going to miss a morning with Harmless. She had too many questions in need of answering. Yesterday, her mother said no sneaking around the cemetery until the Bog Noblin mess was settled. It certainly seemed settled now.

"Breakfast is delicious," Harmless said. "What is it?"

Rye looked sceptical.

"Corn meal mush and molasses," she said.

Harmless spooned it all up with great enthusiasm. Clearly he was not a fussy eater.

When he had finished his meal, he set the bowl on the headstone, stretched and let out a large belch. Rye giggled. Her mother didn't always appreciate her and Lottie's burping contests at the table.

"You know," Harmless said, "there are places where it's considered rude if you don't belch after a meal."

"Really?"

"That's right," Harmless said. "It's how you say 'thank you'."

"In that case, you're welcome," Rye said.

They both sat quietly for a time. Harmless wasn't going to make it easy, and he seemed content to just sit and enjoy the morning sun.

"Everyone is quite relieved that the Bog Noblin has been captured," Rye said finally.

"I imagine so," Harmless said.

"It's been a frightening few days," Rye said. "Weeks really."

Harmless rubbed his stubbly chin. He seemed to be considering things.

"Leatherleaf's behaviour was much unexpected. I'm surprised he ventured on to Mud Puddle Lane. It makes very little sense."

"You said you've been following him," Rye said. "Aren't you glad he was captured by the Earl's men?"

"I'm neither happy nor sad about that. I am, however, troubled by what comes next."

"Next?" Rye said.

Harmless turned to her. "I'm not the only one following Leatherleaf. There are others. Leatherleaf, you see, is running for his life."

"Running from who?" Rye said, her eyes wide.

"His clan," Harmless said. "That's like his family. Although they're nothing like a family you or I would imagine."

"Why would he run from his family?"

"It's a sad and complicated story. But to make it simple, Leatherleaf's clan – the Clugburrow – is one of the oldest and fiercest of the Bog Noblin clans – which is saying something, believe me. They are very mean, and terribly cruel. Leatherleaf was the runt of the clan – the smallest and weakest. He was beaten and tormented mercilessly. Finally, he fled."

The runt, Rye thought, and shuddered. What on earth did the others look like?

"Why does everyone say Bog Noblins are extinct?" Rye said.

Harmless gave her a tight smile. "We often tell untruths to help us sleep easier at night."

Rye frowned and wondered what other untruths she'd been clinging to.

"Anyway," Harmless continued, "Leatherleaf has been running for several months now. I am most surprised he has stopped and dawdled for so long…" Harmless trailed off in thought. "Only something very compelling would keep him here."

Rye's mind jumped to the leather pouch. Could that be the answer? One she knew but Harmless didn't? Rye's excitement quickly soured. If the pouch was indeed keeping Leatherleaf here, it meant his destruction – and any more to come – would be her fault.

"Why is his clan chasing him?" Rye said. She suddenly felt like she'd swallowed a rotten pigeon egg. "Why won't they just let him go?"

"Some of your questions I cannot answer," Harmless said, shaking his head, "because I don't know myself. What I do know, is that Morningwig Longchance is putting this entire village in grave danger so long as he keeps Leatherleaf here."

"Because Leatherleaf's clan will come after him?"

Harmless nodded. "Yes."

"The Earl's men captured Leatherleaf. Maybe they can defend us from the rest of the Bog Noblins as well," Rye said.

Harmless sighed. "As I said, Leatherleaf is young and small. He's not much older than you – in Bog Noblin years anyway. He's also injured. A healthy Bog Noblin, even one as young and frail as Leatherleaf, would never have been captured by the soldiers that way."

"How was he hurt?" Rye said.

"He was injured in a fight. Last week. It was the night of the Black Moon, in fact."

"Was it you?" Rye whispered.

"No."

"Was it the Clugburrow following him?"

"Not this time," Harmless said.

"What then?"

Harmless clasped his hands and leaned forward. "It is somewhat difficult to explain. There are ancient creatures. They've been called many things over the years. These days, humans call them Gloaming Beasts."

"Gloaming Beasts," Rye repeated.

"That's correct," Harmless said. "Gloaming Beasts are the only known predator of the Bog Noblin. Their hide is thick and their bodies immune to the Bog Noblins' infectious bites. Their own claws are laced with toxins that are poisonous to Bog Noblins. To all other creatures, the effect isn't much more than a mild itch."

"Why do they hunt Bog Noblins?" Rye said. "They don't look very appetising."

"Oh, Gloaming Beasts don't eat Bog Noblins," Harmless said. "Well, they may snack on them, but Bog Noblins are not their food. They hunt them for sport. For the sheer joy of it. Even a well-fed, content Gloaming

Beast has an insatiable desire to slaughter Bog Noblins. They are curious beasts indeed."

"They sound dreadful," Rye said. "What do they look like?"

"They aren't as bad as they sound," Harmless said. "They are mostly docile, although fiercely independent creatures. They walk among humans nearly invisible, blending into everyday life. However, to the informed eye, clues of the Gloaming Beast are everywhere. You just need to know how to look."

"Why are you telling me all this?" Rye said.

Harmless looked surprised. "Because we made a deal, of course. I've done many things I'm not proud of, Riley, but I have never broken a deal."

Harmless certainly seemed to know a lot about Bog Noblins. Rye paused before asking the next question.

"Are you a Gloaming Beast?" she whispered.

Harmless smiled and slapped his knee. "No, no. Certainly not."

"But Leatherleaf seemed very frightened of you last night," Rye said.

Harmless did not say anything. He just stared at her,

and she couldn't tell if he was surprised or upset.

"That was you on the street last night," Rye said. "Wasn't it?"

"It was," Harmless said quietly.

"Why was Leatherleaf so scared of you? I mean, you are a little scary. To me. But that was a *monster* running from you as if his life depended on it."

"Let's just say that I too have a history with creatures of his kind."

Now that Rye was rolling, she had no intention of stopping.

"What was that round your neck?" Rye said.

"I'm sorry?" Harmless asked.

"Last night. Something was glowing round your neck."

Rye found that she wasn't waiting for an answer. She was stepping closer to Harmless, probably closer than she should. What did she really know about this strange man who had appeared out of the cemetery – a man covered in scars and tattoos with a history that included things like piracy and chasing mythical beasts through the forest? Well, she knew that her mother had called him harmless, and a friend. She also knew her mother would never put her in danger.

When she was just a step away, she extended her hand towards his neck. He did not move. With a finger, she carefully pushed aside the collar of his cloak. Round his neck, she saw a black leather necklace strung with runestones.

Rye swallowed hard. She looked to his eyes for an explanation.

"Rye!" voices were yelling.

"Rye, are you in the cemetery?"

She recognised them as Folly and Quinn. She still wasn't ready to share Harmless with them.

"You'll be back tomorrow?" she said.

"Of course. I always keep my deals," Harmless said.

Rye ran off to meet her friends.

Grim Green was the great swathe of open, unplanted field just west of the village, separating it from the craggy hill that was home to Longchance Keep. It seemed like an enormous waste of tillable soil, but Earl Longchance did not want his view to be obstructed by crops of any kind.

Grim Green earned its name because it was little more than a depressing field of mud during the spring thaws. On some April days you could sink hip-deep in the muck. The winters and summers weren't much better, when it was either covered under a metre of frozen snow or teeming with mosquitoes and biting flies. The autumn wasn't so bad though, and Rye had heard that long ago Grim Green hosted fairs, festivals and even jousting contests, back when anyone was interested in those sorts of things.

That day the Green was active again as volunteer labourers toiled in the field. The Earl's 'volunteers' were almost always villagers who couldn't afford to pay their Assessment – voluntary work duty being the best of several unpleasant options. Tents were erected. Overgrown grasses were cut and cleared. Rats were chased from the weeds.

Rye, Folly and Quinn made the long walk from Mud Puddle Lane to see what all the fuss was about. It seemed most of the village's children had the same idea.

"What are they doing?" Quinn asked.

"I heard Earl Longchance declared a new festival," Folly said. "The Long Moon Festival – two days from now."

"The Long Moon?" Quinn wondered out loud.

"I think he named it after himself," Folly said. "It marks the tenth anniversary of the night of the Purge. That's what the announcement said anyway – I think his maths is a little off. Anyway, the Bog Noblin will be the guest of honour. I guess he wants to remind everyone that the village doesn't need the Luck Uglies to keep us safe."

"What do they have planned for the Bog Noblin?" Quinn said.

"Nobody knows. Maybe it's a secret."

"Do you think there'll be jugglers?" Quinn asked.

"Jugglers are boring," Folly said. "What about fire eaters?"

"What do you think, Rye?" Quinn said.

"Oh, I like both," Rye said, her mind swimming elsewhere.

Rye was thinking about her secrets. One of them anyway – she seemed to have been collecting them lately. The one troubling her at the moment smelled like swamp cabbage and currently resided in the best hiding place Rye could think of – inside her dried-lizard collection, a spot much reviled by her mother.

Rye was still staring at her boots when the afternoon

sun sent shadows creeping across her feet. She looked up. The shadows were cast by the tall, spidery towers of Longchance Keep, rising up like skeletal fingers digging out of the earth.

Groups of children and several adults wandered along the path to the Keep.

A boy shouted, startling them as he skipped towards the hill. "Don't you want to see the Bog Noblin? The Earl's got it in a cage outside the gates."

Quinn and Folly both got to their feet.

"No one's ever captured a live Bog Noblin before," Folly said.

"Maybe that was a good thing," Rye said.

Folly and Quinn exchanged curious glances.

Rye leaned forward. "Did you ever stop to think that where there's one Bog Noblin, there might be more? What if it has friends?" *Or enemies*, she thought to herself. She still hadn't shared her discussions with Harmless with them.

"They don't strike me as the friendly sort," Folly said.

"Come on, Rye," Quinn said. "Let's have a look."

After all she'd heard about Leatherleaf, Rye didn't

feel like being part of the spectacle. She'd been thinking about monsters. What was a monster? Many villagers still believed Folly's twin brothers were monsters. Just because they were different. She'd heard, when the twins were born, soldiers came to the Dead Fish Inn to take them away. Needless to say, the Floods didn't let them. Soldiers hadn't been welcome in the Shambles ever since.

She'd also been considering what Harmless had said – about what could have been so compelling that it kept Leatherleaf here. Leatherleaf surely didn't want to be in Drowning. He was alone, running from the unimaginable cruelty of his own family, and now he was trapped. He must be terribly frightened himself. Could it have something to do with her? The pouch she took from his camp on the night of the Black Moon?

"You go," she said. "I need to get back home."

"OK," Folly said. "We'll see you tomorrow?"

"Of course," she said, and the three friends parted ways.

Rye trudged back across Grim Green alone, the shadow of Longchance Keep now heavy on her back.

Rye cut through town and made it to Mud Puddle

Lane by late afternoon. Her neighbours were cleaning up Leatherleaf's mess from the night before, and Mr Pendergill was busy repairing his roof. Inside, Abby was cutting carrots into a pot with Fair Warning. Its sharp blade was as useful for making supper as it was for chasing thieves out of The Willow's Wares. Abby had let Rye chop leeks with Fair Warning once. It took fishing line and a sewing needle to eventually stop the bleeding. Rye still had the crescent-shaped scar across her thumb.

Rye helped Abby with some of the safer supper preparations while Lottie and Shady took turns swatting a goose feather they'd torn loose from Rye's pillow.

They were all interrupted by an unexpected – and not entirely friendly – knock at the cottage door. Abby wiped her hands on her dress and set Fair Warning on the table. She opened the door carefully. Staring back at them was the unpleasant face of Constable Boil. He was joined by the two burly soldiers who seemed to accompany him everywhere he went.

Boil raised a dustball eyebrow.

"Miss O'Chanter," he said, by way of greeting.

"It's 'Mrs'," Abby said. "How can I help you, Constable?"

Rye and Lottie both pressed themselves to Abby's legs and stared from behind her hips.

Boil squinted at Rye, as if he recognised her, but continued on to the business at hand.

"We were hoping to have a word with you, Mrs O'Chanter," Boil said. "Inside."

He placed a leathery palm on the door. With a pang of disgust, Rye noticed the blue hair ribbon tied round his bony wrist. It was the one he'd taken from her mother at The Willow's Wares.

"You may certainly have a word with me, Constable," Abby said. "Right here."

She adjusted her stance in the doorway, making it clear that the Constable and the soldiers were not welcome in her home. Boil did not seem to like that one bit. Across the street, Mr Pendergill stopped repairing his roof to watch. The other neighbours took notice as well.

Boil raised his voice and spoke sternly. "Mrs O'Chanter, it has come to the Earl's attention that last night, during the altercation with the Bog Noblin, multiple eyewitnesses sighted yet another troubling thing, here on Mud Puddle Lane."

"Really?" Abby said. "Did someone report the soldiers stealing my neighbours' hens or napping in our doorways? Because I can assure you that those accounts are absolutely true."

"No, Mrs O'Chanter," Boil said coolly. "It has been reported that a Luck Ugly walked these very streets."

"How exciting," Abby said, without enthusiasm. Rye, on the other hand, could not believe her ears.

"That's right, Mrs O'Chanter," Boil said. "And we have reason to believe that it was not just any Luck Ugly. No, indeed. We very much believe that it was one of the most notorious of their kind."

Abby just stared at the Constable.

"No witty response, Mrs O'Chanter?" Boil asked.

Much of the neighbourhood had now gathered on the street. Constable Boil raised his voice in his most authoritarian Constable-like way.

"Mrs O'Chanter, by declaration of the Earl, you are hereby ordered to produce the criminal sometimes known as Grey the Grim, or Grey the Ghastly, or Grey the Ghoul, or Grey the Gruesome—"

"I have no idea who you speak of," Abby said

matter-of-factly.

"Son of Grimshaw the Black," Boil continued, "brother of Lothaire the Loathsome, and last known High Chieftain of the outlaws known as the Luck Uglies."

"Are you finished?" Abby asked.

"I can continue if you need further clarification," Boil said.

"I know not who you speak of and therefore I cannot produce him."

"We have good information," Boil said, "that you are harbouring said criminal in your very home."

"Your information is not only bad, it's preposterous."

"In that case, Mrs O'Chanter," Boil said, "you won't object if we look inside – to clarify the misunderstanding."

"You shall do no such thing," Abby said.

She pulled Rye close to her.

"Mrs O'Chanter, my patience for pleasantries has run out," Boil said. "Step aside or these men will knock both you and your scrawny boy out of the way."

"Hey," Rye said.

"You are not welcome in my home, Constable," Abby said, "lest you've forgotten where you are."

Boil laughed and gestured to a soldier.

"Move them aside – Aaaaaaargh!"

Boil let out a blood-curdling scream and looked towards the ground. Abby, Rye and the soldiers did too. Lottie O'Chanter had wandered off and retrieved Fair Warning, and she was in the process of slowly burying it eight centimetres deep into the Constable's foot.

"You mean! Mean! Mean!" Lottie said.

Boil wrenched his foot away and grabbed it with both hands, Fair Warning still impaling his boot.

"Grab that red-headed bog spawn," Boil yelled, gesturing to Lottie. "She's coming to the Keep for a lesson she'll never forget."

"Me no spog bawn, me Lottie," Lottie clarified, with a stomp and a pout.

The first soldier lurched for Lottie. Both Abby and Rye jumped in front of her. Abby put a thumb in his eye and Rye left teeth marks in his shoulder before he roughly knocked them aside with swats from his thick arm.

He grabbed Lottie hard by her little shoulders and her face went from anger to sheer terror. Lottie's eyes welled with tears.

Struggling to her hands and knees, Rye saw something

large fall from the roof. It landed with barely a sound behind the Constable and the two soldiers.

"I prefer Grey, thank you very much," it said.

The Constable and the soldiers all turned round. It was Harmless. Both of his hands were empty and he pointed a finger.

"Put the child down," Harmless said.

The first soldier looked to Boil but held Lottie fast.

"That wasn't a question," Harmless said, and hit the soldier with such speed and ferocity that Rye barely saw him move. She did see the soldier's head snap back and his feet swept out from under him. Harmless landed on top of him with a bone-crunching crack, and he safely deposited Lottie within arm's reach of Abby. The next soldier quickly advanced upon Harmless with his sabre drawn. Harmless's two swords appeared in his own hands and he nearly disappeared behind his cloak as he whirled and slashed. In an instant, the soldier was disarmed and lay in a moaning heap on Mud Puddle Lane.

Constable Boil had extracted Fair Warning from his foot, but quickly dropped it to the ground when he saw Harmless eyeing him with bad intentions. Harmless cleared the ground between them in two strides and contorted the Constable's arm behind his neck in a way that looked like it might snap it right off.

"Two men?" Harmless hissed into Boil's ear. "On top of everything else, Longchance tries to insult me? Next time bring twenty. Or don't come at all."

He released the Constable from his hold with a shove that sent him stumbling. The soldiers picked themselves up and all three crawled, shuffled and limped away from Mud Puddle Lane as fast as they could. The neighbours watched with mouths agape.

Harmless dusted himself off, although he did not seem the least bit rumpled from the scuffle. There was a fury in his eyes Rye had never seen before. It seemed to fade when he saw them. Harmless offered a hand to Abby. She ignored it and got both Rye and Lottie to their feet. Abby pushed back her hair behind her ears and wiped a smudge off Lottie's cheek.

"Riley," Abby said, "there's no easy way to explain this so I'll just say it. Please invite your father inside for dinner. We have many things to cover and little time to do it."

16

THE SPOKE

WORDS COULD NOT adequately describe what Rye was feeling. After all, for her entire life she had been told that her father was a soldier of the Earl who had disappeared Beyond the Shale. Now, it turned out, her father was a mysterious stranger named Harmless, or Grim or Gruesome, among other not so nice things. He skulked around in the night and chased monsters through the bogs for fun and profit. He was called a criminal and an outlaw by the Earl and seemed to prove it by pummelling the Earl's soldiers in the streets. And not just any criminal – no, he was the High Chieftain of the notorious Luck Uglies. It was certainly more interesting than having a father who fished for cod or shoed horses. But what did that make her? It was all just too much, too fast. The fact was, deep down, excitement stirred in Rye's stomach, but it was buried beneath waves of confusion and frustration.

Lottie, on the other hand, was swinging on Harmless's arms as if they were vines and began to climb up his back as nimbly as a tree squirrel. Harmless smiled awkwardly. His eyes bulged as Lottie threw her arms round his neck and hung there with her full weight.

Shady also took an immediate liking to Harmless, pressing his face into Harmless's wine goblet and depositing himself in his lap, purring like they were old friends.

Harmless wiped Shady's whiskers and chuckled to himself. "I see Shady still likes the good stuff."

As they sat down to supper, Abby deposited a bowl of potato stew in front of each of them, but didn't join in herself. She darted in and out of their bedrooms, putting clothes and supplies together in small packs. Rye hadn't spoken a word to her since they'd come inside. For the first time she could remember, it was her own mother who had made her ears burn red in anger. What else had she lied to her about?

Harmless, as usual, was quick to clean his bowl and compliment.

"Abigail," he said, "the stew is quite delightful. You should really eat some yourself."

"No, Grey," she said with annoyance. "I really need to get these things together. Now."

"There's time," Harmless said, sipping from his goblet. "We have time."

Rye fumbled at a potato with her spoon.

"Why does the Earl dislike you so much?" she asked Harmless finally.

"My family – that is, our family – has a long history with the House of Longchance," Harmless said. "Your grandfather was a bit brash in his youth. He and Morningwig's father got into a dispute – several disputes really – and, well, your grandfather burned the village to the ground."

"This village?" Rye said.

"I'm afraid so," Harmless said. "Twice, actually."

"Twice?" Rye said.

"Yes. You notice that the newer buildings are all made of stone and brick? You can thank your grandfather Grimshaw for that."

"What was the dispute about?" Rye said.

"Well, that particular one was about your grandmother," Harmless said. "Ascot Longchance locked her in a tower at Longchance Keep."

"Grey," Abby said, shooting him a glare, "you really don't need to cover all of this right now."

Rye scowled.

"The girl has a right to know her history," Harmless said. "Haven't we kept her in the dark long enough?"

He turned back to Rye.

"Longchance had it coming. Although, in retrospect, your grandfather may have overreacted just a bit. Particularly the second time."

"They call you an outlaw and a criminal," Rye said. "Why?"

"Well, we were of course," Harmless said. "It's in our blood. A farmer's son toils in the field. A fisherman's son casts his nets. A Luck Ugly's son waits until dark then takes both the corn and the fish."

"A delightful first message to share with your daughter," Abby said dryly.

"Perhaps a poor analogy. Farmers and fishermen were never the Luck Uglies' marks," Harmless said, sitting back. "In any event, for generations the Luck Uglies were worse than any beast that ever roamed Beyond the Shale. When your grandfather was made High Chieftain, he was as fearsome and malevolent a spirit as the Shale has ever seen. But something happened as he got older. Most high chieftains don't live to see the age of forty you see. Historically, it's been a position of great honour, but also a great curse."

"Grey," Abby said, her tone more severe.

Harmless grew reflective. "Your grandfather was the first to live to a ripe old age. And as he aged, he grew wise, more tolerant. Certainly he was still fearsome, but he was fearsome with purpose. He was willing to set aside his differences so that his grandchildren might not have to follow his path into the shadows. So why does Longchance still call us outlaws? Because he needs the village to hate us. If they don't, it makes him weaker."

"Harmless," Rye said quietly, "how old are you?"

Harmless smiled. "I will be forty in just a few days."

"Enough," Abby said loudly, and this time they both went silent.

Rye noticed that her mother was clutching a soup

spoon with white knuckles. She looked like she might put it through Harmless's eye.

A frantic knocking at the cottage door jolted Rye from her seat. She recognised Quinn's voice from the other side.

Abby moved to the door and opened it. Quinn was trying to catch his breath.

"Quinn, what is it?" she said.

"I was just in Nether Neck," he said between gasps. "The Earl's men… they're heading this way… I ran here as fast as I could, but they're only a minute behind me."

Abby's face went calm. "Thank you, Quinn."

"Mrs O'Chanter," Quinn said and looked at Rye, "there are lots of them."

Abby put a hand on his shoulder. "You go home and bolt the door. Don't come back here."

Quinn looked confused.

"Go now," she said. "Run."

She closed the door behind him. Harmless clasped his hands on his stomach.

"My," he said, "they are an eager lot, aren't they?"

Abby hit him in the chest with a heavy pack that nearly knocked the wind out of him. "I told you," she said. "You and your ego. You just had to bait them."

She was already helping to put a pack over Rye's shoulders. She had a smaller one for Lottie.

"Where are we going?" Rye asked her mother, breaking her silence.

"Somewhere safe," Abby said. "Just for a while."

"Will we be coming back?" Rye said.

"Yes, of course," Abby said, although she didn't sound convincing. She adjusted Fair Warning under her dress and slung her own pack over her shoulder. "Come on, let's get going."

"What about Shady?" Rye asked.

"We can't take him. It will be too easy for him to get lost," Abby said. She must have seen the look of horror on Rye's face. "Don't worry," she added. "We have a problem with mice and a leaky roof. He'll be just fine with food and water for some time."

"Wait," Rye said, and ran to her and Lottie's room.

"Riley!" Abby yelled. "There's no time. Get out here now!"

Rye reappeared with Mona Monster. She handed the doll to Lottie.

"Tu-tu, Rye," Lottie said.

"You're welcome," said Rye.

No one noticed that Rye had stuffed something else into her own pack.

"Now," Abby said and shuffled them towards the door.

Harmless shook his head as he peered out of the window. "It's too late." He looked at Abby and the children. "They're already on the street. The boy wasn't kidding. There must be thirty of them."

"Into the hidden chamber," Abby said, and hurried the girls back the other way.

"Should we bar the door?" she asked Harmless.

"They'll just break it down anyway," Harmless said. "Leave it. Save us the trouble of fixing it later."

The O'Chanter family pushed through the paintings on the wall.

What Rye and her family anticipated, but couldn't see, was the gathering of soldiers outside the cottage. On the count of three, two soldiers rushed forward and put their shoulders into the door. Of course, it was unlocked and slid gently open, sending them tumbling on to the cottage floor. Three more rushed in behind them, peering from behind their shields as they charged first into Abby's bedroom, then the girls'. They checked under the beds and in the wardrobes and found nothing more than an enormous, bored-looking cat that didn't even bother to hide.

Once they determined that the cottage was empty and sent word outside, a most unexpected visitor ducked through the front door of the cottage. Morningwig Longchance himself stepped delicately over the threshold, consuming the room with his height. His war helmet and plated boots shone and bore not a single scuff or dent. He held a sword as long and thin as his legs. With its jewelled handle and engraved blade, it looked like it had been pulled from a display over a castle fireplace.

Longchance looked down at Constable Boil, who had hobbled in to join him. Boil used a walking stick and his foot was heavily bandaged.

"You're certain this is the correct house?" Longchance said.

"Yes, yes, my Lord," Boil said. "Quite certain."

Longchance beckoned to an attendant, who extended

a purse of orange slices. He sucked one and squinted his black eyes to examine the room.

Longchance pulled at one of the thin tails of beard that dangled over his throat and paced from door to window. After a few moments, his eyes narrowed further. He cast the orange peel on the floor and pointed his sword towards the far wall.

"There," he said, waving at a torn painting. "Bring a lantern."

Longchance and two soldiers approached the wall. Longchance pressed his face against it and examined the cracks. He removed a glove and ran his finger along them. He sniffed it. Then, with a shove, he pushed open the hidden door.

The lantern light bounced off the walls of the windowless workshop. The table was still cluttered with countless trinkets. But, aside from that, nothing or no one was in there.

"Someone warned them," Longchance said to Boil, who was studying the mysterious little room. "This cow path has always been a haven for Luck Ugly sympathisers. Drag the other Puddlers from their hovels. Find out who it was."

*

Moments earlier, when Harmless, Abby, Rye and Lottie had huddled into the secret workshop, Rye had turned to her mother with a great deal of concern.

"Mama," Rye said, "do you really think they won't find us here? I mean, even Lottie found this place."

They heard a great commotion in the main room of the house. It sounded like soldiers knocking in the front door.

"Riley," her mother said, with some amusement in her voice, "you really didn't think that *this* was the hidden chamber, did you?"

Harmless was on his hands and knees under the worktable, fiddling with a small iron tool. He popped open a square panel in the floor that had blended in seamlessly with the dust and dirt. He took the lantern from the table and peered through the hole.

"Abby, you first," he said. "Then Riley. I'll lower Lottie down after you."

Rye couldn't believe her eyes. A narrow wooden ladder extended down from the mouth of the trapdoor into what looked like a dirt tunnel below.

"Stay close," Harmless whispered as he helped Rye

through the trapdoor. "The Spoke hasn't seen much use in the past ten years. Several tunnels are flooded. Others have caved in. If you get lost in there you may never find your way out."

Harmless climbed down last. As he descended the ladder, he sealed the door shut behind him.

Harmless hurried them down a short stretch of tunnel. He told them to stay put – and quiet – when they arrived at a slightly wider chamber. Then he went back towards the ladder briefly, taking the lantern with him. It was dark and damp, and everything smelled like decaying wood and stagnant water. They all remained quiet. Even Lottie.

When Harmless reappeared with the light, he said, "It's quiet up above. They've left the house, but they're not far."

He used a spark from the lantern to light something on the wall. When the torch flared, Rye could finally make out her surroundings. The chamber was carved from the earth itself, with rotting beams supporting the dirt ceiling. Roots and stones jutted through the walls and floors. Abby could stand, but Harmless had to duck when he walked. From the chamber, dark tunnels snaked off in every direction.

"Where are we?" Rye whispered.

"There's no need to whisper, darling," Abby said. "No one can hear us down here."

Abby reached into her pack and unwrapped two chocolates. She handed one each to Rye and Lottie.

"It's called the Spoke," Harmless said. "It's an old tunnel system that runs under the village. Your mother's right. I've been down here for weeks and haven't run into anyone. It looks like no one's used it in years."

"Where does it lead?" Rye asked, biting at a fingernail. Abby gently pulled Rye's finger from out of her mouth and swapped it for the hand with the chocolate.

"All over the village," Harmless said. "This chamber is called the Hub. From here, each tunnel will take you to a different part of Drowning. Unfortunately, half the tunnels have fallen into disrepair."

Harmless pointed with his finger. "That way, of course, leads back to the cottage. This way goes to Miser's End Cemetery. Over here is the tunnel to the basement of The Willow's Wares."

Rye looked at her mother, wide-eyed. There was a short cut she could have taken on snowy and rainy days?

Abby just shrugged.

"This one over here is called the Long Way Home," Harmless said. "It's quite a hike, but it leads to the deepest, darkest dungeon of Longchance Keep. Needless to say, the Spoke leads to some places you will never want to go."

"The Long Way Home? That's a funny name for a tunnel," Rye said.

"The men who built these tunnels spent as much time in the dungeons as they did with their wives," Abby said flatly.

"The cemetery, The Willow's Wares' basement, the dungeons of Longchance Keep…" Rye said. "People say those places are haunted."

"What a peculiar coincidence," Harmless said, and gave her a wink.

"So who built these tunnels?" Rye said.

"Riley, my dear, I am glad to see that your curiosity has got the better of your nerves," Harmless said. "However, we really must be going now. We're going somewhere safe. The tunnel we'd normally take has been flooded by storm water, so we'll need to take the long and not-so-scenic route. We can talk more on the way. Now stay close. If we misplace you, I fear your mother's sweet mood is going to sour."

Rye glanced at her mother, whose glare at Harmless had all the sweetness of an overripe lemon.

Harmless adjusted his swords, hoisted Lottie on to his back and carried her as they set off through the underground caverns. He led the way, lighting torches with the lantern as he went. Abby was close behind, with Rye sandwiched between them for safety. Rye always struggled to keep her footing even under the best of circumstances; these narrow pathways lined with rocks and hidden roots did her no favours. She fell several times and the old scabs on her knees that never had a chance to heal stung under her leggings. One hard landing sent her pack flying. Rye snatched it quickly before anyone could help, and slipped her hand inside to make sure Leatherleaf's pouch had not fallen loose. As her parents hooked their arms through Rye's elbows to lift her up, she heard Harmless sigh heavily. She feared he was growing frustrated with her.

"We need to get you some new boots, I think," he said. But when he noticed what she had on her feet, Rye saw his eyes change at the sight of the boots he'd worn himself so long ago.

"Come on," he said, "I'll make room." He placed Lottie in Abby's arms and hoisted Rye on his back.

They soon came to one spot that Harmless and Abby seemed eager to avoid. There was a wide, iron door with a small grate at just about an adult's eye level. It was bound shut with the thickest chains Rye had ever seen and more heavy locks than she could count. The metal door was gouged with thick grooves that looked to Rye like claw marks, but from a beast much larger than Shady. This section of the tunnel was much colder than the stretch that ran under their cottage. It made Rye shudder. She could see her breath.

"What's that?" Rye asked Harmless.

"That's the door to Beyond the Shale," Harmless said quietly. "Behind it lies a passage that, for many, is the start of a one-way trip."

It was not lost on Rye that, despite what her mother had said earlier, Harmless was whispering. Abby kept walking without a word.

Rye found the rest of the journey more exciting than scary. Occasionally dirt would fall on their heads from the ceiling and more than once something unseen scuttled by their feet. From time to time they would pass old ladders or worn stone steps leading up to the world above. Rye knew these were the secret exits and entrances that Harmless spoke of. Before long, the tunnels all appeared to be the same. Rye certainly wouldn't want to get lost down here. Then she heard a strange but steady sound. A whoosh that became a roar. The tunnel widened and before them stretched a small rope bridge over a wide body of fast-moving water.

"Is it flooded?" Rye asked.

"No," Harmless said. "It's a branch of the River Drowning. It flows underground here."

"Are we crossing it?" Rye said with some alarm.

"Don't worry," Abby said. "Hold on and you'll be fine."

Rye watched the water rush below them and disappear into the darkness.

"Isn't there another way?" Rye said, as Abby set Lottie down and they all joined hands to navigate the rope bridge.

"It's the only way to get where we are going, Riley," Abby said.

"And where's that?" Rye said, trying not to look down.

"A wine cellar," Harmless said, as he expertly tiptoed across the rope.

Rye turned to her mother. "Mama, do you really have to stop for wine right now?"

Abby frowned. "Riley, my darling, we are not stopping for wine. We're going to the Dead Fish Inn."

17

LAST ROOM AT THE DEAD FISH

HARMLESS MOVED THREE casks, some old wooden crates and countless cobwebs to access the Dead Fish Inn's wine cellar from the Spoke. There certainly was a lot of wine down there, along with plenty of ale, grog and other popular village drinks. It was cold and dimly lit and Rye could understand why people said it was haunted, although Folly had said her parents made those stories up themselves to keep the barmaids out.

The watchdog in the cellar was an old hound whose belly barely cleared the floor. He didn't bark when he saw the four strangers appear from the mysterious passage in the wall, but he scampered up the stairs, dragging his ears behind him as fast as his short legs would take him. He returned with both Fletcher and Faye Flood.

The Floods quickly ushered the O'Chanters up the stairs and into the main room of the inn, where they set themselves up to dry by the enormous fireplace. They had been in the tunnels of the Spoke for longer than any of them had realised, and most of the inn's guests had retired to their rooms. A few slumped in chairs at the bar, and several more were playing Hooks. Rye recognised Jonah and some of the other barmen. The sinister-looking man who had followed Harmless and her mother out of the Dead Fish after the Black Moon Party was back. His eyes twitched from Jonah to his own cards, then to the other players. His surly little monkey dealt another hand.

Faye brought spiced plum cider for Rye and Lottie. Only after sitting and sipping the warm drink did Rye's exhaustion creep up on her. Soon she heard Lottie snoring, her head buried on Abby's shoulder. Rye curled up under Abby's other arm and, despite her efforts to keep her eyes propped open, fell in and out of slumber.

Her dreams blended in with the adults' conversation until she had trouble telling the two apart. It seemed to Rye that Abby, Harmless and Folly's parents talked over their glasses into the early morning. They were joined by

Fitz and Flint, who drank ale from four tankards spread out in front of them. At one point, Leatherleaf sat down beside them on the floor. The Bog Noblin hunkered over a steaming pot of stew. He poured it straight down his gullet and used his black tongue to lick the remains from his ropey orange beard. When he had finished, he cast a hungry look at Rye.

Rye forced her eyes open, her heart racing. Thankfully, Leatherleaf was just in her dreams this time.

"The poison," Abby was saying to the Floods. "Do we know who Longchance sent to poison Grey?"

"Not for certain," Fletcher said. "But we've narrowed it down and we're keeping a close eye on them."

Harmless glanced at the table where the men were playing cards. His jaw tightened. Through her fog of sleep, Rye thought she saw the man with the monkey glaring back at him.

"The Dead Fish is safe," Fitz said.

"Once we find Longchance's eyes and ears—" Flint said.

"—we'll cut them out ourselves," Fitz finished.

"Boys," Faye chastised, "must you always be so crass?"

"Sorry, Mum," they said together. Fitz sipped his ale sheepishly.

"Until then—" Flint said.

"—no new guests get in," Fitz finished.

"As safe as the Dead Fish is, the village is running out of time," Harmless said. "The Clugburrow are at our doorstep. At least three travel by night."

"Longchance will see us all dragged into the bogs before he seeks help again," Faye said with rising anger.

"He thought he'd buried the Bog Noblins and the Luck Uglies years ago," Abby said. "If not for this wayward juvenile, maybe he'd have been right," she added bitterly.

"Nothing stays buried forever," Harmless said quietly, as if speaking only to her.

"He's gone mad," Fitz said. Rye noticed that the twins even sounded alike.

"This festival is madness," Flint said. "Keeping a live Bog Noblin in the village—"

"—only invites catastrophe," Fitz added.

"He's drunk with ego," Harmless said. "This is his opportunity. Once and for all, he's out to prove that Drowning doesn't need the Luck Uglies. He may truly believe it himself."

Harmless turned back to Abby. "You and the girls should be safe here with me gone. If I stay, everyone will be at risk."

Abby pressed her goblet to her lips and said nothing.

"We can hold our own regardless of what Longchance throws our way," Fletcher said.

"I know you can, my friend," Harmless said, putting a hand on Fletcher's arm. "I won't be far. But there are other old acquaintances I must speak with before this mess is said and done."

Fletcher sighed. "Well then, if you must leave in the morning," he raised a glass, "we drink now."

They all raised mugs and clinked them together. The twins had enough to clink with everybody.

Rye pretended to be asleep, but more dreams would not come easily. She had only just met her father and he was already leaving again. She reached up and gently placed her hand over his.

Rye woke to the sparkle of sunlight on coloured glass. She was surrounded by hundreds of bottles in all shapes and sizes. Sitting up, she realised she was lying on thick blankets on the floor of Folly's room. Someone must have carried her there during the night.

When she ventured downstairs she discovered it was already midday. People sat in small groups at tables eating, drinking and talking loudly. There was always loud talk and whispering at the Dead Fish Inn, but not much in between. Nobody used their 'reasonable' voices, just as Rye and Lottie didn't at home, despite Abby's urging. Rye looked for Folly or her mother. She heard a familiar, unreasonable voice rise above the general noise of the Inn.

"Mean sker-rell take my monster!" Lottie yelled. "You mean!"

Rye found her little sister on the floor by the bar. Lottie was engaged in a tug of war with the small black monkey Rye had seen before. The monkey clutched Mona Monster's feet and Lottie grasped her by the arms. Eventually, Lottie won the battle and gave the monkey's tail a pull for good measure. The monkey yelled and clambered up the wall, taking refuge in the enormous chandelier of candles three floors overhead. It screeched angrily at Lottie from its perch.

"Mean sker-rell," Lottie said when she saw Rye. "Take

Mona. Humph," she added, and stomped off towards their mother by the fireplace.

"Your sister's made herself right at home," Jonah said to Rye with a broad smile. He was tidying up behind the bar. "Although she's been fighting with that hairy nuisance all morning."

"Oh. Hi, Jonah," Rye said. "Where did that monkey come from anyway?"

"Name's Shortstraw. At least that's what he calls it," Jonah said, pointing to the sinister-looking man in the corner. "It showed up with him. Three weeks ago."

Rye could see now that the man had pale blue eyes the colour of robins' eggs. He picked a callous on his thumb with the point of a sharp knife.

"His name's Bramble," Jonah said. "Nobody knows where he came from or where he's going. Between you and me, Rye, I'd avoid him. Both he and his monkey are card cheats, if not worse. I don't trust him one bit."

Bramble was watching someone intently. Rye followed his gaze and swallowed hard. His eyes were fixed upon her mother.

"Thanks, Jonah," Rye said and hurried off to the

Mermaid's Nook, where her mother was sitting.

Rye joined Abby at the table, glancing over her shoulder as she sat. Bramble conveniently turned his attention elsewhere.

"Hello, my sleeping dragon," Abby said with a smile.

"Hi, Mama," Rye said. Lottie was playing at their feet. Rye looked around for Harmless. "Is he gone?" she asked.

Abby nodded. "Yes, darling. For now."

"Will he be back?"

"I don't know," Abby said.

"Oh," Rye said, and looked down at the table. Abby reached out and took her hand.

"You have questions," Abby said. "Maybe it's time we talked."

And, for the first time in a long while, they did.

"I told you your father was a soldier who had gone off to fight for the Earl Beyond the Shale because, in many ways, it was true," Abby said. "Your grandfather, your father and others had brokered a peace treaty with Ascot Longchance – Morningwig's own father – years before. The Luck Uglies agreed to provide a most useful and honourable service. To rid the Shale of the Bog Noblins.

They did this so their crimes would be pardoned, their bounties lifted and – most importantly – so that one day their children might have a better life.

"I make no excuses for the horrors Grimshaw once brought upon this village," she continued. "But I remain grateful for what he tried to do for his grandchildren – even though he never met you. It was not without its price, even among the Luck Uglies themselves…"

Rye saw the look of sadness in her mother's eyes. It was strange to hear of sacrifices made for her and Lottie long before they were even born.

"Your grandfather met his demise not long after signing the Treaty of Stormwell, but your father completed his work after he assumed the High Chieftain's crest. Unfortunately, Ascot Longchance also died before the Luck Uglies' task was finished, and his heir, Morningwig, proved to be most dishonourable – even by Longchance standards."

Abby explained that the new Earl had grown wary of the Luck Uglies' success. The villains remained feared, but they were no longer reviled. Bards belted drinking songs in their honour. Maidens batted their eyelashes at them. Village children set out crumb cakes on the night of the

Black Moon. Nobody made crumb cakes for Morningwig Longchance.

Rye had heard much of that before. Abby leaned forward, her voice now tart as she spoke.

"Official village history would tell us that despite their uneasy truce, the Luck Uglies were unable to change their nature, stealing away the Earl's bride, the mother of his only child, during the night. Tragically, Lady Emma was never seen again."

"They chained her to a stump…" Rye said quietly, her eyes on the table as she recalled her discussion with Quinn.

"No," Abby said. "Riley, look at me."

Rye did.

"No," Abby said firmly again. "The Luck Uglies did no such thing. Your father would *never* allow it. The Luck Uglies have never had many scruples, but they live by an unbreakable code. Their rules are secret, and even I do not know them all. But one pillar of their beliefs is that the women and children of their enemies must not be harmed."

Rye felt a break in the dark cloud that had been shrouding her.

"Why would Longchance say such a thing to the village?" she asked.

"Because he cares for his own stature above all else," Abby said, her voice rising. "If the Luck Uglies could protect the village where he had repeatedly failed, how long before the village would decide it had no need for the House of Longchance? It was without warning that Longchance doubled their bounties and declared the Luck Uglies to be outlaws once again, banishing them from the Shale."

Abby paused and took a breath to compose herself. Her voice softened, but the fire in her eyes remained.

"Even your father doesn't know what became of the unlucky Lady Longchance, but blaming her disappearance on the Luck Uglies was just what Morningwig needed to turn the village against them. If the Luck Uglies were so brazen as to steal his bride from the armed Keep, what hope did the villagers have in their own cottages?"

Abby took Rye's hand. She held it firmly and looked her daughter in the eye.

"Morningwig Longchance lives by no code. He would have undoubtedly bargained with the throats of every last wife and child of a Luck Ugly if he knew who they were. He agreed that those families who were suspected would not be persecuted, so long as no Luck Ugly ever returned to Drowning."

Abby explained that, to drive the point home, Longchance assembled an army the likes of which the village had never seen. He borrowed soldiers from his neighbouring nobles, retained fierce mercenaries with promises of gold and pardons from the gallows. Under a full moon, they marched through Drowning, purging the village of all Luck Uglies who had not yet left. Some of the Luck Uglies, blind with rage, ravaged the streets and terrorised the villagers – innocent and otherwise.

Abby shook her head when she said, "This short-sighted act of vengeance only reinforced the lies that Longchance had fed the village."

Abby was silent for a moment, and seemed to weigh her words carefully.

"Homeless and family-less," she continued, "the remaining Luck Uglies disbanded, disappearing far and wide to make new lives doing the only things they knew how – which, unfortunately, were a lot like the troublesome things they'd tried to stop doing in the first place."

Abby stared off into the shadows, and Rye knew that those lost years had taken their toll.

"However," Abby went on, "after many years, your father did return – much to my surprise. The lure of a family left behind proved too strong for even his rakish heart. He began coming and going in secret, bringing me the exotic treasures he collected on his travels so that I might sell them at The Willow's Wares."

Abby shrugged her shoulders when she explained that Lottie was a product of one of those visits.

"I met your father when I was young," Abby said. "He was a puzzle even then, but he was, and still is, charming. I knew who and what he was and, for a long time, I was convinced I might change him." Abby shook her head sadly. "When I first told you he had disappeared Beyond the Shale, I truly believed we would never see him again. It was never my intention to deceive you."

"And what about after he returned?" Rye asked.

"It was too dangerous, Riley," Abby said, looking her in the eye. "That type of secret is too much for any child. Keeping it from you was not the easy choice. I knew if you ever found out, you'd never forgive me for lying."

"Then why did you?"

Abby put a hand on Rye's cheek. "I'd rather have you hate me forever than put you in harm's way for a single moment."

"I don't hate you."

Rye picked a fingernail. Abby reached across the table and gently took Rye's hands in her own again.

"And if he doesn't return this time? What then?" Rye said. "We can't stay here forever, can we?"

Abby shook her head. "No. But don't trouble yourself with that part just yet. I'm making arrangements. There is another place we can go, far away from here..." her voice grew distant. "If we have no other option."

Rye nodded. "OK."

"In the meantime, these secrets you have learned, Riley," Abby said quietly, "the Spoke, the mysteries of the Bog Noblins your father has told you – you must keep them to yourself. They must not be repeated. These secrets put not only him, but all of us in terrible danger."

"I understand, Mama," Rye said. "I won't tell."

"Good," Abby said, and kissed her head.

Rye hugged her mother, and it felt as if a great weight had been lifted.

Of course, when Rye found Folly, she dragged her into Folly's room and told her everything about Harmless, the Spoke, Leatherleaf and the Clugburrow, and the O'Chanters' narrow escape from Mud Puddle Lane. Rye threatened to revoke her friendship if Folly told another soul, but she knew she had nothing to worry about.

"How could you not tell me?" Folly yelled.

"I just did," Rye said.

"Let's go in the Spoke!" Folly said.

"Absolutely not," Rye said. "You can never go down there. You promised."

"Oh, I hate promises," Folly said, biting her lip.

The next morning the inn seemed alive with energy. That afternoon would bring the Long Moon Festival at Grim Green and most of the village was expected to attend. At first, Rye's mother had flatly refused to let her go with Folly and her brothers. Rye argued that none of Longchance's soldiers would know what she looked like. Even if they did, Grim Green would be so filled with villagers, there was little chance any of them would spot her in a crowd. Abby still said no.

As the day wore on and the younger Flood children's excitement grew while Rye's sulking worsened, Abby relented – much to Rye's surprise.

When Abby took her aside, Rye could tell something else was weighing on her mother's mind.

"You may go, but there's one thing you must do," Abby said.

A hitch, Rye thought. She knew her mother wasn't one to give in without good reason.

"You'll see Quinn?" Abby said.

"I can't imagine he'd miss it."

"Tell him that if things get bad – with the soldiers or anything else – he and his father should come here. There'll be a safe place for them at the inn."

Rye nodded. That was a relief.

Abby made Rye promise to stick close to her friends at the festival.

"Always," Rye said.

Abby told her to get out of there at the first sign of any trouble.

"Like the wind," Rye said with a smile.

Abby just nodded with a look of exhaustion that made Rye wonder whether her mother believed her, or if she'd just resigned herself to some unspoken truth.

"You are more of your father's daughter than I could have ever expected," was all Abby said.

Later that day, Rye and Folly took positions in the alley behind the Dead Fish. At one end was the scarecrow Folly's brothers had built to practise knife throwing. Folly removed a corked bottle from the pack slung over her shoulder. It was tied with a string and a label.

"Are you ready?" Folly said, as she prepared to throw it.

"Ready," said Baron Nutfield, who sipped wine and leaned against the scarecrow.

"What's it supposed to do again?" Rye asked.

"It creates a deafening bang and a blinding flash of light," Folly said with excitement. "I actually knocked myself down when I tried it last week."

"Will it hurt him?" Rye asked.

"Not permanently, there's no flame. The flash will just knock him stupid for a while." Folly looked at Nutfield, who was trying to balance on one foot with his eyes closed. She raised an eyebrow at Rye. "I think he'll be fine."

"Commence the experiment," Baron Nutfield bellowed and raised his cup, spilling wine on his ample belly.

Rye looked sceptical. "All right, go ahead."

Folly took aim and threw the bottle down the alley towards Baron Nutfield. The bottle hit the ground at his feet and shattered, sending a little puff of smoke into the air. There was no bang. No flash.

"That was extraordinary!" Baron Nutfield yelled and raised his wine again. "Well done, Lady Flood!"

"Pigshanks," Folly said. "I don't know what happened. Let's try another."

She rummaged through her bag.

"Are you girls ready?" Fifer Flood said, tramping into the alley with Fowler and Fallow, Folly's youngest brothers. "We should go soon if we want a good spot on the Green."

Rye turned away so Fifer wouldn't see her blush. They all carried packs filled with jars of stinging ants, rotten goose eggs and other items they found useful for making mischief. The boys knew better than to attempt such shenanigans in the Shambles where, if caught, they might be sealed in a barrel and tossed in the river. The rest of the village was fair game, though.

"Wait," Rye said, pulling the remnants of her fingernails as she mulled over a decision. The Flood boys' bags of mischief had planted an idea in her mind. "I just need to run upstairs and get a couple of things first."

Rye hurried inside and up the stairs, carefully retrieving the small pouch she'd hidden in Folly's room. On her way back down, she borrowed a decoration from the wall when no one was looking. She rejoined Folly and her brothers in the alley. The group marshalled their nervous energy as they prepared to go.

"Boys!" Faye Flood's voice called from above. "No picking pockets tonight! Understand?"

They all looked up. Abby and Faye leaned out from a third-storey window.

The Floods hooted and hollered in reply, strutting down the dirt street. Rye lingered behind and caught her mother's eye. Uncharacteristically, Abby wore her concern on her face. Rye kissed her fingertips and opened them, letting the invisible kiss flutter up to the window above. Abby pretended to catch it. Rye and Folly quickly caught up with the Flood boys and, aside from Rye's occasional stumble in her father's boots, they didn't miss a step.

18

GRIM GREEN

RYE AND FOLLY met Quinn at the far side of Grim Green, near the treeline of the western woods. Colourful tents had sprung up all over the Green like giant mushrooms. Smoke filled the air, carrying with it the smells of the grilled lamb and fish stew sold by festival vendors. The leaves had fallen from most of the trees and a flock of black rooks lined the spindly branches. Their dark silhouettes eyed the large crowd as the late-afternoon sun dipped in the sky, ready to swoop at the first opportunity to scour the Green for scraps. Folly's brothers had already disappeared into the masses in search of mayhem and amusement.

With some hesitation, Rye told Quinn all the secrets she had already shared with Folly – it was only fair. He was understandably shocked by the stories of Harmless, the Spoke and the Clugburrow. Rye was still overwhelmed herself, and she'd had days for it to sink in. Most importantly, she conveyed her mother's message.

"You and your father should come to the Dead Fish. You'll be safe there."

"Yes," Quinn said without enthusiasm. "I'll let him know that."

"Quinn, this is important. Come to the inn, just for a little while."

"I don't think he'll be keen on hiding behind the Luck Uglies," Quinn said.

Something was off. From his tone, Rye didn't think Quinn was eager to join them at the inn either.

"You're not hiding behind anyone," Folly interjected. "We're your friends. We're just trying to help."

Quinn had tightened up again with the talk of Luck Uglies, and Rye decided once more to change the subject. She asked him to look in on Shady.

"Rye, why do you always ask me to do these things?" Quinn said crossly. He seemed uncomfortable, and Rye worried that the news about Harmless had truly rattled him. "I can't sneak into your house. There are guards outside the door every hour of the day."

"The Earl's soldiers are lazy dolts," Rye said. "What do they do all day?"

Quinn thought for a moment. "Well, they spit. Scratch themselves. Nap a lot. Throw dice."

"I just need you to check on him," Rye said. "Bring him something to eat. Make sure he's OK."

"I don't know…" Quinn said. "Your favours always seem to get me bitten, scratched or pooped on."

"Please, Quinn. He's part of my family."

Quinn sighed. "All right, I'll see what I can do."

"Thank you," Rye said. "Now, I need to get up to the front. Are you both coming with me?"

Folly and Quinn looked at each other sceptically. Rye had explained her plan earlier. Neither of them thought it was a good idea.

"Rye, do you really think you need to do this?" Folly said. "I mean, even if you are right, what difference does it make now?"

"Yeah," Quinn said. "What if the Constable recognises you?"

"I am doing this," Rye said, "because it is the right

thing to do. Leatherleaf stayed here for a reason, and it may be my fault."

Rye reached into a pocket and showed them something in her hand. It was the small leather pouch she had found by Leatherleaf's campfire – the item she had taken from her room the night the O'Chanters fled their cottage.

"These things don't mean anything to us," she said. "But they might mean the world to him. I had no right to take them."

"It's probably just junk," Folly muttered.

"Well if it's not junk to him, it doesn't really matter what we think," Rye said hotly. "If I'd never taken this, maybe the Bog Noblins would have stayed where they belong – disappeared."

Quinn sighed. "If we aren't more careful, we're all going to need to disappear."

"As far as being recognised," Rye continued, returning the pouch to her pocket, "I need you to keep an eye out for the Constable… and, just to be safe, I brought this."

She pulled her cloak tight round her shoulders, brought its hood over her head, and took a step away from Folly and Quinn.

From her cloak, Rye removed a small purple mask of a leathery, hook-nosed imp. She'd taken it from the collection on the wall of the Dead Fish Inn. She slid it in place over her face. It was like looking through the cracks of a fence.

Folly nodded enthusiastically. "Excellent."

"Rye," Quinn said with alarm, "you'll get yourself arrested."

"Look around," Rye said, taking it off and returning it to her cloak. "Nobody's going to worry about a girl in a mask."

Indeed, the number of festival-goers far outnumbered the soldiers patrolling Grim Green. Consistent with village festival custom, almost everyone seemed to be flouting at least one Law of Longchance or another. At first, soldiers had hauled away the most boisterous offenders, but they seemed to quickly recognise the impossibility of the task and now were turning a blind eye.

Quinn just shook his head. "I'll do what you need me to."

"Let's go," Rye said. "If anything goes wrong or we get separated, we meet back here. Agreed?"

"Agreed," Folly and Quinn said together.

The three friends walked down the hill into the maze of tents, performers and villagers. They proceeded carefully and with great focus, as their goal was to reach the far side of Grim Green undetected. Their ultimate destination was the giant iron cage that sat alongside Earl Longchance's great stage and banquet table. It was the cage that housed Leatherleaf the Bog Noblin.

Longchance's banquet table stretched the length of the elevated stage that had been erected on the castle side of Grim Green. Torches and makeshift fire pits blazed at either end, keeping Longchance and his guests comfortably warm on the crisp autumn afternoon. To the south, behind the stage and table, rose a steep rocky hill lined with jagged pine trees. On top of that sat the walls and towers of Longchance Keep like an ugly black crown.

Morningwig Longchance lounged in a gilded chair at the centre of the table, his cold eyes watching the stage performers and the Green full of villagers beyond. He had taken the strands of his beard and knotted them into one skinny little braid for the occasion. He stroked it as one might pet the tail of a cat. He wore so many rings on his fingers that they clattered each time he picked up his goblet of wine or sucked another orange slice from the bowl at his side. Longchance's table was filled with his special invitees, most of whom looked to be the youngest and fairest maidens from throughout the village. The exception was his daughter on his left. Lady Malydia had donned her most depressing black dress and customary scowl for the occasion. She pecked at the piles of fine food on her plate like a constipated hen.

The stage saw a steady stream of dancers, jugglers and jesters, and a wall of soldiers lined the front of the stage to keep the masses from troubling the Earl. Of greater interest, however, was the hideous creature chained and caged in the enormous iron chamber to one side of the stage. The chamber looked like a massive birdcage on wheels, large enough to house a small family, and tethered to it was a team of draught horses nibbling nervously at the grass.

Most villagers had never seen a Bog Noblin up close before. Bog Noblin sightings in the village had historically consisted of screaming, yelling and running away at breakneck speeds. Here, villagers could press right up to the wooden barriers just metres from the cage. Close enough to see the residue of the beast's last meal embedded under its claws. Close enough to smell the stink of rot on its breath. For a small fee, they could purchase a stone from one of the Earl's minions and play 'Knock the Noblin'. There was no real object to the game or prize to be won, just the satisfaction of hitting the Bog Noblin with the stone as hard as you could throw it. Villagers' animosity towards the creature ran deep and business was brisk. At one point someone was dispatched to the dry riverbed to restock the supply of stones. Nobody was willing to go into the cage to collect them.

Leatherleaf sat in a bed of straw at the back of the cage, his dirty, hairy arms wrapped round his knees. His ankles and wrists were bound together with thick chain. In captivity, he had become more withdrawn than fearsome. He stayed motionless as the villagers' stones bounced off his knotted head and shoulders. His bulging eyes darted around, though, at the shadows playing on the horizon of the darkening sky. His long, upturned nose twitched, as if he had caught a familiar scent on the wind.

Rye, Folly and Quinn huddled by the queue to purchase

throwing stones. Rye pursed her lips as her ears began to burn. The village had never captured a live Bog Noblin before and all they could think to do was abuse him with rocks? Rye studied her surroundings carefully, wanting to make sure she'd absorbed every detail. Finally, she nodded to herself and said, "I think it's now or never."

"Are you sure you still want to do this?" Quinn said.

Rye nodded. "Are you?"

"No," Quinn said, "but don't worry. I'm still the fastest runner on Mud Puddle Lane."

"I see the Constable," Folly said, pointing to the far end of Longchance's banquet table.

Boil was on the other side of the stage from where they stood. He was hobbling on his bad foot, grudgingly trying to carry some wood to the fire. Good. Now they knew where he was.

"Then we're ready," Rye said. "Folly, you stay here where you have a good view. Quinn, if you need to run, don't stop until you're back in the village."

"OK," Quinn said. He turned to her and said quietly, "Be careful, Rye. You're not a Luck Ugly." He hesitated. "If you ask me, I hope you stay that way."

He quickly joined the queue before she could respond.

A troupe of step dancers ran out on to the stage in a carefully organised line. The musicians broke into a high-spirited folk song that involved flutes and pipes. The dancers' shoes clattered and clacked.

Rye and Folly stayed put while Quinn inched forward, waiting his turn. When he got to the front of the queue, Rye whispered, "Here we go."

She buried her head in her shoulder and carefully slipped her mask in place.

"I'll take six, please," Quinn said, handing the stone broker his bronze bits.

"Six!" the stone broker boomed. "We have a boy who intends to do some damage. Give it your best shot, lad. Make us proud."

The stone broker handed Quinn half a dozen nicely weighted grey stones. Quinn closed one eye and measured the distance to the cage. He cocked his arm and threw with all his might, missing wildly to the left. The stone landed on Longchance's banquet table and skipped across several plates, spilling wine into one of the maidens' laps.

"My apologies," the stone broker called to the table

nervously. "Lad, you must be more careful."

"Sorry," Quinn said. "Let me try again."

This time Quinn's stone bounced off the leg of dancer.

"Enough, boy!" the stone broker shouted. "Stop!"

Quinn threw two more, breaking three goblets and knocking a spoon right out of a diner's hand.

Now the nearby soldiers had taken notice and moved towards the source of the disturbance. Quinn ran along the grass in front of the stage, the stone broker in hot pursuit, and hurled the last two stones haphazardly. The first knocked a flute out of a performer's hands. The second just missed the hat of Longchance himself. After he let the last stone go, Quinn nimbly darted into the crowd, the stone broker and a handful of soldiers pushing through behind him.

The brief diversion was all Rye needed. Still in her hood and mask, she darted under one of the wooden barricades and scrambled directly for the iron cage. When she reached it, she ducked down and rolled underneath, disappearing between its wheels and the bottom of the cage itself.

Rye caught her breath and crawled on her hands and knees through the grass. In the darkness, she noticed a faint glow from where the collar of her cloak dangled away from her neck. She peeked down. Her choker was glowing blue. Rye looked up. Leatherleaf must be right above her. Only rotting straw and the iron grates separated them. Rye took a deep breath when she got to the back of the cage where she had last seen Leatherleaf sitting. Mustering her courage, she dragged herself out from underneath it.

Crouching behind the cage now she could smell the nervous horses that had been forced to drag Leatherleaf in his prisoner's chariot. Peeking up, she saw the grey flesh of Leatherleaf's broad back just metres from her face. The ridge of his spine jutted up through his skin like craggy stones from the bog itself. His back was etched with unhealed claw marks that looked infected, oozing pus. Rye wondered if they were the work of the Gloaming Beast Harmless had told her about. Leatherleaf was close enough for her to touch him. More troubling, Leatherleaf was close enough for him to touch her.

Rye reached inside her cloak and felt for the small leather pouch. Without warning, Leatherleaf sprang around in his cage so that he was facing her. For a fleeting moment, the Bog Noblin and the hook-nosed imp stared into one another's eyes. Rye leaped back when he pressed his hideous face against the bars, his nose snorting at the air. She could see sticky mucus dripping from it. His bulbous eyes twitched and squinted through the shadows, but they were bloodshot and swollen. It occurred to Rye that Leatherleaf could probably smell her, but he was having a difficult time spotting her. They'd temporarily blinded him with a paste of onions and pepper.

Rye looked towards the stage. The dancers clattered furiously as the musicians picked up their tempo. Villagers clapped along to the festive beat. She glanced through the cage and could just make out Folly's head of white-blonde hair in the crowd on the other side. Folly's job was to watch out for the Constable and to send Rye a signal if he was near.

Rye still had her hand in her cloak and her fingers round the bag. If nothing else, maybe having his pouch back might bring Leatherleaf some comfort. She could probably just drop it into his cage and get out of there. It's not like she was expecting a thank you. She took a step forward.

There was a blood-curdling scream from the stage.

"Bog Nooobliiiin!" a dancer yelled, as if her life depended on it.

The music stopped and an unsettling silence fell over the crowd. No one moved. Then a wave of hysterical cries and flailing limbs spread across Grim Green like a summer fire.

Leatherleaf jolted round to face the villagers. Rye first assumed the screams were in response to Leatherleaf himself, but that wouldn't make any sense. He was still secured inside his mobile prison. She pressed the pouch back into her pocket and ran to the side of the cage where she could get a better view. Villagers were fleeing in all directions, clearing a path for the creature rapidly approaching the stage and the banquet table. The creature bore a resemblance to Leatherleaf, but it was immediately and terribly clear to Rye what Harmless had meant when he said Leatherleaf was small and weak.

This Bog Noblin was a metre taller than Leatherleaf. Where Leatherleaf's arms and legs were long and sinewy, this creature's limbs looked as powerful and dense as tree trunks. Its lower teeth had grown so long that they extended past its mouth and over its upper lips like the tusks of a boar. Its nose had been smashed flat and its face was pierced full of metal nails and bolts, like iron warts. Its filthy orange hair was matted into long flattened coils and strung with bones. Instead of Leatherleaf's bulging, twitching eyes, this monster's eyes were focused black coals of pure malice.

At the Earl's table maidens hitched up their dresses and screamed off in a variety of directions. Soldiers who had patrolled the Green rushed back to reinforce the perimeter in front of the stage.

The Bog Noblin that Rye would later come to know as Iron Wart purposefully made its way to the front of Grim Green, dragging its huge clawed hands behind as it walked. It only stopped when the small army of soldiers raised their swords and shields, barricading the front of the stage. Archers assumed positions round the Green and took aim at the creature's head. It examined the soldiers with little concern, then glanced towards the shadows of the western woods more warily. Satisfied for the moment, it looked up at the banquet table where Longchance sat with the few members of his dinner party who had not already disappeared. The dancers had frozen in mid-step.

Rye glanced around the Green and beyond. Harmless must be out there somewhere. She wondered if the creature sensed it too.

Iron Wart opened its terrible mouth and gurgled something that sounded like an old man choking on a chicken bone.

Longchance stared back, dumbfounded.

Iron Wart roared. It sounded like a cave bear being torn apart by a pack of wolves.

"Well, this is unexpected," Longchance said aloud to himself. He shifted in his chair uneasily. "Boil, come here."

Constable Boil stumbled over the fallen chairs without taking his eyes off the beast.

"Yes, my Lord?"

"Boil," Longchance said, "you speak Noblin, don't you?"

"Well, uh, just a few words." Boil rubbed his face nervously. "I mean, it's been many years. I wouldn't say I'm fluent."

"What's he saying?"

"I'm, uh, not familiar with the exact dialect..." Boil stammered.

"Boil!" Longchance screamed, and grabbed him by the

scruff of his collar. "What is the beast saying?"

"Well, he's demanding that we send down a… translator." Boil swallowed hard. "Someone who speaks Noblin."

"Well get down there then," Longchance said, giving him a shove.

"But, my Lord—"

"NOW!" Longchance commanded.

Boil limped down the stairs at the front of the stage, taking even more time than his injured foot would require. Everyone on the Green seemed to hold their breath. Leatherleaf took no further interest in Rye. He huddled in a corner of the great cage, panting.

The villagers watched as Boil shuffled up to the protective barrier of soldiers and stopped. Iron Wart extended a clawed finger and waggled it, beckoning him closer. Boil glanced up at Longchance, who was perched on the edge of his chair, ready to make a run for it at any moment. Longchance gestured him forward with two hands as if shooing a child. Malydia sat next to her father, her brow furrowed and her goblet frozen in both hands.

Boil eased past the soldiers and took small steps forward

until he stood in the shadow of the monster, averting his eyes. The bent, crooked Constable only served to accentuate the enormous proportions of the Bog Noblin. Rye, like the rest of the villagers, couldn't look away.

Longchance stood at the table.

"Boil," Longchance called in a cracked voice. He cleared his throat and tried for something more authoritative. "Tell this beast to be gone or he shall suffer the same fate—"

Iron Wart hissed the sound a schoolmaster would make to shush a small boy, that is, if the schoolmaster was a toothy, drooling menace and wore a necklace of human feet.

Boil translated. "He says, 'shh'."

Iron Wart cocked his head and listened. Grim Green had fallen eerily silent. He looked towards the trees again. The villagers craned their necks to look. There was nothing there – the shadows remained still. Suddenly, Iron Wart grabbed Boil by the throat and lifted him to his toothy mouth. Boil's spindly legs kicked in the air. Iron Wart grumbled, then loosened his grip enough for Boil to speak.

Boil's words came between gasps. "He says – and forgive me, my Lord, for he insists that I translate this literally –

he says, 'Little princeling, do not think that I'm here to engage you in conversation. I am not. I care not what you have to say. I care only what you will do and expect that you will do it soon.'"

Iron Wart spat forth more terrible sounds. Boil translated them expertly.

"You hold in that cage something that belongs to me. As worthless and weak as it may be, you are not permitted to keep it. Only the Clugburrow can make slaves of our own kind."

Boil's face grew red from the strain of hanging in the air by his neck. He struggled on.

"You will return the young one to us sooner or later. But we know, from experience, that humans are slow learners. You will come up with many reasons to refuse to do what I demand. We have come far and are weary, but we'll indulge your stubborn behaviour for only so long."

Lady Malydia leaned towards her father in alarm.

"Not now," he spat.

"Father," she said, tugging his sleeve. "He said 'we'."

Longchance shook his arm from her grip with a

dismissive wave.

Iron Wart's upturned nose sniffed the top of Boil's balding head as if it were a bouquet of wild flowers. A few grey wisps of hair danced on top of Boil's skull. He craned his eyes up, voice cracking as he proceeded.

"You have two moons to release the young one we call Leatherleaf. Set him free at the edge of the forest, where we will wait to collect him. If you do not, should you doubt our convictions, we will return to this spot in two nights' time."

Rye was still hiding behind the cage. She studied the shadows herself now. *Where in the Shale was Harmless?* she wondered. *Isn't this exactly why he came back? To save the village?*

Iron Wart stuck out the tip of his black tongue and touched Boil's ear. It reminded Rye of a giant snail exploring a rock. Boil shuddered and closed his eyes. Iron Wart seemed to catch himself mid-taste, as if sampling a forbidden treat. He coiled his tongue back into his mouth and narrowed his eyes into cold slivers.

Boil forced himself to continue his translation after Iron Wart refocused and uttered more terrible words.

"First," he said, "we level the walls. Second, we sack the village. Then, we take the Keep…" Boil gulped hard as he spoke, "… and your feet."

Iron Wart fingered his necklace as Boil translated the last of his words, showing Longchance the chain of decomposed human feet strung round his neck.

"That's quite enough," Longchance yelled, although his voice was far from commanding. "As loathsome as you may be, you are but one beast—"

Iron Wart raised a clawed hand and for the first time gurgled in heavily accented, but understandable, human language.

"These are your lips," Iron Wart said, waving dismissively at the soldiers. "Where are your *teeth*?"

"What?" said the Earl, bewildered.

"I'll show you mine…" Iron Wart taunted.

"Wait a minute, what?" Boil asked, wide-eyed.

And with that, Iron Wart bit off Constable Boil's arm from the elbow down, and dropped the rest of him on to Grim Green.

The crowd on Grim Green broke into hysteria. Fleeing and screaming, the villagers knocked one another to the ground in their desperation to escape, as the Earl's archers launched a barrage of arrows at Iron Wart. Most of them landed among the scattering mob with unfortunate results.

Those who fled west for the woods were stopped in their tracks by a second Bog Noblin as fearsome as Iron Wart. The brute had knotted horns like a ram and a coarse orange beard so long that it was tied round his waist like a sash. It appeared from behind a mountain of brush and gleefully grabbed armfuls of villagers unfortunate enough to be leading the pack.

Those who fled east for the village were surprised by a third Bog Noblin that scrambled from a canal on its webbed hands and feet, steam rising off its damp, hairless skin in the cool night air.

On the stage, Longchance grabbed Malydia and shouted for all the soldiers to gather and escort them back to the Keep. Once again, it seemed clear that the villagers would have to fend for themselves.

From behind Leatherleaf's cage, Rye spotted Folly. She frantically waved for Folly to run. Folly just stood where she was, peering through the panicked crowd. Rye realised that Folly was looking for her. Rye pulled off her hood and loosened her cloak. She tore the mask from her face. Pushing all fear of Leatherleaf aside, she jumped and climbed up the rungs of the cage so that she was high off the ground. She dangled from the side and waved her free arm.

"Folly!" she yelled. "Over here!"

Folly turned her head and saw Rye. She waved back.

"Run, Folly!" Rye yelled. "I'm fine. Meet me at our spot."

At precisely that moment, Iron Wart, who was surveying the mess with great delight, caught sight of Rye too. More particularly, he seemed to focus on the cage. He moved towards them now with haste, and Rye feared that Iron Wart had decided to take Leatherleaf without further delay.

The beating of drums overhead stopped everyone in their tracks, including the Bog Noblins.

Rye looked up. The sky's twilight glow went dark behind a rapidly moving storm cloud. The black cloud descended in a funnel and the noise grew louder still. It wasn't drums. It was the beating of thousands of wings. Blackbirds. Rooks. More than Rye had ever seen. If you believed the old wives' tales, this must be at least fifty years of bad luck. They hurtled low across Grim Green *en masse*. Leatherleaf hurried to a corner of the cage and wrapped his arms round his head, crying out in his terrible beast-baby wail.

Iron Wart crouched low to the ground, his fearsome face contorted in alarm. The cloud of birds seemed to consume him before rising. The flocks broke ranks only to regroup and dive again. Iron Wart roared and thrashed as they circled him like a cyclone.

"Two moons," he growled at Longchance again in garbled language, shielding his eyes from the storm of grey beaks and claws.

He pulled a staked torch from the ground and hurled it towards the stage before heading off for the treeline at an urgent pace. The spilled alcohol caught fire and the stage burst into flames.

The spooked draught horses tethered to Leatherleaf's cage lurched forward and began galloping away in terror.

The cage jolted so sharply that Rye lost her grip and fell backwards, hitting the ground with her full weight. The impact knocked the wind from her lungs, but she threw her arms over her head as the cage wheels rumbled past her ears. The cage skittered off behind the horses, up the rocky path to Longchance Keep, the only safe place the animals knew. Leatherleaf let out another bone-chilling wail as he, the horses and the cage disappeared.

Rye opened her eyes. She was in a clearing of matted grass where the cage had sat. By a stroke of luck, each of its four heavy wheels had missed her. Through the smoke and storm of wings she could see soldiers leading Longchance and Lady Malydia off the burning stage, ushering them to the steps on the side nearest Rye. As they did, Malydia looked down, directly at her.

Rye fumbled through the grass, searching for her mask without success. Without her hood and with her cloak hanging off her shoulders, her choker was blazing blue like a beacon.

Rye watched helplessly as Malydia grabbed her father's arm and pointed. Longchance paused and blinked his eyes. He gestured and two soldiers jumped from the stage and ran towards Rye.

At the treeline by the western woods, Folly and her brothers gathered. They were joined by Quinn, who hadn't needed to run back to the village after all. They all sat in a circle, examining something in the grass. It was the pieces of Rye's mask Folly had found on the Green, now carefully reassembled into a broken face.

Grim Green was burning. Tents were collapsed. The stage was in cinders. After terrorising the villagers, the three adult Bog Noblins had disappeared into the night as suddenly as they'd arrived. The big black rooks covered the field now, picking through the broken farmers' carts and smouldering food stands with opportunistic beaks.

The friends waited, and waited some more, their hearts growing heavy. They waited for as long as they possibly could. But Rye never returned to meet them.

19

THE KEEP

THE DINING TABLE was as long as the O'Chanters' entire cottage. Rye sat at one end, staring at the food on her plate. It all looked delectable – the cheeses and grapes, the cinnamon twists and raisins – but Rye had no appetite. A fire crackled in the fireplace of the Great Hall. Thin slivers of light peeked through each of the hall's windows.

Malydia Longchance sat at the opposite end of the table, plucking crumbs from the bread in her hand and placing them in her mouth. She never took her mismatched brown and blue eyes off Rye. There were at least two dozen chairs between them, all of them empty. A nanny came in and out of the Great Hall silently, clearing plates and refilling their glasses. An uncomfortable-looking guard stood by the door, staring blankly at the ceiling while shifting his weight from foot to foot.

"Do you always eat alone?" Rye asked in a loud voice. She'd already learned that she needed to shout in order to be heard at the other end of the table.

"Father never eats with me," Malydia said. "He's very busy."

Rye looked at the enormous oil painting of Earl Longchance hanging over the fireplace. The artist had taken certain liberties, as the Longchance in the portrait had a delicate nose and much more luxurious hair. Dwarfed next to it, in a frame no larger than a book, was a portrait of a regal, silver-bearded man in a crown.

"Is that a relative of yours?" Rye asked, pointing to the smaller picture.

"You know very little of the world, don't you?" Malydia said, smoothing a strand of hair that had escaped her tight black bun. "That, of course, is the King."

Rye knew that the Shale was, in fact, an island – an expansive island full of forests, fields and mountains so vast that those who lived in certain towns might go their whole lives without ever seeing the ocean. But it was nonetheless part of a larger Kingdom. The House of Longchance and a few other noble families had divvied up control of the Shale long ago but, at least in theory, they were subject to the rule of some faraway King who lived O'There. Rye had heard of O'There, but didn't know anyone who'd ever been. It was on the other side of the sea.

"Where is your father now?" Rye asked.

"I suspect he is meditating in his chamber," Malydia said, with a roll of her eyes. "Most of his important decisions require a lot of wine and sleep. The villagers are calling for him to let that hideous Bog Noblin free."

"So, why doesn't he?" Rye said. "Have you made it your pet? It would seem to suit you."

Malydia scowled back at Rye. "Clearly you know even less about leadership than my father. If he bends to the demands of the Bog Noblins now, they will only come back with greater demands next time."

"So the Earl will sit by and see the village burn?" Rye said.

Malydia tapped a finger on her chin. "If necessary."

"And what about this Keep?" Rye said.

"I don't expect it will come to that," Malydia said.

"Those Bog Noblins seemed pretty convincing last night."

"That's why we have you," Malydia said with an exaggerated smile. She put her chin in her hands and leaned forward on her elbows. "We didn't bring you here for your table manners and fascinating thoughts on world affairs. It seems, for whatever reason, that the outlaw Grey the Grim has some kind of strange affinity for you."

"I don't know who you're talking about," Rye said, remembering how her mother had responded to a similar question.

"Is that so?" Malydia said, taking her napkin from her lap. Rye thought she saw Malydia look quickly at Rye's neck. "Something tells me that nothing will happen to me or this Keep so long as you remain in it."

Rye didn't say anything more. That certainly explained why, after some initial pushing and shoving by the soldiers last night, she had been treated reasonably well. They had provided her with a luxurious room and comfortable bed to sleep in, not that she'd slept a wink all night. She had been given the freedom to walk the halls, albeit shadowed by a guard at all times.

"Come," Malydia said. "You make a dreadful guest, but a Lady Longchance is nothing if not hospitable. I'll show you the rest of the Keep."

Rye narrowed a suspicious eye.

Malydia's nanny rushed over and pulled out Malydia's chair for her. Malydia didn't acknowledge her. The nanny then ran to Rye's chair and pulled it out for her too.

"Thank you," Rye said.

The nanny just nodded and turned her eyes to the floor. She was probably younger than Rye's mother, but had a face that bore the pocks and scars of harsh treatment. She seemed uncomfortable being spoken to.

The corridors of Longchance Keep were long and dark despite being lined with torches. The idea of living in a castle occupied only by an army of soldiers and silent servants struck Rye as lonely. Malydia enthusiastically pointed out things of interest – to her anyway – as they went, almost as if she'd been rehearsing this for years. Rye sensed that Malydia didn't get many visitors. The nanny and the guard trailed several paces behind. On the walls, in garishly ornate frames, were paintings so primitive that it seemed to Rye that only the troublesome monkey at the

Dead Fish Inn could have made them. Lottie's works were masterpieces by comparison.

Rye stumbled over a jagged stone in the floor, but caught herself before she fell. She knocked over a tartan tapestry covering a gaping crack in the wall. It depicted a rather unpleasant scene: a frightened man in chains stood knee-deep in what looked like a bog, surrounded by a ring of hooded figures with candles. She quickly hung it back up – crooked.

"Who did all these paintings?" she asked.

"Father did," Malydia said. "These are some of his better works."

Rye raised an eyebrow.

"He's been taking lessons from a master painter," Malydia said and couldn't stifle a smirk.

Rye smiled too. They both looked at each other, then broke into a little giggle.

Malydia composed herself and her smile quickly disappeared. She stopped at a set of heavy double doors. They were engraved with the crest of the House of Longchance, the sharp teeth of the slithery eel creature fanning out in all their menacing glory.

"This is where I have my lessons," she said.

Rye carefully ran her finger along the door's dark surface.

"What is this thing anyway?" Rye asked, poking her finger between its jaws. "A sea worm?"

"It's a hagfish," Malydia said, as if that should be readily apparent to anyone. "They secrete slime to escape their enemies and eat the corpses of rotting fish. They're quite resourceful."

"Yes," Rye said dryly. "They sound like noble creatures."

"You may go in," Malydia said.

Rye hesitated.

"It won't bite," Malydia said, a mischievous glitter in her eye. She pushed the door open and stepped aside.

Rye entered carefully. Beyond the door was a library, its carrels covered with pens, inkwells, paper and parchment. She couldn't conceal her wonder as she took in the walls. She had never seen so many books. They lined the shelves from floor to ceiling and filled her nose with a scent that was part mildew, part magic. She strolled slowly around the library and stared up at the patchwork cavern of multi-coloured bindings.

"I've read most of them," Malydia said self importantly, following Rye in.

"What's this one about?" Rye asked, marvelling at the texture of a book bound in the hide of an exotic reptile.

"Well, a lot of them, anyway," Malydia added with a frown.

The guard stayed by the door looking anxious, as if there couldn't be anything worse than being stuck in a room full of books. Malydia probably thought she was playing a cruel trick by bringing Rye into the library. After all, only Daughters of Longchance were permitted to read under the Laws. But, thanks to her mother and Quinn, Rye had certainly learned enough to read the titles on the covers and spines. She spotted books of maps and books of fairy tales, and books about nature and its creatures. She tried not to allow her eyes to reveal that she knew what they said.

After further perusing the shelves, she came upon something familiar. On a high shelf, in a cluttered corner, was a thick, leather-bound tome. It was in much better condition than the copy that was tucked under Quinn's bed at this very moment but, without a doubt, it was the banned book: *Tam's Tome of Drowning Mouth Fibs, Volume II*. Rye noticed the gaps on either side of the shelf, space where *Volumes I* and *III* should have been. Her eyes must have lingered for a moment too long.

"That's an interesting one," said a voice in her ear.

Rye whipped round and found Malydia hovering behind her. "My father's spent hours with it himself. When he finally puts it down, he'll stomp off to his chamber and sulk over his wine."

Rye just returned her stare, as if she didn't know what Malydia could possibly be talking about.

"The author… Tam, is it? He apparently has some truly awful things to say… about my father… my family. Lies, my father would tell you, all of it. He's searched the hills for him – even Beyond the Shale – but with no luck. I'm sure he'll cut off Tam's fingers should he ever find him – bury his quill in his neck. Yet it's almost as if Tam is a ghost or… something worse."

Malydia crossed her arms and leaned in close.

"I've told him… these stories date back over a hundred years. If Tam's not dead already, he must be a withered old husk. Why not let time and the worms have their way with him?"

Malydia brushed past Rye and reached an arm as high as she could, her long fingers adorned with fine silver rings, their nails chewed down to jagged nubs.

"The prattlers say another copy has found its way into the village." Malydia shook her head as she pulled *Tam's Tome* from the shelf. "He'd no doubt be going door to door, emptying the village cupboards, if not for the more immediate… priorities."

Rye swallowed. She happened to know the illicit copy of *Tam's Tome* wasn't in a cupboard.

Malydia's eyes flashed and a tight smile crossed her lips. She placed the book on a table and placed her hands on either side of its closed cover.

"I've read it, you know," she said, her voice hushed. "Do you know what I think?"

Rye shook her head.

"I'm not so sure it's lies at all. I know my father… and what he's capable of. And I think that certain little clovers of truth could be very dangerous if fed to the sheep of Drowning."

Rye took little comfort in Malydia's smirk.

"So tell me, Riley, what do you think? Fibs, truth or lies?"

Malydia's conspiratorial tone set Rye on edge. She'd never met anyone quite so puzzling. Rye just returned a blank look and said nothing. For once, she was going to win the who-could-stay-quiet-the-longest game.

Malydia must have mistaken Rye's mask for stupidity. Eventually she sat back and gave Rye a condescending smile.

"Of course you wouldn't know," she said. "You can't read." It almost sounded like a hint of disappointment in her voice.

"I imagine it must be difficult to be ignorant," she said, tapping her fingers on the table.

Rye frowned, but held her tongue as her ears began to burn.

"Then again, my nanny can't read or write and she's made a decent enough life for herself," Malydia pondered. "You'll be here for a while. Maybe she can teach you to wash my dresses or file down the callouses on my feet."

The blood rushed to Rye's face faster than she'd ever felt it. Her urge to lash out at Malydia was uncontrollable, even though she knew it was likely to get her skewered by the Earl. Malydia raised an eyebrow and actually took a step back. Rye couldn't tell if the older girl was regarding her with surprise or a new-found respect. The look passed quickly.

"I have other things to tend to around the Keep," Malydia said, her tone dismissive. "Stay here if you want, you can always look at the pictures."

Malydia pulled the folds of her dress from under her heels and disappeared from the library, the nanny close behind. *Tam's Tome* sat alone on the table.

Rye glanced over at the guard. He seemed entirely uninterested in what she was or wasn't reading. As she cracked open the book, she wanted to read, but found herself reluctant. Her afternoons with Folly and Quinn rushed back to her. She thought of the three of them crowded round the book, reading *Tam's Tome* aloud in the back of her cottage, a home she might never see again. She thought about her mother and sister. She thought about her father, whom she had only recently come to know.

The stories in *Tam's Tome* weren't just tall tales any more. In part, they were the stories of her family, the blacked-out portions of her own past that she never knew. Rye didn't want to read them alone in a library. She wanted to hear them first hand from the people who had lived them.

"I'm ready to return to my chamber now," Rye said to the guard.

He led Rye up a winding staircase to the tower where Malydia's room and the guest quarters were located. He opened the door to the guest chamber and Rye went in first.

Malydia was sitting on the bed. Spread out in front of her was the leather bag and its contents – the iron anklet, the tiny skull, the stick figure and the string with the yellow tooth. She must have taken them from Rye's cloak.

She looked up as Rye came in. "What are these?" Malydia asked.

"Are you going through my things?" Rye said. She could feel the anger coursing through her veins again. Her ears were on fire.

"I could smell them," Malydia said. "They stink like skunk cabbage."

Rye remembered how much she disliked Malydia the

moment she'd met her at The Willow's Wares. Nothing had changed.

"Yuck," Malydia said, picking up the string. "Is this a tooth? What *is* all this? More junk from your mother's shop?"

"Yes," Rye said, "that's exactly what it is."

Malydia threw the tooth on the bed in disgust. She wiped her hands on the blanket and stepped closer to Rye.

"And that necklace you wear," Malydia said, craning her head to see if she might catch a glimpse of it. "Is that from the shop too?"

"Yes," Rye said.

"Does it protect you in some way?"

"No, just another beaded trinket."

"Is that so?" Malydia's whisper sounded like the hiss of a serpent. She hadn't taken her eyes off Rye's neck. "Your mother said it was one of a kind."

"My mother's an excellent salesperson. She makes fools believe that her rubbish is their gold."

Malydia narrowed her mismatched eyes.

"I saw it glowing last night," Malydia said.

"Glowing?" Rye said with a laugh. She pulled down her

collar so Malydia could see the choker. "I like the stones too, but I can assure you they do nothing extraordinary."

Malydia examined the runes. Indeed, they were not glowing.

"Is it comfortable?" Malydia asked. "I mean, you must take it off when you sleep."

"No," Rye said. "I wear it all the time."

"I see," Malydia hissed again. She stepped away. "Well, speaking of sleep, I think I shall rest my eyes. I'll be back to collect you for supper."

Malydia turned on her heel and walked out of the guest chamber. Rye could hear her footsteps echo down the corridor. The guard shut the door, but she didn't hear him walk away. She was certain he was posted outside.

Rye went for the windows. Even if she squeezed through them, the tower's smooth walls would ensure a fatal drop. Thin plumes of black smoke drifted into the sky from Grim Green, where Rye could see the shapes of people sifting through the remains of the disastrous Long Moon Festival. She could see the far-off rooftops of the village. The Clugburrow promised to return tomorrow night. If Malydia was to be believed, Longchance was prepared to see the village burn. She was terrified for her mother and Lottie. Folly and Quinn too. What would happen to them in the village when Iron Wart and the other Bog Noblins returned? Harmless had disappeared into the woods again. For another ten years? Forever this time?

Only when she returned to the bed did she realise how fast her heart was racing. She carefully placed the items in the leather bag. Instead of returning it to her cloak, she tucked it inside her oversized boot. It wasn't comfortable, but it fitted. For the first time in a long time, Rye had no idea what else to do. She buried her head in the pillow and shut her eyes tight. It was clear she was no guest here. She was a prisoner.

Her sombre thoughts were interrupted by the throaty caw of a rook.

20

A BLACKBIRD CALLS

RYE SAT UP and listened closely. The bird had to be on top of the tower's turret. Its coarse song was soon followed by loud voices and yelling in the courtyard below. Rye went to the window. Through the glass, she saw that several soldiers had assembled in the courtyard. She opened it so she could hear more clearly.

The gates of the Keep were flung wide open. From the tower she watched a solitary horse make its way up the rocky path towards the Keep. It came at a slow trot. More soldiers appeared in the courtyard as the horse and its rider approached. As it drew near, Rye could see that the horseman was draped in a black cloak and hood.

The soldiers let the horse and rider pass through the gates and into the courtyard; they surrounded them in a half-circle at a safe distance only when the horse drew to a stop. The horseman dismounted, his black cape billowing as he leaped to the ground.

The soldiers stood alert, following the horseman's every move. Several flinched as the horseman slapped the horse on its rump. The animal reared up and whinnied, then galloped at full speed out of the gates and down the path from where it had come.

A few soldiers slid behind the horseless rider, blocking his path to the gate. He was now surrounded by a full circle of soldiers that filled the courtyard.

Finally, the doors to the Keep opened and Earl Longchance appeared, dressed in wrinkled sleeping robes in the middle of the day, his long ornamental sword at his side. He sucked on an orange slice wedged between his teeth. It was the first Rye had seen of him since the previous evening. He stood at the top of the Keep's steps, well behind the circle of soldiers.

"We scour the village looking for you for weeks to no avail," Longchance said, "and yet here you arrive at my door." He clucked his tongue. "Fate is a strange mistress."

The rider lifted both hands to his hood and pulled it back from his head. Rye's heart jumped.

"Harmless," she whispered.

"These towers are lined with archers," Longchance said. "I warn you, any companions you may be hiding will be greeted by the kiss of their arrows."

Rye scanned the perimeter of the Keep's walls. They were indeed populated by soldiers with longbows, their quivers filled. Their eyes were focused on Grim Green and beyond.

"I bring no companions and no tricks," Harmless said. "What I bring is an opportunity. You have put yourself and this village in grave danger."

"Is that so?" Longchance scoffed. "It seems we've done quite well so far without your interference. Or have you not seen the beast we captured?"

"He's a juvenile," Harmless said, "and an injured one at that."

"Since you know him so well, perhaps I'll allow you to share his cage," Longchance said.

"You and I both know that the Bog Noblins who appeared last night are the real threat," Harmless continued. "Iron Wart, Dread Root and Muckmire. They are the fiercest of their clan. Even if you could defeat them, the village would be destroyed in the process."

"Thank you for your expert opinion," Longchance said without sincerity. "I will gladly pay you for it by way of fifty lashes with a bull whip."

"The Clugburrow do not yet know you've forsaken our protection. Surely even you must realise it's the only reason they didn't simply take the juvenile from you last night? That was not sport you witnessed on the Green, it was a test. They have been cautious, but they will understand soon enough. What I offer to you, Morningwig, is one last opportunity to preserve the peace that was once brokered between us. Honour your father's bargain. And we will again save this village."

"We?" Longchance spat with a laugh. "Who are 'we'? You and a handful of other criminals who have nothing better to do than reminisce over grog at that illegal tavern by the river? Everyone knows you are the last of your kind. The Luck Uglies are ghosts. Bugaboos conjured up to haunt children at night. When did you start believing your own lies?"

Harmless didn't say anything. Rye wondered if Longchance's words could be true. Was Harmless really the only Luck Ugly left?

"Grey, you have made a mistake coming here. But I will extend you this courtesy. You can live out your fantasies of grandeur in the dungeons. It is dark there and I understand the silence does wonders for the imagination."

Longchance pitched his chewed orange peel into the courtyard, where it landed centimetres from Harmless's boots. He waved his soldiers forward.

"Take him alive," he said, and retreated into the Keep with his long, loping stride.

Harmless extended his arms to his sides in surrender and bowed his head. "As you wish."

As the soldiers approached, they noticed two metal rods in each of his hands. Spiked iron balls dropped from Harmless's palms to the ground at his feet. They were connected to the rods by lengths of chain.

The soldiers paused. One looked to the other for explanation.

"Devil's flails," the other soldier yelled, but too late. He was instantly knocked senseless as one of the iron balls collided with his head.

The deadly weapons soared higher in flight, whirling through the air as Harmless whipped the chains around him in circles, one high and one low. The first length of chain slashed through the legs of the soldiers, knocking half of them to the ground. The other spiked ball hurtled through the air at head height, the remaining soldiers ducking to avoid being struck. As they lowered themselves, the first ball flew past again and bounced off each of their faces.

The archers held their fire for fear of striking their comrades in the confusion, or worse, missing a sneak attack from outside the Keep's walls.

His enemies now stunned, Harmless dropped the devil's flails and drew his two short swords from the scabbards on his back. The soldiers who could still move clambered back to their feet. Rye watched in awe as Harmless became a moving, striking shadow in his cloak, appearing and reappearing, diving between legs, cutting down one soldier after another until they piled up in groaning heaps. As more soldiers poured into the courtyard, he fended them off two and three at a time, fighting with a grace and flair that rivalled any dancer.

Then, Harmless looked up. His gaze met Rye's and she became aware she was leaning out of the window. Rye thought she saw a twinkle of relief in her father's eyes, and the slight curl of a smile at the corner of his mouth.

Harmless lowered one sword just a little, enough that a soldier was able to break past his defences and grab hold of his arm. He then lowered the other, just a bit more, and a soldier caught hold of his wrist. A mass of bodies quickly set upon him. Rye gasped and took a step back. If she hadn't, she would have tumbled right out of the window. Harmless kept eye contact with Rye as they pulled him to the ground, until she couldn't see him any more beneath the bodies of the soldiers.

Rye threw her hands over her face as the soldiers spared no time in exacting their revenge, pummelling Harmless with fists, boots and the hilts of their weapons. Once they'd exhausted themselves, they dragged him through the courtyard by his feet, right up the stone steps and through the heavy doors of the Keep, slamming them shut behind them.

Rye sat with her head in her hands for a long while. She was horrified by the terrible beating the soldiers had given Harmless in the courtyard, but Longchance had commanded that they take him alive. That meant Harmless would be somewhere in the Keep.

She removed her palms from her wet eyes. Her father had come back for her.

Rye shovelled chunks of bread and spoonfuls of stew into her mouth. Malydia watched her with a crinkled nose, barely pecking at the food on her own plate. Rye's appetite had returned with her realisation that Harmless was also somewhere within these very walls. He would have come with a plan of some sort, although she didn't expect that being beaten half to death and captured was part of it.

Rye hadn't said more than a few words to Malydia all meal, although that hadn't stopped Malydia from quizzing her about Harmless – how Rye knew him, where he'd come from? Rye had absorbed much from her mother and the folk around the Dead Fish Inn over the years. When pressed about anyone's identity, the correct answer was 'Who? Don't know him.'

The less Rye said, the darker and more sour Malydia's mood became.

Rye sopped up the last of her stew with a piece of bread and washed it down with a gulp of fermented cider. When she swallowed, she let out an enormous belch.

Malydia looked horrified. The nanny lowered her eyes and stifled a giggle.

"How vile," Malydia said.

"In some cultures, that's how you say 'thank you' after a good meal," Rye said. "I'm surprised you haven't read that in one of your books."

Malydia just shook her head and threw her napkin on the table.

After supper, Malydia marched to her room in silence and the guard and the nanny escorted Rye down the hall to the guest chamber. The nanny turned down her bed while the guard waited in the hall.

"Don't let the dark fool you," she whispered without looking at Rye, as if she were just thinking out loud. "The Keep can be a restless place at night. If you sleep at all, I'd do it with one eye open – the Lady of the Keep has a way of gettin' what she wants."

"Thank you," Rye said. "But—"

The nanny had said all she was willing. As soon as

she closed the door, Rye peeked through the keyhole. As she expected, the guard had set up watch on a stool right outside.

Rye felt her choker round her neck. Somehow, she did not expect that she had seen the last of Malydia for the night. She didn't intend to stick around long anyway. She was going to find Harmless.

Rye wrapped her cloak round her shoulders, pulling the hood over her head. She curled up carefully in a dark corner where she could keep an eye on the door.

Rye stayed awake for as long as she could. It wasn't difficult at first. The floor was cold and uncomfortable, and outside she could hear the wail of Leatherleaf, caged somewhere on the Keep's grounds. From time to time, she got up to check the keyhole. The guard was still awake each time, tapping a boot, scratching his back with a dagger or, once, digging around with a finger lodged halfway up his nose.

It had been an hour or more when her eyelids began to sink as the round, glowing moon rose in the night sky. Exhaustion was winning its battle and eventually she nodded off to sleep, her cheek pressed against the hard stone floor. She dreamed of a slithering serpent – a creature she now recognised as a hagfish. She sat with it in the bogs peacefully for a long while, but just as she reached to touch it, the nasty creature snapped open its mouth to bite her. Before she could pull her arm away something grabbed her by the neck. An enormous, orange-bearded Bog Noblin sprang from the muck, dragging Rye and the hagfish down with him under the bog.

Rye woke up coughing, the imagined feel of peat in her throat so realistic that it made her choke.

She opened her eyes, and there were the mismatched brown and blue eyes staring back at her just centimetres from her face.

Rye lurched, but a gentle finger moved to her lips and the night-time visitor said, "Shhhh."

Rye blinked several times to make sure she was seeing clearly.

"Truitt?" she whispered. "Is that really you?"

21

COLD, DARK PLACES

Truitt would not let Rye speak until they were well past Malydia's room and on their way down the tower's darkened staircase. Rye held the back of his shirt as he led the way, navigating only with his fingertips against the Keep's walls, as if each crack and groove told the next direction.

"Truitt," Rye said, "what are you doing here?"

"Quietly. Please."

"Where are we going?"

"Someone asked me to find you."

Rye's heart jumped at the prospect. Then she grew wary.

"We should be careful. The Earl's daughter – she may come looking for me in my room."

"I doubt she'll leave her chamber until morning. The

Keep's halls frighten even her after dark."

"I hope you're right," Rye said, unconvinced. "I'd be glad if I never saw that terrible girl again."

"Malydia's not all bad," Truitt said. "She's just been living with the Earl for too long. It's made her heart black round the edges. It still beats warm inside, though."

"You know her well?" Rye asked in surprise.

"Yes," Truitt said, and then paused. "I mean, as well as anyone can under the circumstances – she's my twin sister."

Truitt paused and looked back at Rye with his brown and blue eyes. "You may have noticed the resemblance."

Rye's jaw dropped. She was glad at that moment that Truitt couldn't see her. If he could, he might be offended by the look of disgust on her face.

"Longchance is your father?" Rye said, stopping in her tracks.

"No," Truitt said firmly. "He's no father to me."

He must have felt the tension in Rye's grip on his shirt.

"Let's keep moving," he said. "I'll try to explain as we go."

Rye's grip relaxed and Truitt pressed on. He paused to

listen carefully as they reached the bottom of the stairs. After a moment he kept going, leading them down the corridor.

"I don't understand," Rye whispered as they walked. "Do you live here in the Keep?"

"No. This is a terrible place. I come here only to speak with Malydia. My home is underground in the tunnels beneath the village."

"You know of the Spoke?" Rye said.

Truitt cocked his head. "I've heard them called that by those who speak of the tunnels, although few do. Most would think it a dreadful place to live. But, obviously, I don't mind the dark, and it's not as lonely as you might think. I live there with an old man who took me in and cared for me, and others like me, when I was an infant. He's sick now and I look after him as best I can. If I have a father at all, it would be him."

They came to an intersection between the corridor they were travelling down and a narrower one. Truitt stopped and pressed them against the wall.

"Rye, I smell something," Truitt said. "Lean out – carefully – and tell me what you can see."

"Truitt, you should know that bad things tend to happen when I try to be careful."

"It will be fine. Just look."

Rye leaned her head round the corner of the wall, peeking out from under her cloak and hood. There, sleeping in the middle of the floor, was the most enormous grey dog she had ever seen. It was larger than a wolf and it wore a heavy leather collar, but no leash. Its paws rested on a half-chewed bone of disturbingly large size. Rye leaned back.

"You're smelling a calf's leg or a damp dog. Either way, it's bad news."

"So we take the long way," Truitt said, and they slunk off in the other direction.

This stretch of corridor was darker and narrower. Judging by the texture of the stone floors and walls, it seemed to lead to an older part of the Keep.

"Rye," Truitt said, as they reached the top of a passageway so steep that it seemed to disappear beneath the earth itself. "We're about to enter the dungeons of Longchance Keep. I don't know if you scare easily – something tells me not – but things have occurred here that have left their impression on these passageways forever. Take a torch from the wall. Its light may give you some comfort. And don't let go of my shirt."

Rye took his advice. Truitt started forward.

"Truitt," Rye said, her hope rising. "It was a man who sent for me?"

Truitt nodded. "I don't know his name. But he knows yours."

Rye had never been in a dungeon before, and it was every bit as awful as she expected. Interconnected stone passages and cells formed a labyrinth of catacombs meandering beneath the earth. It was cold and damp, and the smell of decay rose from puddles of stagnant water. There wasn't a soul in sight.

"I thought there'd be more people here," Rye whispered once they'd stopped.

"The Earl set all the prisoners free," Truitt said. "He thought it would be cheaper to let the Bog Noblins loose on them in the village than to keep feeding them here."

Truitt removed a long, bone-white key from a shabby pocket and unlocked a metal door as quietly as he could.

Rye raised an eyebrow with interest.

"Except for him," he said, and pushed it open. "He's the only one left. Excuse me, but I think it's best if I wait out here."

Rye peeked inside. There, chained upside down by his boots in the middle of the cell, was a man. The long hair hanging from his head grazed the floor. His arms dangled. It looked like a most uncomfortable position, but the man didn't seem to be in any torture. He swung ever so slightly. Like a bat.

He craned his neck and shoulders when he heard Rye step inside the cell and rotated his body to face her.

"Riley," Harmless said, "is that you?"

Rye pulled the hood from her head and stepped closer. Harmless flashed a warm, upside-down smile and immediately grimaced. His cheeks were red and purple and one eye was nearly swollen shut.

"It's me, Harmless. Are you in much pain?" Rye wanted to reach out to touch his face, but feared she might hurt him.

"Well, remember I told you I'd broken nearly every bone in my body? It turns out I've found another. There's a tiny little bone in your ear right about here," he said pointing to the one ear he still had.

"I'm sorry," Rye said. "That sounds terrible."

"Could be worse," Harmless said. "More importantly, what about you? Have you been harmed?"

"No. They're unpleasant, but they've treated me OK – for now anyway."

"I'm relieved. Come, give me a hand, would you?"

Rye stepped forward and lifted Harmless by the shoulders so he could bend upwards at the waist. He grabbed the chains at his ankles with his hands and pulled himself into a more upright position.

"Much better," he said. "Too much hanging gives me double vision."

Rye looked towards the door. "How do you know Truitt?"

"The boy? I met him down here. He found me, actually. He seems to know every corner of this Keep."

"He says he lives in the Spoke," Rye said.

"He may indeed. I hadn't come across him in my recent travels, but there are tunnels I have not revisited. In any event, he has brought you here, and for that I am most grateful."

"Harmless, what was your plan in coming here?"

"Well, first, it was to find you," Harmless said, and Rye again saw that flash in his eye. "Second, as you probably heard, I was trying to save the village one last time."

Rye looked around at the cell. "So what's your plan now?"

"Well, I've found you at least. I imagine you heard Longchance in the courtyard. Given the circumstances, I suppose we let the Bog Noblins raze the dreadful place once and for all."

"What?" Rye choked and took a step back. "You can't possibly mean that."

"Don't worry," Harmless said, gesturing in a way that was meant to be reassuring, but didn't seem so when made hanging from chains.

"Harmless, no, you can't."

"Your mother and sister will be fine," Harmless continued. "So will your friends as long as they stay in the Dead Fish Inn. As for us, when the Bog Noblins arrive at the Keep, that will be our opportunity to escape..."

Harmless's voice trailed off as he looked at Rye. He

reached out and touched the choker round her neck.

"I know your mother explained to you what this does. Or some of it, anyway." Harmless measured every word as he held her eyes with his stare. "You must not remove these runestones in the coming days. Do you understand?"

"Yes, but—"

"Listen."

"The village—"

"Riley, listen," he said firmly, and she stopped. "You must guard them as if your life depends on it. Understand?"

"I understand," Rye said. "But what about the rest of the village?"

"What do you mean?" Harmless said.

"You can't let the Bog Noblins destroy the village and everyone in it!"

"I don't have much of a choice, Riley. Longchance broke the Treaty long ago. What good is a treaty without consequences?"

Rye grabbed him by the tattered and torn collar of his shirt. He lost his grip on the chains and fell upside down again.

"Harmless," Rye said, "Drowning is the only home I've

ever known. You said that my grandfather burned this village to the ground twice because of his fight with the House of Longchance. You're going to do the same?"

"Now, Riley, there is in fact a difference—"

Rye's ears were as hot as her voice. She shook him by the fabric clutched in her hands. Harmless grimaced.

"No, there isn't. Ten years ago, the Luck Uglies – you – burned the bridges and terrorised these villagers because the Earl had wronged you. All the good you had done – completely ruined."

"Not all of us," Harmless corrected in between grunts of pain. "We're not all cut from the same cloth."

"You can stop this. We can escape this dungeon together right now. Didn't you say the Spoke had a tunnel leading to the deepest, darkest dungeon of Longchance Keep? The Long Way Home?"

"I did."

Rye looked around the cell. "We'll find a way to break your chains and then we'll look for it."

"You won't find it here," Harmless said. "This isn't the deepest, darkest dungeon of Longchance Keep."

"What?" Rye said, looking around. "It gets worse than this?"

"Most certainly yes. This is the upper dungeon. It's actually rather nice as far as dungeons go. Riley, would you… please?"

Harmless placed his hands over hers. They still gripped his collar, its folds pinched tight round his throat. Rye let go as soon as she realised what she was doing, examining her hands as if they didn't belong to her.

"Thank you," Harmless wheezed, and sucked in a lungful of air.

A thin gash had reopened under his eye. Rye tried to blot the droplets with a trembling finger.

"I'm so sorry." Her eyes welled.

"Riley," Harmless said, touching her cheek gently. "I'll confess to you that I want to see the Earl get what is coming to him – I'd shed no tears over the destruction of this Keep. However, your point is not lost on me."

Harmless had caught his breath.

"You are a very persuasive young woman, Riley O'Chanter," Harmless said, rubbing the fresh welts on his throat. "You remind me much of your mother when she was young. Despite my better judgement, I can think of one way that we might – just might – save the village. It is fraught with uncertainty though, and I cannot do it alone. Are you prepared to help me?"

Rye nodded enthusiastically.

"Very well," Harmless said. "Let's call in our new friend. We shall need his help too."

Truitt joined them in the cell at Harmless's beckoning, and offered to share his plunder from the Keep's pantry – a stale loaf of bread he'd wrestled from a kitchen rat and a large flask of rice porridge. Rye declined. Harmless, of course, ate it all and seemed quite at ease using a spoon while hanging upside down.

"Marvellous snack, thank you very much," he said, and wiped his mouth with the back of his hand. He burped when he was finished.

"That means thank you," Rye said.

"Oh," Truitt said. "You're welcome."

Rye and Truitt helped Harmless up so that he could reach his chains and dangle more comfortably.

"Truitt, are you still willing to accept the deal we discussed earlier?" Harmless asked.

"I am," Truitt said.

Harmless reached round his neck with his free hand and unclasped his runestone necklace.

"Come," he said, and Truitt stepped towards his voice.

Harmless pressed the necklace into Truitt's hands. Truitt reached into his pocket and handed his bone-white key to Harmless.

Rye's eyes grew wide.

"Don't worry," Harmless said, recognising Rye's concern. "The Clugburrow are well aware of who I am, with or without the runes. This key, on the other hand, will allow me to unlock my chains – and the necessary doors – at a time when Longchance least expects it."

Truitt clasped the necklace round his neck and carefully covered it under his collar.

"Riley, I have something you will need as well," Harmless said, and with his index finger and thumb, he dug deep into his mouth. He tugged and pulled, grimacing as he worked at his gums. Harmless shut his eyes tight and, with a pop, something came loose. He reached out and handed Rye something smooth, wet and shiny.

"Is that… your tooth?" Rye said opening her palm with hesitation.

"No, but the gap left by a tooth long forgotten has proved to be a safe hiding place for this. I was afraid I'd swallowed it after the guards so warmly welcomed me."

Rye examined what looked to be a metal figurine. She squinted to make out its tiny details. It was short, stubby and cast in the shape of a wailing banshee. Just touching it gave her a sense of dread.

"It too is a key of sorts," Harmless said. "A puzzle piece actually. Although it fits a puzzle unlike one you've ever put together."

"What does it open?" Rye asked.

"Do you remember when we escaped through the Spoke? The locked door that we passed?"

"The door to Beyond the Shale?"

"That's the one," Harmless said.

Rye was quiet for a moment.

"You're going to tell me to open it, aren't you?" Rye said, with a tremble in her voice.

"I'm afraid it's the only way."

"Can't you just unlock your shackles with Truitt's key now?" Rye said. "We'll go together?"

"If you wish," Harmless said softly. "But dawn is almost

upon us. We would probably need to fight our way out and, I'm sorry to say, I'm not at my finest. Even if we escape undetected, Longchance will quickly discover we're gone. Rest assured he will come after us."

Rye considered the odds of a girl and one unarmed, injured man – Luck Ugly or not – fighting their way out of a castle full of soldiers.

"Defeating the Clugburrow would be difficult enough without his interference," Harmless continued, "but if we must battle the Earl's soldiers in the streets as well, I'm afraid the village is doomed. No, if we are intent on saving Drowning, we must bide our time. And I must stay behind."

Rye bit her lip.

"We will be safe here at least until tomorrow night," Harmless said. "By then most of the soldiers will be preparing for the Clugburrow. That's our chance to get you out."

Harmless read the concern on her face.

"Saving the village is not the easy choice," he said and paused. "There's no shame in changing your mind."

Rye swallowed hard and nodded. "Tell me what I

need to do."

Harmless smiled just a little. "First you need to know where you are going. The gate to the deepest, darkest dungeon is guarded at all times. Tomorrow night Truitt will get you into the Spoke by way of an alternative passage. The Earl and his soldiers will be too preoccupied preparing for the Clugburrow to stop you. For those who are not–" for just a moment, Rye saw a predatory glint flash in Harmless's unswollen eye– "well, I'll have had a day of rest. I'm sure I can keep their attention away from you for a little while."

Rye wondered if, in fact, Harmless was looking forward to that part.

"Once you are in the Spoke, you will have no one to guide you. You'll need a map."

"Where do I get one?"

Harmless had a twinkle in his eye. "If you don't mind, go and gather the bone dust from that poor fellow in the corner."

"You're joking," Rye said. The skeletal remains of the cell's former inhabitant sat in a pile of decomposed clothing. Rye thought she might gag.

"Go on, he won't mind," Harmless said. "Grab his trousers too."

After Rye had torn the fabric into a makeshift canvas, found a long, slender bone for her quill, and collected a pile of chalky dust of origins she cared not to imagine, Harmless lowered himself so that he hung upside down again, his back facing her. He untucked his shirt and let it fall to his shoulders. Laid over the long, faded scars on his back was a circular pattern of tattoos that looked like the spokes of a ship's wheel. Rye looked closely. It wasn't just a design. It was a map.

"Here is everything you'll need to find your way."

Rye gritted her teeth and began to copy the map on to the trousers using her disgusting quill.

"If we are waiting until tomorrow anyway, why can't you come with me?" Rye said as she worked. "We can do this together."

"We can't be in three places at once," Harmless said. "The road to saving the village ends here. This is where I must be."

"I can't be in three places either," Rye said.

"No, but you're fast. Resourceful. And you have friends

if you need them," Harmless said. "Two friends you would trust with your life?"

Rye looked Harmless in the eye. It was a serious question that begged a serious answer.

"Yes," she nodded. "I would."

"Then I shall trust them with mine," Harmless said. "Now draw with care, Riley, and I will explain everything you need to know."

Rye hurried to copy the map in as much detail as she could, all the while listening intently to Harmless's plan. It covered three stops: the door to Beyond the Shale, the bridge over the River Drowning, and the Dead Fish Inn – in that order.

First, she must enter the Spoke and take it to the door to Beyond the Shale. She was to use the puzzle piece Harmless had given her to unlock the door, but he said this step could be tricky. Luck Ugly puzzle locks were designed to frustrate and bewilder, and the Luck Ugly locksmith who had made this particular puzzle lock was the most devious of his kind. Harmless warned her that, once the door was opened, she would need to get away as fast as she could. The forest Beyond the Shale was unpredictable. It might attack ferociously or beckon to her with promises – its effect was different on everyone, but its intentions would not be pure.

Second, she was to take the Spoke to the bridge over the River Drowning. He pointed to her map and a tunnel that ended at the bottom of an abandoned well. There she was to light the Luck Cauldrons on top of the bridge. Harmless described them for her and said that any torch or spark should do the trick.

Finally, she was to return to the Dead Fish Inn, where she should tell her mother and the Flood family what she had done and everything Harmless had planned. There she was to stay, with Abby and Lottie, and let the night run its course.

Harmless told her that if she did all those things, in that order, there just might be a village left in the morning. It sounded overwhelming at first, but Harmless's voice was so calm and confident that, by the time he had finished, Rye was convinced that maybe, just maybe, they might be able to pull it off.

After Rye had repeated the instructions back to him three times, Harmless tilted his head towards Truitt and said kindly, "Truitt, could you give us just a moment?"

"Of course," Truitt said. Letting the touch of his fingertips guide him, he stepped outside the cell.

"Riley," Harmless said, "the steps we've discussed are very important. You must complete them in order, as quickly as possible, for everything to work the way we hope. Your timing must be precise."

"I understand," Rye said.

"I did not want to speak of this in front of Truitt, but you must know – the Luck Cauldrons are a signal. A call as old as the Luck Uglies themselves. Once lit, any Luck Ugly who sees them is bound by duty to answer."

Rye swallowed hard. So it was true. The Luck Uglies were really coming. Or were they?

"But Longchance said you were the last one. Are there any Luck Uglies left to answer?"

"The cauldrons haven't been lit in more than ten years. The Luck Uglies have been flung far and wide but, yes, there are still some out there – nearby. That's where I've been since I left the Dead Fish. That's why I wasn't at Grim Green."

"Why didn't the Clugburrow finish us all when they had the chance?"

"Fortunately for us, the Clugburrow are a superstitious

lot," Harmless said. "To them, a blackbird that flies by night brings bad luck. The ugliest kind." He smiled. "Remarkable birds, the rooks. Be kind to them. They always repay their debts."

Rye was dumbstruck. "You sent the flocks? How?" Harmless's skills seemed to defy logic.

"Practice," Harmless said with a smirk. "But never mind that now. The Clugburrow won't be fooled again."

"I hope the others will answer the call."

"I believe they will. Once a Luck Ugly, always a Luck Ugly. Until the day you take your last breath."

Harmless smiled wryly. "That said, time can do strange things to men. They may come, but I can't guess what other troubles the call might bring with it. That, however, is a problem for another day."

Rye nodded.

"Stay in the Spoke as much as you can. Once you make it to the Dead Fish Inn, do not leave there. And do not, under any circumstances, return here to the Keep."

"Harmless, what about you?" She was sure there was more to the plan that he wasn't telling her.

"I've been doing this sort of thing for many years.

Whenever I feel I've grown weary of it for good, my ears – well, ear these days – starts to burn. I come to my senses and realise I have one more in me."

"I mean," Rye said, moving closer, "what happens here at the Keep?"

"The worst monster dwells within these walls. When he seals himself off from the threat outside, I'm the twist of fate who'll be waiting."

Rye would have asked what Harmless meant, but deep down, she already knew the answer. Instead, she asked, "Will I see you again?"

"One way or another, we will have breakfast together again on the morning of my birthday. Three days from now. At our favourite spot." Harmless reached out and touched Rye's cheek with his palm. "You are an extraordinary young lady, Riley O'Chanter. It has been my greatest pleasure getting to know you these past few weeks."

Rye hugged Harmless round the shoulders. He hugged her back.

"Now go," he said. "The guards will be coming. And there's a village in need of your help."

22

A LADY'S LAST RESORT

RYE AND TRUITT made their way back towards the tower, carefully avoiding the team of guards patrolling the Keep's halls.

"Truitt," Rye whispered, "what is that key you traded?"

"It's called the Everything Key," Truitt said. "It opens every lock in the Keep."

"Where did you get it?"

"Malydia gave it to me," Truitt said, and must have heard the surprise in Rye's breath. "I told you she's not all bad."

"I know she's your sister," Rye said, shaking her head, "but she doesn't strike me as the generous sort."

Truitt paused at the echo of footsteps in the distance, then moved forward again once they'd passed.

"Malydia used to wear the Everything Key round her

neck," Truitt said. "To this day I have no idea how she came by it, but she gave it to me as a gift."

"Why?"

"Malydia knows that my life is not an easy one. She wanted to be sure that I could get into the storerooms and pantries if I needed to. It was only later that I discovered it opens other doors in Drowning. I use it to take care of the link boys and girls who live in the streets and sewers. Link *rats* you call them."

Rye now felt ashamed for ever using the term.

"Malydia knows what I use the key for and doesn't stop me. Say what you want about her, but if it wasn't for Malydia, most of those children would have starved."

"So why sneak through these halls after dark?" Rye asked. "Can't you just live here with her?"

Truitt stopped and turned to Rye.

"When I was just an infant, my father threw me into a sewer. He considered me broken – because my eyes didn't work. He blamed his imperfect son on my mother, and I won't speak of what he did to her."

His eyes might not see, but they still conveyed emotion. Rye thought of Lady Emma. She sang part of the illicit rhyme in her head: *Emma bore a child and tongue too loose, then she was of no further use.* Truitt was Longchance's dark secret – a secret no mother would be willing to keep. Rye swallowed hard. She couldn't believe any father could be so evil.

Rye was quiet for the remainder of the way. Truitt paused as they approached Malydia's room. He heard no sound and waved Rye forward. Further ahead, Rye's guard was snoring loudly on his stool, his chin slumped on his chest.

"Truitt," Rye whispered. "You're risking much by helping us, but it seems you have little to gain."

Truitt sighed.

"Rye, I don't wish to live in the tunnels and sewers forever. And when it is time for me to come back into the light, I want there to be a village left to come out to."

It occurred to Rye that Truitt reminded her a lot of Harmless. His words always seemed deeper than their plain meaning. Rye's feelings were easier to express.

"Thank you, Truitt."

Truitt bowed his head.

"I will see you in the Chamber of the Lost Lady

tomorrow night," he said, and disappeared down the stairs.

Rye made it back to her bed, but found herself staring into the dark night. The fat moon was sinking in the sky and would soon be replaced by dawn. She was too anxious to fall asleep, and she kept running over Harmless's plan in her head. The steps were simple enough, but the number of things that might go wrong seemed limitless.

Rye finally began to drift off only to be awakened by Leatherleaf. He was out there, in his cage, wailing as loudly as she had ever heard him.

Rye woke late the next day, and was surprised to find that the guard was no longer outside her door. However, outside her window, the courtyard of the Keep was filled with more soldiers than she had seen during her entire stay. They gathered weapons and barked orders.

Rye scouted the hallway. The nanny was knocking on Malydia's door. The door opened and Malydia's unpleasant face emerged.

"Earl Longchance is using the Great Hall, my Lady," the nanny said, eyes to the floor, and offered a plate to Malydia.

Malydia looked it over and accepted it.

As the nanny turned to leave, Malydia gave her an awkward smile. The nanny seemed stunned by the simple gesture. Then Malydia saw that Rye was watching and scowled, slamming the door shut.

The nanny continued down the hall to the guest chamber. Rye raised her eyebrows and the nanny did the same.

"I guess even Malydia can be pleasant with enough effort," Rye said.

"It seems so," the nanny said with a giggle and offered a similar plate to Rye.

"Thank you," Rye said. "What's going on in the Great Hall?"

"Earl Longchance and his advisors are planning for the night."

"Of course," Rye said. "Will you make plans for yourself?"

"I'm afraid there's little hope for me." The nanny shook her head. "My fate lies with the House of Longchance."

"Must it?" Rye asked. She hoped her enthusiasm didn't betray her secrets. "What of the Luck Uglies? What if they return?"

The nanny smiled sadly. "I don't suspect the Luck Uglies care about my wellbeing any more than the Earl. I've been around long enough to remember that the Luck Uglies don't look out for anyone but themselves."

Rye's face fell.

"But," the nanny added, "it's always nice to hope."

"Yes," Rye said, dispirited. It was easy to forget that the Luck Uglies – and her father – had a history she was only beginning to discover.

"Be well, miss," Rye said.

"You as well, my Lady," the nanny said. She bowed her head and disappeared off down the hall.

As Rye wandered the Keep during the day, she realised why her guard had disappeared. Every exit and entrance to the Keep was heavily guarded by multiple soldiers, and the stairways to the dungeons and each tower were being patrolled. While the soldiers kept giving her unfriendly glances, it was clear that they had bigger concerns on their minds. It was also clear that, for now, nobody was getting in or out of the Keep except by order of the Earl. She hoped Truitt knew what he was doing.

Rye spent most of the day at the window, examining

the sky and the distant village, trying to estimate how long it would take her to make her scramble through the Spoke. She noticed that, as the day went on, jarred dragonflies and beeswax poppets began to appear in each of the Keep's other windows. The dragonflies, of course, were all dead. Rye recognised them as the very items that Longchance had taken from The Willow's Wares – the talismans believed to ward off Bog Noblins. Malydia kept her distance from Rye, but once, when Rye had poked her head out of the door to the guest chamber, she caught Malydia pacing the hall while pinning a dead dragonfly to her dress.

It was mid-afternoon and Rye was on her way back from stocking her pockets in the pantry one last time when she heard a conversation echoing in the Great Hall. One voice was clearly that of Longchance. The other was familiar, but she could not place it.

"You're certain that they are there?" Longchance was saying.

"Yes," the familiar voice said. "The woman. The young girl. The Floods are busy securing the inn for the night. There will be no way to enter once they've finished. That is, unless someone lets you in – from the inside."

"Is there a back door?" Longchance asked. "Away from the street, where they won't see my men coming?"

Rye's heart jumped. They were talking about the Dead Fish Inn! It must be Longchance's informant. The man who had poisoned her. Could it be Bramble?

"Yes," the familiar voice said. "I can slip away and unlock the door to the alley. The soldiers will be able to enter undetected. Inside, they'll be so focused on preparing for the Bog Noblins they'll be taken by complete surprise."

"You had better open that door," Longchance said with menace. "If my men are left stranded in the street, I shall hold you personally responsible."

"I'll be there. I guarantee it will be opened."

Rye had to find out who it was. The door to the Great Hall was guarded, but she would only need a quick glimpse.

"You had better," Longchance said. "If you hadn't bungled the poison, we wouldn't be worried about this. Mess this up and the next drink of Asp's Tongue will be yours."

Rye took a deep breath and headed towards the door.

When she reached the guard, she intentionally dropped a piece of bread to the floor, bent down, and peeked past his legs.

Longchance was sprawled in his chair at the head of the table, a goblet of wine in his fist. His hair hung in his face and he had dark circles under his sunken eyes. The table was littered with gnawed pieces of orange peel.

Longchance reached into his pocket and tossed a small pouch across the table. It sounded like it was full of gold grommets.

The familiar-voiced man caught the pouch and looked inside.

"You get the rest after the soldiers are in the Dead Fish Inn," Longchance said.

Rye couldn't believe her eyes. The man who caught the pouch was her friend, Jonah the barman.

"Hey," the soldier at the door said. He nudged her roughly with his boot. "Push off. This doesn't concern you."

"Sorry," Rye said, and ran back to her room in a cold sweat.

Rye's heart and mind were each still racing when the sun began to set. Jonah changed everything. Longchance was sending soldiers to the Dead Fish Inn. By the time she got there, after unlocking the door to Beyond the Shale and lighting the cauldrons, it would be too late. Her and Folly's families would be captured by Longchance's soldiers – or worse. What good would a message do then? Talking to Harmless was impossible, as the dungeons were securely guarded by now. All she could do was meet Truitt at the arranged time and escape the Keep. From there, she'd have to work it out on her own.

As the sky grew darker, Rye nervously packed up everything she intended to bring. She made sure the puzzle piece and Leatherleaf's pouch were safely tucked inside her boots. Her hand-drawn map of the Spoke was in her pocket. She touched the choker round her neck.

As the time drew near and the castle grew quiet, she looked down to the courtyard, where a large group of soldiers had gathered. The walls were again lined with archers, and soldiers stood guard at every corner. Leatherleaf had gone eerily quiet. The gates creaked open as the soldiers marched out, then quickly closed shut behind them. Torchlights twinkled in the village far away. Rye couldn't be certain, but she suspected those soldiers were on their way to the Dead Fish Inn.

Rye couldn't wait any longer. She threw her hood over her head and set out into the Keep. It wasn't as quiet as the previous night. She could hear the sounds of heavy boots and the calling of guards, but the darkness was her friend as she made her way to another tower. At the top was the Chamber of the Lost Lady. Truitt had told her about it the night before. It had once been Lady Rory's room. Rye remembered the rhyme about Lady Rory: *Rory came third and seemed just right, she snuck away after just one night.*

Lady Rory had a little secret, Truitt said. One that had been shared with the other Ladies Longchance who followed her. As Rye reached the top of the tower, she saw that the door was ajar. She stopped at the unmistakable sound of arguing voices.

Rye approached the door and carefully opened it more fully. A large four-poster bed fit for a queen had been pushed aside to reveal a crude opening chiselled in the stone wall. It was just large enough for a small person to fit through. The small but sturdy door that must have sealed the space was standing open. Truitt stood at the entrance to the opening, as Rye expected. But she hadn't counted on finding Malydia there too, blocking her brother's way. And Rye's own.

"Sister," Truitt pleaded, "please let her go."

Malydia turned and glared at Rye. She then looked back at her brother.

"What shall become of me?" Malydia said. "Who's going to protect me?"

"You have the Earl and his army at your disposal," Truitt said.

Malydia clenched her fists and reset herself more squarely in front of the door. "He sacrificed our mother to the Bog Noblins rather than fight them himself!"

Malydia's words seemed to draw the air from the room and the colour from Truitt's face. Rye was stunned.

"Please, Malydia," Truitt said. "Let her go. For me."

Malydia looked at each of them again, but didn't budge. She was silent for a long time.

"Sister," Truitt implored, "she has done you no harm."

Malydia's eyes flared, then softened. Finally, her shoulders sank as if relenting to a great weight, and Malydia stepped aside.

Truitt waved Rye forward. "Come, Rye. We must go."

Rye ran to the opening in the wall. It led to darkness beyond.

Truitt climbed through first.

Rye hesitated, then stepped into the opening.

"Good luck, Riley," Malydia whispered, a glint in her eye.

"Thank you," Rye said, forcing a slight smile in return.

"You'll need it," Malydia hissed, and grabbed Rye's neck. She pulled Rye's choker free and gave her a hard kick in the back, knocking her through the hole in the wall.

Before Rye knew what was happening, Malydia slammed the door shut and Rye could hear it being locked and barred behind them.

Rye clutched her neck where the choker had once been. She and Truitt were now alone in the dark.

23

HOUSE RULE NUMBER FIVE

"**W**HAT IS WRONG with your sister?" Rye fumed.

"Careful," Truitt said. "It gets a little steep here."

"I can't see anything."

"Me neither," Truitt said, chuckling. "Just keep hold of my shirt and take small steps."

The steps – if you could call them that – felt jagged and uneven beneath Rye's feet. They were slippery with moss. Rye's narrow shoulders barely squeezed through the walls of the passageway she could not see. She got the hang of it, though, and they had begun making good progress when Rye's heel slipped off a step that was smoother than the others. She crashed into Truitt, sending them both down a flight of invisible stairs so steep they felt like a slide.

As they tumbled, their surroundings lightened around them. When they landed, it was no longer dark, just dim. Torches smouldered on the walls and the passageway's construction was more familiar. They were in the Spoke.

"She's awful. Just plain awful," Rye said, her ears still hot with fury. "I've never met a more confounding person in my entire life."

Truitt shook his head and lowered his eyes towards the ground. "I'm very sorry for what she has done. At times she's pulled by voices that only she can hear."

Rye saw the pain in Truitt's face. She didn't think it was from the fall down the stairs.

"Don't worry, Truitt," Rye said, softening. "You may be twins, but you're not alike."

Rye touched her knees gingerly. Smashed up again.

"Will you be able to find your way?" Truitt asked.

"I have my map," Rye said. "Let's hope luck is on my side."

"I'd join you, Rye, but I must return to the link children. They are more vulnerable than ever and the Earl's left them to fend for themselves. I suspect it will be some time before we will see each other again."

"Goodbye, Truitt," Rye said, gently touching his face the way he had once touched hers. "Thank you for all that you've done. I'll do everything I can to make sure that, some day, you have a village to come back out to."

"Rye, wait," Truitt said. He reached up and removed Harmless's necklace. "Take this. You'll need it more than me."

He held it out, but nobody took it from his hands.

"Rye? Are you still there?"

She was, but she said nothing. Harmless had told her that he'd done many things he wasn't proud of, but he'd never broken a deal. She wasn't about to make him start. Rye slipped off, without a sound, deeper into the Spoke. She hoped that some day she would see Truitt again.

When she reached a fork in the passage, Rye stopped and caught her breath. She knew she had only minutes to make a decision. Harmless's instructions had been clear. She was to unlock the forest door, light the Luck Cauldrons, and retreat to the Dead Fish Inn, in that order. Any deviation could be disastrous. But Harmless could not have known that Longchance was sending a small army of soldiers to the Dead Fish at this very moment. Wouldn't that have changed the plan? Over the past few weeks, everything Rye knew had been turned upside down. She found herself focusing on the principles that had been hammered into her memory since she could walk. The House Rules.

House Rule Number One: Don't stop, talk or questions ask, beware of men wearing masks.

She'd discovered her own father was the High Chieftain of the Luck Uglies – an infamous secret society known for wearing masks. She'd even donned one herself – with miserable results.

House Rule Number Two: He may run and he may hide, but Shady must never go outside.

She had already broken that one too and look at what had happened.

House Rule Number Three: Lock your door with the Black Moon's rise, don't come out until morning shines.

Clearly there was a pattern here.

House Rule Number Four: Worn under sun and under moon, never remove the O'Chanters' rune.

Thanks to Malydia, she had now broken that one too.

There was one other House Rule that Rye rarely thought about. Her mother hardly mentioned it, because if you were thinking about House Rule Number Five, it meant you were already in trouble. Still, it was a House Rule nonetheless.

House Rule Number Five: If four fails and the bogs again crawl, don't break one, break them all.

It was the first time Rye had really considered all the House Rules together. When you combined them, the House Rules weren't just rules, they were a riddle. The O'Chanters' runes were gone. That meant she had broken House Rule Number Four. But were the bogs crawling? Was that the return of the Bog Noblins? Was she now supposed to break them all? And did it mean to break just the House Rules, or could it mean the Laws of Longchance? Any rules? Whichever were necessary? That last idea put a smile on her face.

Rye pulled her map from her pocket. She couldn't be certain of anything any more. All she could do was take her best guess.

Rye worked her way through the Spoke as fast as she

could. The tunnels looked familiar, but she still feared she had taken a wrong turn. When she came to the flimsy rope bridge over the underground river, she knew she was in the right place. Rye hesitated, watching it sway over the black water rushing below. She thought about Truitt navigating his way through life in darkness. She swallowed her fear, gripped the guide ropes tightly until the fibres bit into her palms, and nimbly climbed across without looking down.

Rye had to use all her strength to push aside the heavy crates barricading the entrance to the wine cellar. As they finally gave way, she fell forward on to her stomach. A small body looked up from scratching itself in the corner. Its two beady eyes and hairy black face seemed just as surprised to see Rye as she was to see it.

Rye gasped. Shortstraw screeched and spun in a circle.

"Wait," Rye hissed. "Quiet."

The monkey screeched more loudly and bared its sharp little teeth. It then clambered up the stairs on all fours.

Heavy footsteps returned. Rye was alarmed to see that they belonged to Bramble. His milky-blue eyes fixed themselves on her. He pushed his black hair behind an ear and crouched down. Rye scrambled to her feet.

"Thank heavens you're all right," Bramble said. "Everyone has been out of their minds with worry. Come upstairs where it's warm."

Rye didn't budge. Bramble must have recognised her concern.

"It's safe, Riley. I'm a friend," Bramble said. "Just come."

He knew her name? She didn't have much choice but to follow as he hurried up the stairs.

"Come quickly," he said, holding the door at the top.

There were no festivities at the Inn tonight. The main floor was empty save for a small band of heavily armed men. They sat close to the fire and, although they didn't speak, Rye thought she saw warmth flood their eyes when they saw her. Rye didn't see her mother or any of Folly's family.

"Where are the Floods?" she asked.

"Most are at the bridge. The little blonde-headed firestarter's around here somewhere, I think. They're quite the herd to keep track of."

Rye didn't know whether she should deliver Harmless's message to just anyone, but she didn't have a minute to spare.

"Wait," she said. "It's Jonah. You must stop Jonah."

Rye explained everything she had seen and heard at the Keep and told him of Harmless's plan.

Bramble set his jaw. "I can't say I'm surprised your father's run off half-cocked and got himself into another stew. Abby's been sick to her stomach over all this."

Rye looked at Bramble in alarm. What was she missing?

"Where's Jonah?" Bramble demanded of the group.

As he said it, Rye and Bramble noticed Jonah at the back of the Inn. He whistled as he wiped down the same table over and over again. Rye thought he seemed nervous. When he heard Bramble, the whistling stopped. Now he seemed panicked.

"Take him," Bramble commanded.

Two of the armed men moved forward and did just that.

"Grab the bows and some boiling pots," Bramble ordered. "Head for the third-floor windows. Step lively now. I hope the Earl's men have packed for bad weather. Tonight they'll be surprised to find it raining bolts and scalding oil."

Bramble turned to Rye as three more men ran up the

stairs with heavy buckets of oil, steam trailing behind them.

"You've done well, child," he said, softening, taking her by the hand. His grip was warm and his fingers gently pressed something into her palm. "Your ancestors smile with pride today."

"You still haven't told me how you know me."

"My apologies that we have not been formally introduced," he said with a bow. "Last time we truly met you were still crawling around your mother's cottage. But she tells me all about you when she writes. Of course, I've also had a chance to admire you and your delightful scamp of a sister around here as of late."

Bramble must have noticed the blank look on Rye's face.

"I'm Bramble Cutty from the Isle of Pest. Where Abby was born."

Rye just shook her head. "Oh."

"We were practically raised together. I can be a bit – protective sometimes." Bramble let her hand go and turned for the stairs. "Your mother's up on the roof with the others. She's gone mad with worry – been organising a party to go out and find you herself tonight. We'll be much better served with her here." He looked back and winked. "She's still as fine a shot with her crossbow as anyone from Pest."

"My mother shoots crossbows?" Nothing surprised her any more.

"Go to her, Riley," he said.

"Wait," Rye said. "What about the Luck Cauldrons? You need to light them."

"Little good it will do us if we don't fend off the soldiers first," Bramble said, taking the stairs two at a time. "The rest of the men are out at the bridge now. We'll send a runner over there as soon as we can."

"Wait, what? No, it can't wait," Rye was saying.

But she was too late. Bramble was gone.

Rye opened her palm and noticed the swatch of black material he'd left with her. She unfolded it carefully. The fabric was cut into the shape of a ragged four-leaf clover as black as a shark's eye.

"Rye!" someone yelled. It was Folly, rushing down the stairs in the opposite direction. She nearly knocked Bramble over as she passed.

Folly's hug almost knocked Rye over too.

"They said you were back," Folly said, without letting go.

"Folly, where is everyone?" Rye said.

"My father and the twins are out on the bridge. Some of the others are with them. They're setting up some sort of blockade in case the Bog Noblins try to cross," Folly said, eyes wide. "The rest of us are up on the roof keeping watch. Come on."

Instead, Rye ran towards the massive doors of the Dead Fish Inn. Not only were the locks bolted and latched, but the doors had been barricaded and nailed shut from the inside.

"Where are you going?" Folly asked.

"The bridge."

Rye checked the windows. They were shuttered and sealed just as tightly. There was no getting in or out this way any time soon.

"Are you crazy? Why?" Folly said.

"Because someone needs to light the Luck Cauldrons," Rye said and explained – as best as she could before stopping for breath – what was going on.

"Rye, those Bog Noblins scare me. They're like nothing I've ever seen."

"You don't have to come, Folly, but you can't stop me," Rye said. "What do you have that I can use to light a fire?"

Folly bit her lip. "Wait, Rye. I'm coming. Let me get my stuff."

They rushed upstairs to Folly's room. Folly examined the contents of her shelves and threw an assortment of supplies into her pack while Rye readied the rope ladder for the window. They both stopped when Fifer, Fowler and Fallow barged into the room.

"Where do you two think you're off to?" Fifer demanded.

"To the bridge," Folly said.

"You can't," Fowler said.

"We have to," Folly said. "Someone needs to light the Luck Cauldrons."

"What are Luck Cauldrons?" Fowler asked.

"We'll explain later," Folly said.

"Then we're coming too," Fifer said.

"I'm telling Mum," Fallow said.

Folly looked like she might punch him.

"You decide who stays or goes," Rye said, pushing past them. "I'll be back in one minute and then we're leaving." This time, she hadn't even blushed around Fifer.

Rye tiptoed into a dark room down the hall. A small body was nestled in the bed's blankets. A raggedy pink hobgoblin lay alone on the floor. Rye picked up Mona Monster and carefully placed the doll back on the pillow. The small figure stirred.

Rye found Lottie's big eyes watching her, blinking away sleep.

"Rye," Lottie said, "you came home?"

"Yes," Rye whispered, and put her hand on Lottie's forehead. She gave her a kiss. "Sleep tight, Lottie."

"No let the Bog Noblin bite," Lottie said.

Rye smiled. Lottie reached up and gave Rye a great hug round her neck.

"Of you," Lottie said in her ear.

"Love you too, Lottie."

Rye desperately wanted to see her mother, who she knew must be tearing apart the place, searching for her at this very moment. But if Abby found her, she would never let her leave the Dead Fish Inn. Abby would never be able to let Rye finish what Harmless needed doing.

"Do they look like cauldrons to you?" Rye asked, craning her neck to see.

"I suppose so," Fifer said.

"They really are awfully high," Folly said.

Rye, Folly and Folly's brothers had climbed out of her window just as the first buckets of boiling oil and crossbow bolts rained down on the Earl's soldiers in the alleyway. With all the commotion, neither Bramble's men in the Dead Fish windows nor the screaming soldiers noticed the five children slip round the corner and on to Little Water Street.

Now they stood where the end of the dirt street met the banks of the River Drowning, looking up at the bridge overhead. Drowning wasn't known for its impressive architecture. Its twisted timber-framed buildings and narrow streets weren't much to look at. But the bridge itself loomed over the Shambles, its three stone archways spanning the river at its narrowest point. The bridge was taller than the four-storey Dead Fish Inn, and on its best days was lined with vendors and their stalls. There were two round, decorative features on either side of the bridge nearest to the village that looked a lot like cauldrons.

Tonight the entire bridge glowed orange. This was not typical. It was on fire.

"That's a creative way to block a bridge," Rye noted.

"I guess the soldiers didn't appreciate the effort," Folly said.

On top of the bridge, about halfway across, a faction of men from the Dead Fish was engaged in a fierce battle with soldiers in Longchance tartan. Rye spotted the telltale blond mops of Folly's father and older brothers. The twins weren't fast on their two legs, but their four hacking, slashing arms made them a force to be reckoned with.

"How do we get up there?" Rye asked.

"Are you sure you want to?" Folly said.

"The vine ladder," Fifer said, pointing to a crude ladder made from the thick roots and vines growing down the side of the stone archway. The problem was, it started at least two metres above their heads.

Rye considered the obstacle. "Is there any other way?"

"We'd have to go back up through the village," Fifer said.

"We can make a pyramid," Folly said. "We'll be our own ladder. If we climb on each other's backs, we can get at least two of us up there."

"It has to be us, Folly," Rye decided. "We're the lightest."

Folly looked back up at the fire. She took a deep breath.

"OK," she said.

Fifer and Fowler knelt on the ground and Fallow got on their backs. Rye climbed up and over the three boys and it gave her just enough of a boost to grab the vine ladder.

"Don't look down," Folly yelled from below her. "I'll be right behind you."

Folly hesitated, but summoned her courage. Climbing over her brothers, she seemed to relish the opportunity to step on Fallow's head as she took hold of the vine ladder herself. Their arms and legs ached from the climb as they both reached the top, and they pulled themselves on to the bridge. Smoke from the fire blasted their faces, burning their eyes and making it difficult to see. Bodies ran past them but, in the confusion, it was difficult to tell whether they were soldiers or allies from the Dead Fish Inn.

"There are the cauldrons," Rye said.

Folly froze in her tracks. "Rye," she said softly, "I think

we'd better move fast."

She pointed.

Rye saw Folly's twin brothers leap off the bridge into the river below. Then Folly's father jumped too. They clearly had no idea Rye and Folly were on the bridge. The soldiers had turned and were now running, swords drawn, towards Rye and Folly.

"Rye, take these," Folly yelled, thrusting something from her pack into Rye's hands. "I'll create a distraction."

Rye examined the two pieces of cold metal.

"What are they?"

"Flint," Folly said. "Strike them together to make a spark. That should light the cauldrons."

Almost anyone else would have leaped from the bridge with the others. Or run in the opposite direction. Folly braced herself, took a potion bottle from her pack and stepped forward, right into the path of the soldiers.

"Folly, no!" Rye yelled. Not another one of her potions.

"Go, Rye! Now!"

The soldiers bore down on Folly, their armour and weapons rattling as they came. When they were within throwing distance, Folly cocked her arm, closed her eyes tightly, and threw the bottle with all her strength.

The bottle sailed well over the oncoming soldiers' heads, hit the bridge behind them with an unimpressive plunk, and rolled harmlessly off the edge, into the river.

"Pigshanks!" Folly cursed with clenched fists, just before the soldiers engulfed her.

The men bowled over Folly and Rye like a wave, knocking them both aside. But, to Rye's surprise, the girls might as well have been invisible. The soldiers stormed past them without further regard on their charge towards the village side of the bridge.

Rye shook off the bruises and dragged herself to the first Luck Cauldron.

"Folly," she yelled, "get the other one."

Rye pushed aside the heavy stone top and looked inside. It was filled with thorny nettles and branches knotted like strings of rope. She flicked the flint together like Folly had instructed. Once sparks caught the nettles, they burned furiously and whipped around like snakes struck by lightning. A thick blue haze flared from the cauldron and flew forth like ghosts released into the night. The blue haze streamed as far into the night sky as Rye could see.

Folly was able to stagger to her feet and, with the help of more flint from her pack, repeated the process on the second cauldron. The sky was now tinged with an otherworldly blue glow.

Rye stumbled over to Folly, her friend's wild blonde hair now singed black and smoking at the edges.

"What do we do n—?" Folly started to ask.

Folly hesitated and followed the stare of Rye's wide eyes. Further down the bridge, through the haze of smoke, Rye had spotted the Bog Noblin. It was Muckmire of the grey-green skin and webbed fingers, the one that had emerged from the canal and dragged an armful of villagers under. Muckmire was what had sent the soldiers running.

Rye touched her bare neck and silently cursed Malydia. The familiar glow of her choker was gone.

"You need to get back to the Inn," Rye said.

She looked over the edge of the bridge, where Folly's father and the twins were helping one another out of the river. "That way," Rye said with a nod downwards.

"What about you?" Folly asked.

"I need to go *that* way," she said, nodding to the end of the bridge where the fleeing soldiers had gathered.

"Then I'm coming."

In the distance, Muckmire examined the flames, seemed to consider them, then roared and charged forward.

"Jump now before I throw you off," Rye said, grabbing her arm.

Rye's eyes told Folly she meant it.

"Take these," Folly said, hoisting her pack of potions over Rye's shoulder before she could object.

They were both trembling as they hugged goodbye. Folly puffed her cheeks full of air, pinched her nose and stepped off the side of the bridge.

Rye heard the splash, but didn't have time to check on Folly. Muckmire was nearly upon her, his damp skin smoking from the flames, and Rye had no choice but to sprint for the soldiers, Folly's potions jangling on her back.

24

A SHADY SITUATION

RYE GUESSED THAT the threat of an exhausted, stumbling eleven-year-old girl would pale in comparison to the one posed by a charging, snarling, soldier-gutting monster. Fortunately she guessed right, and Longchance's soldiers barely noticed her as she slipped through their perimeter. She didn't linger to watch the results of the looming collision.

Rye was back in the Spoke now; she had checked her map and found the entrance in the old well not far from the bridge. She'd been navigating the dark tunnels for quite some time, as fast as her legs would take her, when she felt the sweat go cold on her cheeks. The temperature around her began to drop. She stopped and exhaled hard. She could see her breath. There, just a few steps away, was the wide iron door with the metal grate. Its heavy chains were still fastened. It was the door to Beyond the Shale.

Rye took a tentative step towards it. She measured one of the deep claw marks with her fingertip and pulled her hand back quickly. The door was cold to the touch.

She dug into her boot and retrieved the puzzle piece Harmless had pulled from his mouth. Now came the hard part. Connecting the heavy chains were two dozen locks in different shapes and sizes. They each had a slot wider than a conventional keyhole, with enough space to slide a cast-iron figurine up and inside the lock. She began trying them. The wailing banshee fitted halfway inside some but not at all in others. It fitted all the way inside several of the locks, but it was such a tight squeeze the locks wouldn't click open. Twelve, thirteen, fourteen tries. The piece slid with ease into the fifteenth lock. When she turned the clasp, the lock fell off on to the ground, but the chains remained in place. Rye bent over and examined the lock that had dropped.

"You have got to be joking," she whispered.

The lock had opened to reveal another puzzle piece, this one shaped like a clawed paw. Rye sighed and picked it up.

She began trying the locks again. Six, seven, eight tries. Finally the ninth lock opened and dropped off. Another piece was exposed. Rye repeated the process over and over and over again.

By the fifteenth lock her fingers were aching. At twenty, the chains were sagging and the door seemed to bulge outward towards her. Rye shook her head, thinking her eyes and fatigue might be playing tricks on her. The metal groaned as if straining itself. The sounds became louder and the chains actually rattled when she finally obtained the last puzzle piece. It was an iron four-leaf clover, black as coal.

Rye regarded the last remaining lock. The door unmistakably shuddered in anticipation. Rye hesitated. Something didn't feel right. She eyed the grate. Standing on her tiptoes, she peered through. There was nothing but darkness on the other side.

With a deep breath, she undid the final lock. The lock and the chains clattered loudly into coils on the ground that sent Rye jumping back.

The door was now still. She wondered if she was supposed to open it.

She did not have to wonder long. The door flew open, followed by a cold blast of air that blew the hood right off Rye's head. The air moaned as it rushed forth, as if it had been trapped in a tomb for hundreds of years. The torches on the walls flickered and went dark.

Rye remembered the next part of Harmless's instructions clearly. He had said to get out of there. But as she turned, the cold air around her seemed to pause and change direction. What had been an inward rush from Beyond the Shale suddenly became an outward suction of even greater force. Clouds of loose earth kicked up into the air and skittered through the hungry mouth of the doorway.

Rye struggled for a few steps, but the force was too much for her, and it pulled her backwards. She fell to her hands and knees and clawed her fingernails into the earth, trying to secure her grip. Just as her feet disappeared into the blackness behind the door, she was able to grab hold of its frame. She pulled forward and rolled herself to the side so that her back was pressed against the wall of the Spoke. Folly's lumpy pack of bottles dug into her spine. She looked down and saw her own feet dangling off the ground. The suction pressed her against the wall like an insect against a window in a storm. Her eyes watered. Drool ran from her mouth and across her cheeks.

Then, just as suddenly as the vortex had started, it stopped.

Rye fell to the ground. She looked at the great darkness beyond the door.

She now had another decision to make. She'd accomplished both tasks Harmless had given her, but in the wrong order. If she was going to stick with the plan at all, or what was left of it anyway, she should return to the Dead Fish Inn. But the circumstances had changed rapidly – Muckmire was already in the village and she had only just opened the door. Quinn wasn't at the Dead Fish, which meant that, despite her mother's warning, he and his father had stubbornly decided to ride the night out on Mud Puddle Lane. Was it more important for Rye to follow Harmless's plan, or do whatever it took to save the people she cared about? She kept thinking about House Rule Number Five.

"Oh, pigshanks," Rye whispered as she climbed to her feet. "Break them all."

She ran as fast as she could, down the tunnel, towards

the secret entrance to the cottage on Mud Puddle Lane.

If Rye had stayed longer, she might have seen the masked figures that slipped into the Spoke like ghosts from Beyond the Shale.

At long last, Rye reached the ladder that led to the workshop of the O'Chanters' cottage. It felt like forever since she had first seen it. Rye climbed the rungs and slid aside the trapdoor. She wriggled out from under the workbench, bumping her head on the way up. She clenched her eyes but felt grateful for the sting. It meant she was home.

Rye pulled off her hood and rubbed her head. When she opened her eyes, she found a sharp sword pointed at her face.

"Quinn," Rye snapped, "put that down. You scared me half to death."

Quinn lowered the sword. "Rye, I didn't know it was you. You're OK?"

"So far, assuming you don't skewer me with that thing."

Rye looked Quinn over in the lantern light. He appeared tired and unwashed. His clothes stuck to his thin frame.

"What are you doing here, Quinn?"

"I came to check on Shady, like you asked," Quinn said. "The soldiers left and I was able to sneak in with two mackerel and some goat's milk. They came back while I was still here. It's been getting colder, so they've been spending more time inside by the fire."

Rye did not like the idea of dirty soldiers lounging around her house.

"That was yesterday," Quinn added.

"You've been hiding here for two days? What did you eat?"

"Shady was willing to share," Quinn said. He grimaced and bared his teeth. They were full of silvery scales.

"Your father must be mad with worry," Rye said.

"I'd imagine so."

Rye bit her lip. Something had been gnawing at *her* since Grim Green. It all came pouring out.

"Quinn, I'm sorry about all of this. I know you think the Luck Uglies are terrible, and they are – I mean they were – but you don't know the whole story—"

"Rye—"

"The village has it wrong," she implored. "They didn't

take Lady Emma. Longchance lied—"

"Rye, it's OK."

"I know it's hard to believe. And maybe you can't forgive me for who my father is, but it wasn't his fault. I mean, some things were, but he kept his deal—"

"Rye," Quinn said more loudly. "I know."

"What?"

"I know the truth. I've been reading about it. In *Tam's Tome*. It's all in there – the truth. The good, the bad and the in-between."

"Really?"

Quinn nodded. "*Tam's Tome* tells what really happened to Lady Emma. It was Longchance himself."

No wonder the book was banned, Rye thought.

"So you don't hate me?" she said.

"Of course not." His eyes were kind. "I think I've had my fill of your cottage for a while, though."

Rye felt a great weight fall from her shoulders, one she hadn't realised she was carrying until it was gone. After a deep sigh of relief, that particular burden was quickly replaced by another.

"Let's get you home," she said.

"It's crawling with soldiers out there," Quinn said. "And maybe worse."

"Worse?"

"Yes," Quinn said, lowering his voice. "About half an hour ago. There was – I guess you'd call it a roar – from the bogs. I heard the soldiers run outside to investigate. They haven't been back. I was waiting a bit longer to be certain they didn't return."

"Well we need to get your father and bring him with us," Rye said. She explained, as best she could, everything that had happened that night. She described her instructions, the run through the Spoke, the Luck Cauldrons at the bridge and the door to Beyond the Shale.

Quinn tried to absorb it all. "And what have you got there?" Quinn asked, nodding to her pack.

"Potions. From Folly."

"Well for heaven's sake don't drink them."

They exchanged smiles.

"You said they've been gone for half an hour?" Rye said, moving towards the door.

"More or less."

Rye pressed her ear against the door to the workshop. It

sounded quiet. "Come on, let's go. You first."

"Me?"

"You've got the sword."

They slid open the secret door and looked into the main room of the cottage. A lump rose in Rye's throat when she saw the family chairs round the table and Lottie's paintings on the wall. It hadn't been that long since they'd fled their home, but she'd begun to fear she'd never see it again. Then Rye saw the mess the soldiers had made, and her ears went red with anger. The pots and pans were scattered in filthy piles. Greasy, bare chicken bones were strewn across the floor. She guessed the soldiers had eaten their hens. On the bright side, she didn't see any actual soldiers.

"It looks clear," Rye whispered. "You check my mother's room and I'll look in mine."

"Are you sure about this?"

"Yes, go."

They soon met back in the main room. The cottage was empty, but Rye had a growing pit in her stomach. Something was missing.

"Quinn, when's the last time you saw Shady?"

Quinn thought. "I fell asleep in the workshop for a few hours last night. At least, I think it was a few hours. He curled up with me under the workbench."

"Last night is the last time you saw him?"

Quinn hurried back to the bedrooms. Rye could hear him dropping to his knees and calling Shady's name, checking under the beds. Rye's heart sank as she joined the search, half-heartedly checking Shady's favourite hiding places.

"The soldiers must have taken him," Rye finally said. She had to choke back tears.

"Maybe we can find him," Quinn said, although he didn't sound convinced.

Rye and Quinn peered out of the shuttered windows. The street was quiet.

"I'm sorry," Quinn said, his eyes on the floor.

"Come on," Rye said. She took her friend's hand so he would know she didn't blame him. They creaked open the front door together.

Mud Puddle Lane was completely deserted. Farmers' carts were overturned on either side of the road, and further down there were large wooden rain barrels stacked up like barricades. Rye and Quinn ducked down in the overgrown grass by the door.

"Look," Quinn whispered. "There. And there."

Rye studied the shapes in the darkness. There was movement behind the carts and barrels.

"Soldiers," Quinn said.

More of them huddled in the trees. Rye even spotted one soldier perched on Old Lady Crabtree's roof. Still more soldiers, armed with bows, watched the woods at the far end of the road.

"What do you think they're doing?" Quinn asked.

"Waiting," Rye said.

Alone, in the middle of Mud Puddle Lane, a single torch shone light on a rectangular iron cage large enough to trap a beaver. Inside, something rustled. It was dark, furry and so thick it couldn't turn itself round.

Rye and Quinn squinted through the shadows.

"It's Shady," Quinn said.

Shady licked a paw and used it to wipe his ears.

Rye and Quinn glanced back at the soldiers in their hidden positions. The soldiers hadn't even noticed them. They were fixated on the darkest end of Mud Puddle Lane, the one furthest from the village.

"They're using him as bait," Rye said, anger rising in her voice.

Both Rye and Quinn now knew exactly what the soldiers were hunting for.

"They took all our hens and goats back to the Keep yesterday," Quinn said. "Called it a Special Assessment. Shady must have been the last animal they could find."

"We need to get him," Rye said.

"I'll run out and distract them," Quinn offered. "While they're focused on me, you can go and get Shady."

"The soldiers will turn you into a pin cushion with those arrows."

"I'm fast. Besides, when they see I'm just a boy, they won't fire. Come on, it worked before."

"Those brutes would shoot their own mothers," Rye said.

"We can do this, Rye," Quinn said. "Put your hood on. Here I go."

Quinn tiptoed through the shadows along the houses and then darted out into Mud Puddle Lane a fair distance past Shady, towards the wooded end of the road. The first arrow flew past his head. He had to twist, jump and skip to avoid three more.

"Wait!" he yelled, shielding his face with his hands. "I'm just a kid!"

The soldiers stepped from their hiding places, lowered their bows momentarily, and blinked their eyes. The distraction worked. They exchanged confused looks. Rye ran to the middle of Mud Puddle Lane and grabbed Shady's cage with both hands.

Quinn peeked from between his fingertips and tried to smile.

"See," he yelled, raising both hands in surrender. "Just a boy."

The soldiers yelled in a collective gasp, turning their attention from each other back to Quinn. They raised their bows again and took aim.

Quinn's jaw dropped and he shielded his head with his hands. "Please, no!"

Before they could release their arrows, Quinn was plucked from the ground. It looked like he was hovering in the air, but when Rye blinked and strained her eyes, she could make out the clawed hand gripping her friend by the nape of his neck. In one swift motion, Quinn was cast, bottom first, into the mouth of a Bog Noblin. No one had noticed the horned Bog Noblin known as Dread Root appear silently from the woods behind Quinn. Rye gasped as Quinn struggled to prise himself free, his arms, legs and torso dangling from the creature's mouth.

Dread Root looked from side to side, as if searching for something better to eat, his long beard dragging at his feet. He then bit down hard into Quinn's behind.

Quinn's scream of pain nearly broke Rye's heart. She yelled Quinn's name and ran towards him.

Apparently Dread Root wasn't fond of the taste of Quinn's backside, and he spat him headfirst on the ground near Rye. The soldiers let loose a stream of arrows that bounced off Dread Root's knotted skin or landed in the dirt. It was only by some freakish luck that Rye and Quinn weren't impaled. She dropped Shady's cage and tried to comfort Quinn.

Dread Root pulled an arrow from his forearm as if it were a splinter and cast it aside. His eyes turned towards Rye and the metal cage, which rattled violently on the ground as Shady struggled to escape. Again Rye reached for her choker and found herself shouting in frustration. Dread Root licked his lips with a long, black tongue. He reached down and picked up the cage first, peering inside.

"Stop!" a voice boomed and a huge figure sprinted down Mud Puddle Lane, an axe over his shoulder.

The Bog Noblin dropped the cage.

The voice belonged to Angus Quartermast. He placed himself between Dread Root and Rye and Quinn, using his thick, round body as a shield. On the ground, Shady had knocked the cage on its side and was bouncing it forward, launching his head against the metal bars again and again. His collar glowed so blue it was nearly white.

Dread Root's eyes grew enormously wide as he looked down at the gyrating cage. In a burst of speed, he leaped over all of them and ran off down Mud Puddle Lane towards the village. To Rye's horror, the cage rattled behind him. Dread Root must have landed on it and the cage was now caught in his unkempt tangle of beard.

"Shady!" Rye called out helplessly into the night.

The soldiers let loose another barrage of arrows as Dread Root rushed past, swatting archers from the trees and rooftops. Those who remained unarmed took up the pursuit.

Angus reached down and took Quinn in his arms. "Quinn, my boy, are you all right?"

"I'll be fine," Quinn said with a pained look.

He didn't sound convincing.

Rye remembered that Bog Noblin bites were poisonous. Quinn's face had gone grey, but his eyes sparkled when he said, "Papa, that was amazing. You scared away a Bog Noblin."

Angus hoisted Quinn in his arms. "Riley, come with us where it's safe."

"Quinn, will you be all right?" Rye said, torn between her friend and her pet.

"I'll be fine," Quinn said, his voice weak. "Go."

His father began to protest.

Rye wasn't listening. She chased after the Bog Noblin, the cage and the soldiers before Angus could stop her.

25

LUCK UGLIES

RYE'S PURSUIT TOOK her through Nether Neck and Old Salt Cross, where the deserted streets and boarded windows bore the signs of a village under siege. Rye gawked at the number of tattered black flags shopkeepers had hung over their shuttered windows – ragged clovers – but she had no time to stop for a closer look. Dread Root and the soldiers were moving quickly. She saw neither Bog Noblin nor soldier as she ran, but she could hear their nearby calls as she rounded every corner. Smoke rose from distant roofs.

Rye slowed her pace as she progressed down the last alleyway towards Market Street. She placed her hand on Folly's pack to silence the jingling bottles inside. The men's voices were numerous. Some barked commands, others called for help, and many cried out in pain. The roars echoing through the night were even more chilling. Rye was no expert, but it sounded like they came from more than one Bog Noblin.

She stepped from the alleyway on to Market Street, where the scene almost overwhelmed her. To her left, Dread Root pummelled soldiers with his fists, cracking their helmets like walnuts. She couldn't see Shady's cage, and guessed the Bog Noblin must have shaken it off along the way. To her right, Muckmire plucked a soldier up by his feet and beat him repeatedly against the ground like a big dead fish. Rye guessed he'd made his way through the troops at the bridge without much trouble.

The soldiers who weren't already lying in broken piles attempted to surround the Bog Noblins in vain. Their blades bounced off the creatures' knotted skin as they tried to corner them against buildings. Rye made her way back to the alley, but the mob of soldiers snaking their way through the narrow, twisted street choked off her escape route.

Even with the smoke, the light of the moon indulged no secrets, and Rye felt naked amidst the swarm of dangers.

She needed to find shelter. Except for The Willow's Wares, which was currently on the wrong side of the battle, the shops were all shuttered. She looked up to the roofs. It had worked before.

Rye darted to the walls, desperately digging her fingers into cracks in search of handholds. The soldiers were falling rapidly. One dropped at her feet. The sight of what the Bog Noblin had done to him made her sick to her stomach. She scrambled furiously. She found a crack for her fingers, then one for her foot, and pulled herself up.

Over her shoulder, she saw Dread Root finish off the soldiers on his end of Market Street. Muckmire toyed with the last remaining troop. The cobblestones were now littered with black-and-blue tartan.

Rye pushed upwards, clearing the windows and doorframes. She studied the walls in the moonlight to find a path. The walls suddenly went dark behind a looming shadow. She smelled the Bog Noblin before she saw it.

A quick glance back and there he was. Dread Root. Just below her now, he eyed her as Rye might study a tree frog on a fence. She panicked and dug frantically at the wall's surface until her fingers went raw, clawing her way higher. She cursed Malydia at the top of her lungs, but no one was listening.

Dread Root unfurled his long, black tongue upwards, licking at her feet. She kicked at him with her boot. It only seemed to amuse him.

"Go away!" she screamed, scrambling higher, but she was still nowhere near the rooftops. The sounds coming from his throat sounded like cruel laughter.

Rye tried to push on, but felt herself stuck. She yanked and pulled without success. Then it occurred to her – she wasn't stuck, Dread Root had reached up and taken hold of the pack on her shoulders.

"Stop it," she yelled. "Let go!"

His sickening laughter only worsened. Now Rye found herself digging into the walls, just trying to hold on. One foot slipped. There was a rough tug at her shoulder and, after the initial jolt, she was able to move it more freely. One of the straps on Folly's pack had given way and it now dangled in the crook of her arm. The straps were in Dread Root's fingers.

She wiggled and squirmed, trying to free herself from

the pack in the hope that it might buy her even an instant more of time.

Dread Root reached up with his other hand and took hold of her foot. Rye had no choice. She dropped one hand from the wall and lowered her arm so she dangled by just one set of fingertips. Her grip wouldn't last long, but the pack slid off her shoulder, into Dread Root's claws. He fumbled with it, lost his own grip, and it fell to the street.

Market Street exploded in a white light so loud and bright that it knocked Rye off the wall.

She landed hard and, for a moment, couldn't see or hear anything. Her vision returned first and she looked around – everything filtered through a white haze still burning in her eyes. All was silent except for the ringing of bells somewhere deep inside her head.

The remaining soldiers were on the ground too, trying to climb to their feet without success. Dread Root staggered around blindly, clutching at his eyes and ears. He circled like a dancer drunk on too much wine, and backed into Muckmire, who held his hairless head in his hands.

On the ground near Rye's feet, sizzling fluids oozed from the bottles smashed in Folly's pack.

"Folly, you did it," Rye said aloud, or perhaps in her mind – she couldn't tell. Either way, she couldn't help but smile.

Her smile didn't last. The Bog Noblins started to recover, and they turned their attention towards her again. Rye tried to stand, but couldn't keep her balance. She dragged herself away on her hands and knees as fast as she could, but she knew it would never be fast enough. She kept her eyes straight ahead as she crawled towards The Willow's Wares at the far, smoky end of Market Street.

Rye imagined her mother and Lottie, her newly found father and her oldest, truest friends. These were the images she wanted to hold on to when the end came. The Bog Noblin was close behind her now. She couldn't hear it over the deafening ringing, but she could feel its vibrations on the cobblestones under her body. She would not look back. She would not let its evil black tongue be the last image she ever saw.

Then, through the haze, she saw the pale-blue light. It was at ground level in the distance. Shady? It disappeared behind a cloud of smoke and ash.

Rye squinted through the dark. She could no longer

see a light, but in the distance three figures were coming her way.

She blinked to clear her eyes, but the white haze persisted. The figures drew closer. They were cloaked and hooded, all in a colour best described as dead-of-night. If their boots made a sound, Rye couldn't hear them.

Rye held her breath as they approached. All three stopped when they reached her.

The closest one took a step forward and tilted its head. She could see just a portion of its face from under its hood. Its hairless skin was an inky purple. It had angular black eyes and a long pointed nose that extended out from its face like an angry beak. Its garish mouth was filled with jagged shards of scrap-metal teeth.

Masks.

These masks weren't feathered or bejewelled. They weren't funny. They didn't make Rye laugh.

Suddenly, the ground stopped vibrating under her.

A chill ran up Rye's spine.

The figure extended an arm. Rye carefully took hold of its cloaked elbow – its gloved fist was embedded with claws made of nails and broken glass.

After it helped her to her feet, the figure stooped over so that it was eye level with her. Its strange black eyes studied her. Its terrible beak-like nose almost touched her own.

Rye swallowed hard. *Walk strong and act like you belong...* now she truly did.

"Thank you," Rye said, in the strongest voice she could muster.

The figure lifted its arm like the wing of a huge crow, and quickly threw its cloak over her.

Everything went dark and Rye felt the heavy fabric fall across her body. She closed her eyes, wondering if it would grab her. But the cloak kept going over her head and she felt its weight pass her by. When she opened her eyes, all three of the black figures were gone.

She spun round. They'd reappeared at the far side of Market Street, behind Muckmire and Dread Root.

A movement above made Rye look up to the rooftops.

The gargoyles were coming now. They crawled down the face of the buildings like giant spiders.

She turned to the old well. More masked figures emerged, black and dripping like snakes from a hole.

And, for the first time, Rye understood the fear and the

awe. Because as the legendary villains encircled them like nightmares in the moonlight, Dread Root and Muckmire pressed close to one another in the manner of two warriors prepared to make their last stand. These two terrible monsters seemed to know, without a doubt, that the end had come for *them*.

The Luck Uglies had returned to Drowning.

Rye found the cage, bent and twisted, but still securely shut, in an alley not far from Market Street.

She stared down into it and almost cried out in relief when she found Shady in one piece. He was licking his paws with delight – his sharp claws full of coarse orange hair from where he'd snagged Dread Root's beard and unwittingly hitched a ride into the village. His collar glowed a now-familiar blue. Rye was confident that she'd finally worked out one of Harmless's mysteries. It wasn't Angus Quartermast who had terrified Dread Root on Mud Puddle Lane.

For an instant, Shady's blue collar grew brighter than she'd ever seen it, then the mystical glow faded and it was ordinary once again. Did that mean the Luck Uglies had finished off Dread Root and Muckmire? Perhaps. But even so, Rye remembered there was one more.

Iron Wart had not yet revealed himself.

Harmless had told her that the worst monster dwelled within the walls of the Keep. Rye knew he was speaking of Longchance. That was the real reason he'd stayed behind. To rid Drowning of the Earl once and for all.

Unfortunately, Rye didn't think Harmless would also be expecting Iron Wart.

Rye dragged the cage through the alley behind The Willow's Wares. She picked up a loose brick from the kerb.

"Sorry, Mama," she said to herself, and threw the brick through the shop's rear window.

"Come on," she said, lifting Shady's cage as she cast a final glance towards the dark shadows on Market Street. "Someone else needs you more than the Luck Uglies do now."

Rye sat alone in the dark, with no sounds to keep her company but her own breath and the beating of her heart. There was Shady, of course, but he had chosen now to go silent. Back at The Willow's Wares, she'd taken two leather belts and some old leggings and fashioned a harness of sorts, strapping the heavy iron cage to her back and fastening the straps across her chest with the buckles. No wirry troubled her as she searched the basement for the entrance to the Spoke. Shady didn't appreciate her efforts and yowled and caterwauled the whole way through its tunnels.

This last trip through the Spoke had brought her full circle. She was now somewhere deep beneath the Keep. She didn't return to the tunnel of the Lost Lady, for she knew Malydia had sealed that entrance tightly. There was only one way into the Keep now. She'd studied the map carefully. It was here that the tunnel called the Long Way Home ended. Above her, beyond an unlocked iron hatch with a round, pull-down handle, was the Deepest, Darkest Dungeon of Longchance Keep.

Harmless had forbidden her from returning. But that was before everything had been turned upside down. She hadn't followed the steps in order – not that she'd had much of a choice. But she had a terrible feeling that her choices had put Harmless in grave danger. While the Dead Fish Inn had been spared, her delay might have allowed the last Bog Noblin to make it through the village to the Keep. She suspected that Harmless could manage the Earl and his minions, but Iron Wart on top of all that sounded like more than even a High Chieftain could handle.

Rye couldn't stay still any longer. Her body was beyond exhaustion and if she didn't start moving again soon, she wouldn't be able to.

She reached up and pulled down the door. It opened with surprising ease and she was immediately pummelled as hard, blunt objects rained down on her head. Clouds of dust and debris covered her and choked her lungs. Once things had stopped falling, she reached down and examined one. It was an old bone. She quickly flicked it aside. Rye placed her lantern inside the dungeon and pulled herself up.

The dungeon was the darkest place she had ever seen – or not seen. Darker than Mud Puddle Lane on the Black Moon. So dark that her lantern barely penetrated the gloom. Rye had no idea how she was going to find her way to the Upper Dungeon. The silence felt like it was swallowing her. The scuffling of Shady's claws as he huddled in the cage sounded like trumpets in the vast emptiness of sound and light.

She extended her free hand in front of her and pressed on through the darkness, reaching for something – anything – that might give her a clue of what to do. She searched in a circular pattern, not knowing whether she was going to feel the cold hands of a spectre, the grasp of some hidden dungeon wirry or, worse, nothing at all. Instead, on her fourth or fifth pass she felt rough fibres. It was a rope, hanging down from somewhere above, tied with heavy knots to make for an easier climb.

Rye pulled herself up through the hatch to the Upper Dungeon. The rope was tied to the metal grating, as if someone had been expecting her – or maybe someone else. Once she'd cleared the rope, Rye got as far away as possible from the entrance to the pit. Shady twitched anxiously, rustling the cage on her back.

Rye ran as fast as she could towards Harmless's cell. The cell door was open and three guards lay outside, motionless on the ground. Any weapons they'd once carried were gone. She stepped past them and looked inside. Harmless's shackles dangled empty. He was nowhere to be found.

She followed her map out of the dungeon to the

long central corridor. Where the Keep had buzzed with footsteps and conversation earlier in the night, it was now quiet. She rushed down the hall. The castle looked like it had been under siege. Longchance's paintings hung crookedly on the walls or broken on the floor. Shards of armour and weapons littered the steps. She hoped that Malydia's nanny had made it somewhere safe.

Rye approached the Great Hall. Ahead, Rye heard running, like the gallop of a small horse. It was coming her way. She stopped when she saw the huge, grey watchdog rushing towards her, its teeth bared and tongue flying loose. Rye had no time to defend herself as it met her, but the dog simply continued past, running at full speed and whimpering as it went.

Rye looked towards the doors to the Great Hall. There was whimpering coming from in there too.

Rye stepped inside. The whimpering came not from a dog, but a person. It was Malydia. She sat on the floor facing Rye, her back pressed against the overturned dining table she had clearly been using as shelter. Malydia's black dress was torn. She had lost her shoes and her hair was matted to her face. Behind her, the Great Hall had been destroyed. Chairs were broken and tables smashed. Rye knew that any remaining soldiers were in piles, buried beneath the debris.

Something was moving, though. Something impossible to miss. It was Iron Wart, the monstrous Bog Noblin that had separated Constable Boil from his arm in one bite. He lurched through the Great Hall, knocking aside all obstacles. He must have picked up Malydia's scent.

As Iron Wart drew closer to Malydia's hiding spot, Malydia caught Rye's eye.

"Help me," Malydia mouthed.

Rye waved her towards the door. "Run," Rye mouthed back.

Malydia shook her head.

Rye waved more urgently now, as Iron Wart drew near. He was practically over the table.

Again, Malydia shook her head. Her white knuckles clutched Rye's choker, which she now wore round her own neck.

Rye noticed that the choker wasn't glowing.

"Malydia!" Rye yelled now, as loudly as she could. "Run, you foolish, stubborn—"

Iron Wart reached down and clutched Malydia by her hair. He dragged her from the floor and Malydia screamed.

Rye rushed forward and set down Shady's cage. She really hoped she was right about all of this. She opened the cage and set Shady free to do what he was born to do.

26

THE GLOAMING BEAST

RYE HELD HER breath as Shady slowly stalked out from the cage.

Harmless had told her of the Gloaming Beasts one morning in Miser's End Cemetery.

"They walk among humans nearly invisible, blending into everyday life. However, to the informed eye, clues of the Gloaming Beast are everywhere. You just need to know how to look."

Running after Shady from Mud Puddle Lane to Market Street that night, she'd had plenty of time to assemble the clues in her mind.

"Their own claws are laced with toxins that are poisonous to Bog Noblins. To all other creatures, the effect isn't much more than a mild itch."

Rye looked at her own wrists and arms, etched with Shady's faded scratch marks. They had always itched more than they hurt.

"*They are mostly docile, although fiercely independent creatures.*"

Shady was very lovable, but he spent long hours in quiet places tucked away from the rest of the family, and he seemed eager to escape from the house at every opportunity.

"*They hunt them for sport. For the sheer joy of it.*"

She had never seen Shady as agitated as the night when Leatherleaf had approached Mud Puddle Lane. And what of the night of the Black Moon? Harmless had said that Leatherleaf had been injured in a fight with a Gloaming Beast. When Shady escaped, had he not headed straight for the bog? It occurred to Rye that maybe, just maybe, it was Shady who had rescued her from Leatherleaf, not Harmless or her mother.

That was why Abby had repeatedly told her that they were safest in their very own beds. She knew the secret of the murderous beast that slept at the O'Chanters' feet each night.

The fur on Shady's thick tail now flared as he spotted Iron Wart. He tilted his head and looked at Rye, as if he could not believe his good fortune. His ears were pinned back and she could see his sharp white teeth. Was he smiling?

Abby had always told Rye that it was too dangerous for Shady to go outside. It now occurred to Rye that her mother never mentioned whom it was too dangerous for. Perhaps she meant the O'Chanters themselves, if Shady were to leave them.

Shady's yellow eyes shone and he began to move slowly and silently into the Great Hall. His tail twitched with anticipation.

Malydia's shrieks echoed off the wall as Iron Wart held her close to his face and looked hungrily at her feet. He stopped and sniffed at the air.

"Diffryndown!" a voice commanded.

Rye whipped her head round to see Harmless in the doorway. So did Shady. Harmless was armed with an assortment of weapons he must have collected throughout the Keep. He raised a hand to Shady, and repeated his command. He spoke a language that Rye had never heard before. Shady reluctantly stopped and lowered himself into a crouch, ready to pounce.

"Riley, you're safe!" Harmless said with great relief. "I saw the fires and smoke in the village. Did you open the door to Beyond the Shale?"

"Yes, although I'm afraid there was a detour along the way."

"No matter," Harmless said, eyeing Iron Wart like a wolf. "I suppose I should be upset that you returned despite my instructions… but I'm in no position to object. And I see you have brought Diffryndown – Shady, as you know him. Your timing is impeccable. I feared Iron Wart would give me quite a run on my own. It will be good to have my old friend's company."

Iron Wart now caught sight of Harmless and pitched Malydia aside. She landed in a pile of broken chairs and fallen tapestries.

"Is Shady a… Gloaming Beast?" Rye asked. When she looked back towards him, Shady had silently skulked through the shadows and taken up a position under Longchance's broken throne. His yellow eyes never left Iron Wart.

"He is indeed," Harmless said. "And a most impressive one at that. Still, Iron Wart is the strongest member of the Clugburrow. It will take both Shady's and my best efforts to end our troubles here tonight. And I'm afraid we are both a bit out of practice."

Iron Wart raised his knobbly, bolted chin towards the rafters and let out a blood-curdling roar.

"Ahh, Iron Wart has come to play," Harmless said. He smiled a smile of mischief and bad intentions. He drew two swords and shouted another command. Rye saw Shady dart out from under the throne and take a position behind Iron Wart. Her cat began to circle the Bog Noblin, stalking its prey.

Harmless dropped to one knee and whispered in Rye's ear, "Go now. To the courtyard."

"But—" Rye began to protest.

"Please, Riley. Go. Your father and your beloved pet are about to do things you should never have to see."

Harmless kissed her on the top of her head and stood.

"You have done all that I could ever ask of you and more. Now wait for me at the gates of the Keep. Dawn is near. If I'm not out by sunrise, it means I am never coming. Return to the Dead Fish Inn without me. Now, on the count of three, we all run to our fates."

Rye nodded. Harmless took a step forward and began the count.

"One, two…"

Harmless charged, stepping on the overturned table to launch himself through the air, swords flashing in the torchlight. Shady was even faster, a black flash like the shadow of a shark cutting through the sea. He sprinted forward and leapt in the air – a cannonball of claws, fur and teeth. Iron Wart roared again and flailed his arms to protect himself from their attack.

Rye ran out of the doors of the Great Hall without looking back. She considered stopping for Malydia, but surely the girl was now in better hands than Rye could offer. Rye was uncertain of what awaited her at the gates of the Keep, so she took a side passageway that led to the rear grounds. She opened a door and headed into the night. The outside passageways were narrow and twisty, with little room between the Keep itself and the high exterior wall. She followed one that she expected to loop back round to the main gate, but it came to a dead end in a pile of stale fruit, rotting hay and household rubbish. It was the compost heap.

A smell made the hair on the back of Rye's neck stand on end. It wasn't the compost. It was the smell of the bogs. Rye turned very slowly.

There, filling the passageway from which she'd just come, was Leatherleaf.

He studied her intently, his bulging eyes rotating. He still wore shackles on his wrists and ankles, but they now hung loose. His arms and legs looked red and swollen; he must have battled ferociously to break free from his cage. He was staring at Rye's neck. Of course, there was nothing there.

Leatherleaf stepped forward and leaned down so that he was nearly eye level with Rye. His watery eyes were filled with anger and confusion. He bared his teeth and spittle ran down from his chin. It splattered Rye's face.

Rye knew that Harmless and Shady would not be rescuing her in the near future. Folly, Quinn, her mother – anyone who could help – were all far away.

"Wait," Rye said quietly and held out one hand. With the other, she reached for her boot.

Leatherleaf snorted and lunged at her aggressively.

"No, wait!" Rye implored, and pulled her hand back up. "I have this. It belongs to you."

She showed him the small leather pouch in her hand. Leatherleaf's face contorted.

"Look," Rye said. She untied the pouch and emptied its contents on the ground. "It's all still there."

The iron anklet, the tiny skull, the stick figure and the yellow tooth all tumbled out on to the stones.

Leatherleaf's eyes grew wider as he examined them.

"I'm sorry," Rye said. "I never should have taken your belongings."

Leatherleaf looked at Rye with a flash of anger, then down at the items from the bag, then back at Rye. He reached down and snatched up something in his hand. He clutched it to his chest.

Rye waited, not breathing, while Leatherleaf regarded her. Then he turned, took three steps down the passage and leaped on to the Keep's wall, catching the stones with his claws and clambering up to the top. He looked down at Rye as if to commit her face to memory, then disappeared over the other side.

Rye heard the beast-baby wail from outside the Keep's walls. Leatherleaf's cry grew fainter and fainter, until it disappeared somewhere far in the distance.

Rye finally exhaled when she could no longer hear Leatherleaf's cries. Her legs shook and she sat down on the cold, stone ground. There, in front of her, three items remained. The iron anklet, the tiny skull and the wooden stickman. Leatherleaf had taken only his tooth.

The night sky was beginning to brighten as Rye made her way around to the courtyard. As she emerged from a side passageway, she caught sight of the front gate. There, in its shadow, was a cloaked man on one knee, his head in his hands. He seemed beaten with grief.

"Harmless?" Rye called, running forward. "Are you all right?"

He looked up, and his cruel, dark eyes flashed with recognition. It wasn't Harmless. It was Longchance. His face was pale and skeletal in the early morning light.

"You," he spat and rose to his feet. "You and your kind brought this upon me."

Longchance towered as he rose. With his cloak and

bedraggled hair, he looked like a wirry scare come to life. He stepped menacingly towards Rye and drew his long sword. He pointed it at her.

"I have lost everything," he bellowed, lumbering now with long strides.

Rye scrambled away as fast as she could, darting under a cart filled with wine casks.

"Come out!" Longchance screamed, raising his chin and fists to the sky. "Or I shall crawl under there and drag you out like a rat from its hole!"

Longchance jabbed his sword under the cart. He slashed and the blade snagged Rye's cloak, but spared her skin.

He thrust his arm underneath and his nails bit into her ankle. She felt her body being dragged across the ground.

The large front doors of the Keep kicked open and Harmless emerged, carrying a limp body in his arms. The body was small and frail, covered in a black dress.

Harmless laid it gently on the ground. Harmless's hair was wet with sweat. Fresh claw marks bled from his cheeks and arms.

"Malydia," Longchance whispered. The name drew all the breath from his lungs. He let Rye's leg loose and she scampered back under the cart. His sword dropped to the ground.

Harmless looked at Longchance gravely. In three steps so fast Rye barely saw them, Harmless covered the distance between them and launched himself hard on to the Earl. Longchance fell backwards and Harmless pinned him with his full weight upon his chest. Harmless drew a dagger.

"I deliver your daughter safely to you today. She is frightened beyond imagination, but I suspect she will be fine – no thanks to you," Harmless hissed. "I know you would not do the same for me."

Longchance craned his eyes to see. Indeed, Malydia stirred on the steps.

Rye peeked out from under the cart. Harmless had a look of menace on his face that she'd never seen before. He bared his teeth like a wolf as he spoke.

"You have put my family in jeopardy for the last time. To you, Earl Longchance, I show no mercy. Finally, Drowning can bid farewell to its true monster."

Harmless slid his dagger down from Longchance's chin to the knobby Adam's apple in his throat. He pressed.

Rye gasped under the cart. It was loud enough that

Harmless looked over and caught her eye. Rye held his gaze and something in his face began to change. Harmless looked back over his shoulder. Malydia had sat up and was rubbing her own eyes.

Harmless studied the dagger at Longchance's throat. He grabbed Longchance by his long, plaited beard, and Longchance pinched his eyes shut. With a swift stroke of the wrist, Harmless cut off the beard.

The hair dangled from Harmless's fist like the blackened tail of a possum. Harmless thrust it in front of Longchance's eyes.

"I shall keep this little weed of yours. Should you ever trouble the Luck Uglies or any of their families again, I will deliver these whiskers to the Clugburrow myself, so they can follow your scent wherever you may take it. And I will make certain they know that the Luck Uglies no longer protect the House of Longchance."

Longchance rubbed his sore, naked chin.

"As cunning a warrior as you may be, Grey, you are but one man," Longchance said venomously. "You live on borrowed time."

Harmless stepped off Longchance and laughed loudly

into the dawn.

"But there you are wrong, Morningwig." He raised his blade in the brightening sky and pointed to the walls of Longchance Keep. "Your soldiers have all deserted you in your time of greatest need. But mine, once again, have answered the call."

Rye pulled herself out from the cart so she could see. There, perched along the walls and towers of Longchance Keep, a dozen hooded figures had appeared like ravens. Glaring from under the hoods were sharpened teeth, blackened eyes, and twisted faces. Luck Uglies. They peered down into the courtyard. One Luck Ugly was smaller than a child. It clambered up another's leg with its long arms and perched upon its shoulder. Rye thought she saw a monkey's tail twitch out from under its tiny cloak.

Longchance swallowed and said no more.

"Choose your course wisely," Harmless said with a foreboding smile. "Whether it is from the roofs, or the sewers, or the darkest shadows of your own chambers – we will be watching."

Harmless pulled Riley to her feet and up into his arms. He pressed something into her hand. It was her choker.

"Come," he whispered. "Our loved ones at the Dead Fish must be worried sick. Shady will find us soon enough. I do hope he has not given himself a stomach ache."

Rye closed her eyes. She rested her head on Harmless's shoulder as they stepped through the gate of the Keep under lightening skies.

The masked Luck Uglies disappeared from the towers as mysteriously as they had appeared.

A dark, furry shape darted through the courtyard, catching up with Rye and Harmless before they'd gone too far.

Fingers of morning light spread across the Keep, illuminating the outline of a ragged black clover smudged across its stone walls.

27

THE LUCK BAG

RYE STIRRED THE cooking pots over the fire at the O'Chanters' cottage, staring out of the window at the morning sun. Abby peeled and cored the last apples of the season. The house was quiet with Lottie still asleep and they didn't say much to each other – they didn't have to. It was good to be home.

Abby placed the apples in a bowl and wiped Fair Warning clean with a cloth. She held it to her mouth and fogged it with her breath, then polished it on her dress.

Rye smiled and glanced at the window again before going back to stirring her pans.

"Riley," Abby said, and Rye looked up.

Abby held Fair Warning by the tip of the blade, extending the handle to Rye. "Take it. It's yours."

Rye's eyes sparkled. "Really?"

"You're ready," Abby said. "You've proved it."

Rye still hesitated.

"Don't worry about me," Abby said, with a fleeting twinkle in her eye that reminded Rye – just for a moment – of Harmless. "I've got bigger ones."

Rye carefully took Fair Warning in her hand.

"Promise me you'll stick to cutting vegetables for the time being," Abby said. She reached under her dress and unbuckled Fair Warning's sheath from her thigh. She handed that over too.

"Thank you, Mama," Rye said, then paused as she moved to strap it over her leggings. She rarely wore dresses. It certainly wouldn't be well hidden there.

"Hmmm," Abby said, "we'll come up with something."

Rye placed Fair Warning on the table and pulled something from her pocket.

"Mama," Rye said and extended her hand, "what's this?"

Abby looked up at the ragged black clover on the swatch of fabric between Rye's fingertips. She gave her a knowing smile.

"Did your father give you that?"

"No," Rye said.

Abby raised an eyebrow. She stood slowly and put her hands on Rye's shoulders.

"A stranger? With an unusual pet, perhaps?"

Rye nodded.

"That," Abby said, nodding towards Rye's clover, "can mean many different things. But simply put, it means a Luck Ugly has promised you a favour."

Rye examined the black clover with new eyes.

"Do *me* a favour," Abby said. "Don't mention it to your father just yet. I'm not sure how he'll feel about it."

Rye shot her mother a suspicious glance.

"Don't worry, no more secrets. I'll tell you all about Bramble Cutty – but it's not what you might be thinking."

Rye would have pressed her mother for more information, but familiar voices on the street caught her ear. She peeked out of the window again.

"Go on," Abby said. "I'll finish up here."

"Really?"

"Go ahead."

Rye smiled and hugged her mother. Abby clutched her tightly.

Rye thought about Malydia eating alone at the Keep's enormous but silent table each night. She imagined Leatherleaf out there on his own, running fearfully through the forest. Sometimes it was too easy to take a good hug for granted. She held this one for a long time.

Rye, Folly and Harmless sat on stones in Miser's End Cemetery. Quinn was there too, although his bottom was still smarting from the Bog Noblin bite and he preferred to stand. His recovery had been remarkable. No one on Mud Puddle Lane could remember anybody who had recovered from such a severe Bog Noblin Bite at all, never mind that quickly. Angus chalked it up to the sturdy Quartermast bloodlines. Rye knew better because Harmless told her otherwise.

In addition to their other remarkable qualities, Gloaming Beasts were naturally resistant to the toxic effects of Bog Noblin bites. They could pass this immunity on to others by way of biting or scratching. Harmless, Abby, Rye and Lottie all bore scars from Shady's scratches over the years. As it turned out, the O'Chanters didn't have a bad tempered cat so much as a protective one. Luckily for

Quinn, Shady had given him quite a scratch while he was watching Lottie on the last Black Moon.

The Gloaming Beast in question was now rolling in the overgrown grass of the cemetery, tethered to a long leather leash. He seemed to relish the morning sun and settled peacefully on his back, his scratchy pink tongue hanging from his mouth. Shady had returned to his normal cat-like self. Except for the night he coughed up a metal bolt from Iron Wart's face on to Rye's bed, there was no evidence of the recent events.

Shady, Harmless told her, was at least seventy years old, probably older. He had been part of Harmless's household when he was Rye's age, and of her grandfather's household before that. They called him Diffryndown back then, Harmless explained. But Rye was sure that Shady suited him better. Gloaming Beasts were extremely rare and, because of their striking similarity to cats, unknowing humans might go their entire lives without realising they had one in their possession. Of course, one could never really say he possessed a Gloaming Beast, for at any given moment, it might simply pick up and wander away, never to return again. That was why the O'Chanters cherished him, why Abby would never let him roam free unless the circumstances were absolutely dire.

Rye, Folly and Quinn sipped the apple tea Rye had brought down from the cottage and watched Shady fall asleep in the grass. Rye was relieved to see him drift off. He certainly didn't seem to be going anywhere for the time being. Once they'd drunk their fill, the children gathered round a long flat stone where Harmless had spread out the contents of the small leather bag.

"Bog Noblins are notoriously superstitious creatures," Harmless explained. "They are fascinated by mechanical things, but their minds are too simple to comprehend their workings. So, instead, they lean on talismans to help them explain that which they do not understand."

Harmless picked up the empty leather bag.

"Many Bog Noblins carry luck bags filled with items they cherish or believe will bring them good fortune. The tooth might have been of sentimental value to Leatherleaf. Perhaps it was one of his, or one of his parents'. Much of what goes into luck bags are along those lines – special to no one other than the Bog Noblin who possesses it."

Rye, Folly and Quinn listened to Harmless without a

sound. Harmless motioned to the anklet, the skull and the stick figure.

"But these items are different," he continued. "Over the centuries, the Clugburrow have plundered numerous treasures. Amid the gold and jewels, some extraordinary objects have come into their possession. These, as ordinary as they seem, are three such objects. I wonder if, in fact, they are why the Clugburrow chased Leatherleaf so relentlessly."

Rye raised her eyebrows at the three objects she'd been carrying around in her boot.

"These," Harmless said, "are ancient talismans with the power to bestow great abilities on those who possess them. They were stolen from the Luck Uglies by the Bog Noblins many years ago. It is our great fortune to have found them once again."

He looked at each of the children with great weight in his eyes. "However, it is not safe to keep such powerful items in one set of hands. Are you willing to perform a great service for me? I and the Luck Uglies would be in your debt."

They all nodded enthusiastically, mouths open.

Harmless picked up the wooden stickman between his fingertips.

"These are the Strategist's Sticks. In generations to come, the greatest leaders will not be those who raise the largest sword or fill the heaviest armour. They will be the thinkers. Leaders who can inspire, strategise and lead by example. Who better to hold the Strategist's Sticks than you, Quinn? You proved yourself to be selfless and brave."

Quinn accepted the stickman in the palm of his hand.

"Th-thank you," he stuttered.

Harmless picked up the tiny skull.

"This is the Alchemist's Bone. The study of science and chemicals is beyond all but the most scholarly of men. In fact, some in our very own village would have you believe that girls are incapable of such thinking. You, Folly, without the benefit of any formal training, have proven that with hard work and perseverance, anyone can create magic through science. The Alchemist's Bone is yours."

Harmless handed the tiny skull to Folly and her cheeks deepened to the colour of ripe apples. Her eyes twinkled with excitement. Finally, Harmless picked up the iron anklet.

"Last but not least is the Anklet of the Shadowbender. The wearer of this anklet shall have the power to bend the laws of darkness and light. To scale walls and travel the rooftops under the cover of night. Who better to hold this anklet than a girl who, not so long ago, struggled to stand on her own two feet, but whose legs managed to save an entire village. Riley, this anklet is for you."

Rye took the anklet in her hand. She noticed that the dull iron links were imprinted with familiar-looking runes.

"You must cherish these items," Harmless continued, "but be warned. These charms are not short cuts. Their powers shall only come to you over time, with great practice, skill and dedication. It may take years before they begin to reveal the powers I describe. No charm will make a lazy child great. But it may make a child who strives for greatness extraordinary."

"Thank you, Harmless," Quinn said. "I'll keep it in my pocket every day."

"Yes, thank you," Folly said, staring at the tiny eye sockets of the Alchemist's Bone.

None of them could take their eyes off their gifts.

"Harmless," Folly finally said, "I need to head back to

the Shambles. My parents are having a breakfast feast at the Inn today to celebrate – well, just to celebrate, I guess. Would you like to come?"

"Thank you for your kind invitation, but I have made other arrangements this morning."

"OK," Folly said. "Come on, Quinn. Rye, are you coming?"

"I'm going to stay here for a while."

"See you soon," Folly said.

Rye smiled. Folly and Quinn took off up Troller's Hill together.

Harmless leaned back and stretched out his body in the sun. Most of the leaves had fallen from the trees and it was an unseasonably warm day – probably the last of its kind before the real cold would settle in.

Rye took off one boot and clasped her charm round her ankle.

"Your feet are growing," Harmless said.

"They still don't fill these boots." Rye shook out some straw.

"They don't have to," Harmless said. "There are other boots."

"Are these charms really magical?" Rye said. "This anklet, the skull, the little stick man – you're not making fun of my friends, are you?" She remembered what Harmless told her about manipulating the minds of others.

Harmless smiled. "Magic can mean many things, Riley," he said, and nothing more.

Rye chewed a lip. "And what about our runestones?" she asked.

Rye touched her choker, safely round her neck again. She looked at Harmless's leather runestone necklace, which was clasped back round his neck too. After they'd left the Keep, Harmless told Rye that he'd made an arrangement with Truitt. If they both survived the night, they would exchange their traded items at a secret location. The Everything Key was now back in Truitt's hands. That meant Truitt had survived too. Rye warmed at the thought. The link children would still have their champion.

Rye thought about what the Everything Key could have meant for Harmless and the Luck Uglies. She might have asked Harmless why he returned it, but she already knew the answer. Instead, she considered a more puzzling question.

"Why is it," Rye said, "that my choker didn't glow when Malydia wore it?"

Harmless leaned forward. Rye thought she saw him glance, ever so quickly, at his hands clasped between his knees.

"The choker did not glow to protect Malydia because I did not give it to her. The rune stones cannot be taken; they are a gift that only the High Chieftain of the Luck Uglies can bestow."

"Mama told me our runes were a warning to them," Rye said. "What did you do to make the Bog Noblins fear you so?"

"Everything that was necessary at the time," Harmless said. To Rye, it seemed Harmless's words carried with them an echo of regret.

Rye put her chin in her hand and shook her head.

"I have so many questions."

Harmless smiled warmly. "Don't fret, there will be time to answer them. I think I will stay here and enjoy the day. It may be the finest one we have had all autumn."

"And what about tomorrow and the next day?" Rye asked.

Harmless looked up at the sun. "There's much to do around here. You know now that the Luck Cauldrons serve as our signal. By our code, any Luck Ugly seeing the cauldron fire must answer the call. There are other signals that can be used to summon every Luck Ugly throughout the entire Shale. We have not had to use those in my lifetime."

Harmless turned to face Rye again. "In any event, I had you open the door to Beyond the Shale so that the Luck Uglies could pass into the Spoke and access the village. I have since locked it. But it looks as if other – shall we say – unwelcome denizens from Beyond the Shale may have passed through as well."

Harmless read the concern on Rye's face and flashed a reassuring smile. "Nothing to worry about for the time being," he said. "But I may stay around the village for a while longer, just to make sure nothing comes of it. Besides," Harmless said with a wink, "winter is a poor season for adventure anyway."

Two figures appeared, working their way down the dirt path from Troller's Hill. Shady's ears perked up and he sniffed at the wind.

Lottie O'Chanter skipped along the path, Mona Monster tucked under her arm. Abby O'Chanter wore a red dress and a smile. She carried a large wicker basket.

"What do you suppose she has in there?" Harmless said.

"Your birthday breakfast, of course," Rye said. "Make sure you compliment her on it. She's been cooking all night."

Harmless smiled and placed an arm round Rye's shoulder. "I think this is indeed the finest day we've seen in some time."

EPILOGUE

WHAT TOMORROW BRINGS US

"I S THAT SNOW?" Rye asked.

"It's but a little flurry," Harmless said.

Rye watched the first flakes of winter fall past her nose, then her feet, as they drifted down towards the cobblestones of Market Street far below.

"Won't the snow make this too dangerous?" she asked.

"Just more challenging," Harmless said.

Rye and Harmless stood on the edge of the rooftop. Rising above and below them were the twisty, thorny rooftops of the shops and dwellings on Market Street. Jagged chimneys, gutters and decorative arches jutted out from unexpected places.

Harmless waved his hand at the horizon of roofs. "There's a path out there. Once you've found and navigated it often

423

enough, your legs and feet will find new paths all of their own. Eventually, you won't even need your eyes."

Rye looked sceptical.

"You've come so far since I last saw you up here," Harmless said, and with it Rye fully realised what she had recently begun to suspect. A certain masked gargoyle had been watching over her for a long time.

"But we can wait if you're not ready," Harmless added. There was both patience and a dare in his voice.

Rye didn't answer straight away.

Finally she said, "Where do we start?"

"Right there." Harmless pointed to a tiled roof on the opposite side of the street.

Rye looked down. Villagers and merchants scurried by four storeys below, oblivious to their presence high above.

"Is there a ladder?"

"The Spoke is not the only way to traverse the village in secret," Harmless said. "You've learned to crawl its tunnels. Don't you think it's about time you learned to fly?"

Rye looked wide-eyed at the open air between them and the other roof.

"Harmless, bad things happen when I try to do things

like this."

"Do you have your anklet?" Harmless asked.

"Yes."

"Do you trust me?"

Rye hesitated. "Yes."

"The worst that can happen is you fall," Harmless said. "And we both know you always get up."

Harmless smiled and pulled the hood of his cloak over his head. "Hoods on."

Rye tucked her hair under her hood.

Harmless took five strides back from the edge of the roof. Rye followed.

Harmless extended his hand. For a moment, just a split second, the green circular tattoo on his palm appeared to dance.

Rye reached up and took his hand. His grip warmed her whole body.

"On the count of three," Harmless said. "One, two…"

They began running. As Rye's feet pushed off the edge, a smile stretched across her face. Harmless's smile was even wider.

The O'Chanters leaped off the roof, through the air, and let luck guide their landing.

TAM'S POCKET GLOSSARY OF
DROWNING MOUTH SPEAK

Assessment: Every villager's least favourite time of year. During Assessment, Earl Longchance's officials visit and inspect each and every place of business, levying fines for non-compliance with the Laws of Longchance. Assessment keeps the village's (and the Earl's) coffers full for a rainy day. These days, the Earl's reserves are rich enough to handle a decade of monsoons.

Beyond the Shale: Many a villager longs for the tranquillity of the woods and a nap under the trees surrounded by gentle woodland creatures. Nap under one of this forest's ominous pines and you're likely to get your eyes pecked out by a buzzard.

Bog Noblins: An off-colour village joke: 'What has bad breath, one eye and likes to eat children?' Answer:

A Bog Noblin with a stick in its eye. Villagers' comedic sensibilities still need some refinement.

Cackle Fruit: Nothing fancy, just chicken eggs. They also happen to be Lottie O'Chanter's favourite food.

Daughters of Longchance: Known for their poor cooking, lack of any noticeable sense of humour, and high-pitched voices that traumatise dogs and infants. However, given their status in society, they are useful to have around during Assessment and are therefore highly desired brides.

Gloaming Beasts: These creatures are most likely to be spotted, if at all, stalking through the twilight in search of their unwitting prey. Gloaming Beasts are masters of disguise and clever, wanton killers when inspired. Fortunately, they find humans to be oddly amusing, and may sometimes even adopt one or more as pets.

Hooks: A popular card game that involves the exchange of cards through a series of bluffs, cajoles and threats until, one by one, players are eliminated as they 'swallow the hook'. The best Hooks players can become quite wealthy – assuming they can find anyone willing to play with them. It is widely known that success in Hooks is directly related to one's ability to cheat.

Link Rat: A link rat and a feral skunk are likely to receive the same reception at a villager's door, but a good link rat knows every nook, cranny and hiding place in Drowning. The link rat's services can be indispensible to a villager who has a need to disappear.

Luck Uglies: Who? Never heard of them. Really. Not the foggiest clue who you're talking about.

O'There: The rich and prosperous hub of the Kingdom located on the far side of the sea. Nobody in Drowning has actually been O'There, but it's said that even the sewers smell like apricots, all the men wear shoes, and the maidens have all their teeth.

Pigshanks: A bad word. Use it and your mother is likely to scrub your tongue with soap and a horse brush.

The Pot: Lottie O'Chanter's chamber pot. The youngest O'Chanter has proved difficult to potty train and is just as likely to squat in a pillowcase, a boot or Abby O'Chanter's herb garden.

The Shambles: The roughest district in the village sits along the banks of the River Drowning, bathed in a broth of grog, bog wash and sailor sweat. The neighbourhood is home to the Dead Fish Inn – 'where nobody knows your name' – and that's just how its guests like it.

The Shivers: Neither cure nor cause of this epidemic disease has been determined, although theories have included Bog Noblin bites, going out in the rain without a hat, and pooping too close to the town water supply.

The Treaty of Stormwell: Legend says that the written peace treaty between the Luck Uglies and the House of Longchance earned its name because, in a final act of defiance, Grimshaw the Black (then High Chieftain of the Luck Uglies) threw the hat of Earl Ascot Longchance down a stormwell just before signing.

Turkeyhole: Another bad word. Call someone a turkeyhole and you're likely to get a foot in yours.

Wirry: A mischievous ghost or spirit. Wirries are often said to haunt basements, attics, graveyards and other places where children don't belong.

Wirry Scares: These wooden stick people were originally built by rural villagers to scare away wirries, Bog Noblins and other nasties that go bump in the night. Over time, Wirry Scares have been adopted as traditional Black Moon Party decorations, and for the most part scare only those Black Moon revellers who've drunk too much wine.

Follow Rye and Harmless
on their next adventure in:

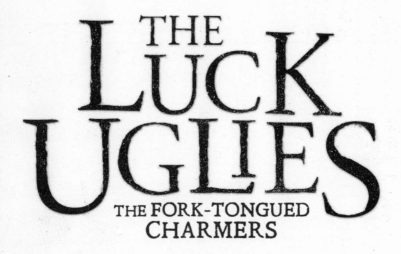

THE LUCK
UGLIES
THE FORK-TONGUED
CHARMERS

Coming Soon